GRASS BEYOND THE MOUNTAINS

GRASS BEYOND
THE MOUNTAINS

*Discovering the Last Great
Cattle Frontier on the North
American Continent*

by

RICHMOND P. HOBSON, Jr.

National Library of Canada Cataloguing in Publication Data

Hobson, Richmond P. (Richmond Pearson), 1907-1966.
Grass beyond the mountains

ISBN 0-7710-4170-5

1. Hobson, Richmond P. (Richmond Pearson), 1907-1966.
2. Cowboys – British Columbia – Biography.   3. Cattle trade – British Columbia.   4. Frontier and pioneer life – British Columbia.   I. Title.

FC3826.1.H63A3 1987   971.1'03   C87-094398-7
F1088.H63A3 1987

We acknowledge the financial support of the Government of Canada through the Book Publishing Industry Development Program for our publishing activities. We further acknowledge the support of the Canada Council for the Arts and the Ontario Arts Council for our publishing program.

Printed and bound in Canada by Webcom Limited

McClelland & Stewart Ltd.
The Canadian Publishers
481 University Avenue
Toronto, Ontario
M5G 2E9
www.mcclelland.com

This book is dedicated to my horse friends—

NIMPO   THE PILEDRIVER
STUYVE   BIG GEORGE
BUCK   LITTLE ROANIE
OLD JOE   THE SPIDER
OLD SCABBY WHITE

—conquerors of the silent lonely trails.

Contents

CONTENTS

Foreword

ACROSS NORTHERN BRITISH COLUMBIA, between the Rockies and the Pacific Ocean, and north of the Fifty-second Parallel, stretches an awesome 250,000 square-mile chunk of mountain, swamp, river and valley.

Although this raw, only partially explored territory is so immense that a number of our states could be submerged within its boundaries, only one railroad track, and a single car road, flanked by isolated villages and cattle-loading pens, splits its vast solitude.

Far beyond these the only visible signs of man's advance is a new frontier—a frontier as tough, as wild and as remote as the West of the early days. This unconquered barrier stands out, unique in this day and age, for it is the last great cattle frontier on the North American continent.

Back in its jackpine forests there are Indians who have never seen a white man, and lonely loon-haunted lakes echo the spooky moans of timber wolves, the splash of beavers' tails and the grunting bellow of the moose.

It is a land of striking contrasts, where the tentacles of great, octopus-shaped, gray muskegs reach into dark, moss-hung spruce jungles; where rolling bunch grass prairies, and flat, yellow-green meadows glide between the fantastic shapes and colors of unexplored mountain ranges that split the sky.

It is a land that drew me like a magnet into its soul.

This story is about that strange land beyond the mysterious crags and canyons of the formidable Itcha, Algak and Fawnie mountain ranges; about the first horses and the first cattle herd to penetrate its forbidding solitudes; and about the fabulous characters that people the surrounding frontier.

GRASS BEYOND THE MOUNTAINS

CHAPTER I

From New York to Wyoming

Like most american and canadian boys, I went through the routine "want to be a cowboy" stage, and like these same youngsters, my visions of far-reaching mountain ranges, cattle herds moving across lonely treeless plains, and the dreamed-up smells of sagebrush and horses and barns were consistently thwarted by the big iron-gated schoolhouse.

But unlike other more normal boys, I was unable to shake these visions loose. They followed me through military academy, into Stanford University, out on construction gangs in California's High Sierras, south to roughnecking jobs in the East Texas oil fields, into the fight ring where I acted as a punching bag for heavyweight contenders, and finally into a New York real estate firm where I peddled apartments and private houses to money-befuddled clients before the 1929 crash.

Not long after the general collapse, my job swapped ends on me. Instead of collecting commissions on sales, I spent my time ducking and dodging cashless clients who angrily demanded lower rents or cancellations.

In 1932, when I could no longer pay rent on my own apartment, I rolled my bed, took a last deep breath of New York's exhaust-filled air and headed west towards Wyoming.

At twenty-four years of age, what ego the New York business and social swirl had not taken from me was quickly and efficiently removed in my Wyoming chore-boy job. I can think of nothing that takes the self-respecting edges off a man more quickly than skinning out dead cows, pulling nails out of old weather-grayed lumber, dunging out barns and packing water and lunches to the branding crew.

Two years and several ranches after my arrival in Wyoming, I had not achieved my cowhand objective, but I had climbed to the dizzy heights of a ranch hand who drew the going thirty dollars a month wages and board.

Late in the winter of 1934, I talked my way into a cattle feeding job at Stanley Blum's Box E ranch near Crowheart Butte, where a hawk-faced, horse-minded character named Panhandle Phillips did the riding.

The wide-shouldered, expressionless Panhandle—whose horse-breaking and cowpunching ability was exceeded only by his ugly practical-joking offenses against humanity—was a hard man to lay your fingers on. Wherever cowhands and ranchers met, in taverns, bunkhouses, and around the campfires from Dubois to Hudson, the talk would drift to the daring exploits or the shady deeds of Wild Horse Panhandle.

Five years before my arrival in the Wind River district, this long-faced, eagle-beaked, narrow-eyed individual had ridden into Charles Smith's ranch on a tall, trim-legged, vermilion-colored gelding, driving a pack animal and four loose saddle horses ahead of him. These horses were all dished-faced, short-backed bays, with a strange red undershading, and showed definite signs of Morgan and Arabian breeding.

Once after a beef drive, when Stanley Blum and Pan were drinking it out at a bar in Hudson, Wyoming, Panhandle casually mentioned that the left hip brand on his horses was an Arizona one—and that's about as close as anyone got to Pan's or his horses' origin.

One night, coming home late from a poker game at a neighboring ranch, George Pennoyer's, I surprised Pan who was sitting in the middle of the bunkhouse floor, surrounded by maps and papers.

He looked up startled, grinned sheepishly, considered a moment, then said, "Sit down, and I'll show ya something."

I closed the door and squatted beside him on the floor.

"I was keeping this here business to myself," he explained easily, "but you've caught me with a cold deck. This detail map here has a big blank space on it—do ya see?"

I said I did, even though my eyes couldn't penetrate the dim lamplight and the cigarette smoke.

"Now look here," said Pan.

He pulled out another large sheet about four-feet square and laid it on top of the first one.

"See this map—look at those little dotted lines ending with arrows."

Now I could see the big sheet well enough. There was practically nothing on it. At one corner a dark winding line had printed along it: "Blackwater River." I looked at Pan then.

"What's the idea?" I said. "Is this a map of a hidden treasure or a gold mine?"

Pan cut in quickly.

"Yes," he said, "a gold mine."

The veins stood out on his forehead. His face was flushed and his deep narrow eyes gleamed out at me like live coals.

"So that's what all this fuss is about," I said. "Where is this bonanza, in Arizona or Old Mexico?"

"No," he replied, "it's in British Columbia."

"British Columbia! You're nuts, man. British Columbia! A gold mine near the North Pole—and waiting for you. That's really good."

Pan was still staring at the map. I had a package of tailormades in my pocket, and straightening up, offered him a smoke.

He reached over and pulled one out of the package, then walked to the stove, pulled open the hinged door and grabbed out a live coal. Rolling it about between his hands, he finally managed to get his cigarette lighted, then threw the coal back into the stove and closed the door. I watched him.

"What kind of gold is supposed to be there waiting for you, Pan?" I asked. "Placer, hard rock or just gold coins buried up there?"

Pan snorted loudly. He inhaled, then let loose a cloud of smoke through his nose. He looked at me and answered slowly.

"Those maps show all that is known of the south tip of a country as big as Wyoming with Montana throwed in. There's reports of a grass country in there some place that reaches as far as the eye can see.

"Yeah—that's my gold mine. Grass! Free grass reachin' north into unknown country. Land—lots of it—untouched—just waitin' for hungry cows, and some buckaroos that can ride and have guts enough to put her over."

He paused, flipped the ashes off the tailormade, and looked down at the pile of maps and papers on the floor.

I didn't say anything. I walked over to my bunk, sat down and looked across the room at the black curtain of night in the bunkhouse window.

"Here it is," I thought. "That new frontier."

Pan took another long drag from his cigarette and continued.

"I talked to a guy this winter who got as far as the Chilcotin country in British Columbia, a big cattle country, rimmed in by a high uncharted mountain range to the north of it.

"Chilcotin is grass country, he said; it's frontier ranch country, cattlemen creepin' their herds back further all the time.

"But those Itcha Mountains—they don't know what's over the other side. Maps don't show. Ya see, Rich, I sent to the B.C. government for maps and any pointers they got on the country."

The Wild Horse stooped over and picked up one of the maps. He packed it over to the bunk I was sitting on and spread it out between us. I turned the lamp wick up. The room brightened. I looked at Pan.

"When are we leaving?"

CHAPTER II

North to the Frontier

A FEW DAYS AFTER we had made our decision to tackle the unknown country, Pan and I rode home from a cowboy reunion at Dubois, and stopped to feed and rest our horses at Stanley Blum's brother-in-law's TL Ranch, where both of us had once worked.

Heavy-shouldered, rock-faced, good-humored, sixty-year-old George Pennoyer, one of Wyoming's most admired and respected cattle ranchers, had once been the general manager of the Rocky Mountain Cattle Company, the largest cattle company combine in Wyoming.

Pan and I told George about our plans for breaking into the wild unexplored country beyond the Chilcotin.

It was after dark when we led our horses out of the barn to the light-flooded porch steps of the ranchhouse. Pennoyer stood iron-jawed before us.

"Boys," he said, "I'm not yet grown so old or so set in my ways that your trip doesn't get my blood stirring up. If the layout up there looks big—if it's really big and you think it's a cattle company proposition—I'll come up there and throw in with you fellows—and we'll start a real frontier cattle company.

"So long, fellows—good luck and good riding!"

On October 15, 1934, with Pan at the wheel of "Old Bloater," an obsolete panel delivery Ford, distinguished by large printed letters across its body, "BOLOGNA—BLOATERS—BLOOD SAUSAGES," we rattled across the Canadian border.

From government officials, we ascertained that Tatla Lake, five hundred miles north of Vancouver, was the northwestern frontier of existing ranches. West of it lay the little-known Anahim country, walled in on the north by the wild, unexplored Itcha and Algak ranges. Beyond the mountain barrier lay our objective, the mysterious Indian taboo land on the unmapped headwaters of the Blackwater River.

Some distance beyond the village of Hope, which is a hundred miles northeast of the city of Vancouver, we came to the historic Cariboo highway, the famous Trail of '98. At the present time this road has been greatly improved, but then it was a bush road, though referred to as a "highway" in British Columbia. It narrowed down on the turns to a single lane with a washboard base that shook the Bloater up badly and gave me a rough time.

This road wound its way for more than a hundred miles along the face of a cliff, with the Fraser River twisting like a tiny thread through the rocky gorge a thousand feet below. In places small slides blocked the highway, and we shoveled enough rock out of the way to carry on.

Once a driver, whom we nearly pushed over the bank, found it necessary to back up a hundred yards to a place in the road where we could squeeze by him. We thanked him.

"That's all right," he said, "but watch it ahead—the road narrows up."

Certainly there was every indication that we were leaving barb-wire fences and farm country behind us and at last getting into the frontier.

At Cache Creek a branch of the highway swung east towards Kamloops, a sunny healthful town of some five thousand people who mixed trout fishing with cattle ranching. Back of Kamloops, thousands upon thousands of head of cattle grazed across the Douglas Lake Cattle Company and the Guichon ranches' million acres of bunch grass hills, meadows and mountains.

The following day the Bloater forged into Clinton, a typical, single-street, one-story cow town on the edge of the Cariboo.

We were now on the border of a grassy world where cattle grazed across some of the largest ranches in Canada or the United States. Fifty miles northwest of us, strung along the east bank of the Fraser River, the vast Dog Creek and Alkali Lake ranches were dwarfed by their neighbor across the river—the fabulous Gang Ranch, the largest ranch in North America, whose four million or more acres covers a land area more than three times the size of the Klebergs' famous King Ranch in Texas. The Gang Ranch is so immense that there are different climates at opposite ends of its range.

We carried on to the north and stopped for lunch at a quiet little lodge on the banks of Lac La Hache. The proprietor told us that for many miles we had been driving through property belonging to an Englishman, Lord Martin Cecil's 100 Mile House Ranch.

After driving for more than an hour through the eye-straining yellowish twilight of October 17, Pan steered the Bloater into a colorful, board-sidewalked, false-fronted little cow town called Williams Lake. Here, on parklike benchland, 370 miles north of Vancouver, six hundred pioneer souls were banded together dispensing the various businesses that centered around the well-kept plank-and-lumber stockyards, where three thousand head of beef cattle could be handled at one time. Williams Lake, one of the biggest cattle-shipping points in British Columbia, is the outlet of the wild, sparsely settled Chilcotin cattle country to the west—the country that Pan and I hoped to leave far behind us in our push into the unknown.

We engaged a room in a small, partially finished frontier hotel, and after a tough but successful battle with two extraordinarily well-muscled T-bone steaks, shoved our way into a beer parlor.

This dark pine-paneled room held a twenty-foot bar at one end, and about sixteen six-chair, rough-hewn log tables. The room was filled with friendly, white-bearded old cattlemen, remittance men from England, and ragged and patched cowhands who grinned and laughed and drank British Columbia's eight per cent beer on a large scale.

The happy-go-lucky company, all of whom seemed to know each other, kept buying Pan and myself beers until the table was covered with glasses. The bartender was a former cowhand. The atmosphere of the place was different from any western saloons or bars that I had ever been in. It was clublike, colorful and generous. In two hours' time we knew half the men in the room, and I counted the unbelievable number of seventy-two glasses of beer, in all stages of demolishment, on our table.

The following morning, slightly hung over, we walked down the main street through groups of buckskin-clad and beaded Indians, cowpunchers, and city-suited travelers. A number of our Stetson-hatted, riding-booted friends of the night before nodded and waved at us. Pan was grinning from ear to ear when we entered another beer parlor, called the Log Cabin, and sat down in a booth.

"This is our country, friend," he said. "Real cowman's country. The boys all comin' to town on their business, and out to have a good time, and that's all. Nobody tryin' to hide anything except the tough, long-houred, hard-ridin' jobs they've left behind 'em."

Working out our plans, we found that. after the purchases of grub, gas and oil necessary for our first push, our finances would have dwindled to about $400 cash between us.

How we would be able to buy the necessary string of horses, pack saddles and equipment needed to outfit and carry through with the exploration of a new country, located hundreds of miles beyond railroad and town, was a problem that looked insurmountable to me, but it didn't seem to worry Pan in the slightest.

"There'll be nothin' to it, friend," he said. "Just let me lay my hands on a few cayuses to start with, and I'll show these boys up here how to make it just by trading horses."

Big, ruddy-faced Pete Slavin, the proprietor, joined us in the booth. He told us that there was a road of sorts to Tatla Lake, at the far end of the Chilcotin, some 175 miles west of Williams Lake. He was satisfied that if we had no bad luck we could get the car that far.

Pete also told us that, after freeze-up in the early part of November, a snowfall usually terminated any further use of the road by car until spring. Obviously we were about to plunge into a back country, where distance and inaccessibility would compel us to remain for at least six months, before we would be able to get back to town again for equipment and supplies.

We worked out our list. We went over it many times, making changes and additions, and finally walked down to a store with the completed article.

Pan explained to me how much this list meant to us. Not a single article could be overlooked; even such small items as a sewing kit or extra repair leather, if forgotten, would cause us a hell of a lot of inconvenience. We have since used the same list with some additions as a check on necessary equipment, essentials to a pack train breaking into remote areas.

Here is the list:

2 double-bitted axes and extra handles
1 four-pound poleaxe
2 curved-backed, take-down model, Swede bucksaws
1 carpenter's saw
  claw hammer
  wrecking bar
  auger and assorted bits
  files and whet stone
50 pounds' assorted nails
5 pounds' horseshoe nails
  horse rasp and hoof cutters
  first-aid kit and sewing kit
  assorted leather snaps and pieces
  extra buckles and snaps and rings
  leather repair outfit
  half dozen gunnysacks
  pliers, cold chisel, blacksmith hammer
  horseshoes, kitchen utensils, water bucket

Grub

bacon	cornmeal
coffee	beans
sugar	dried apples
salt	dried milk
raisins	chocolate
macaroni	yeast
flour	soap
oatmeal	baking powder
rice	matches
cheese	candles

Early on the morning of October 20, the Bloater, loaded to the springs, crept westward into the Chilcotin. Tatla Lake was our objective. We didn't have the vaguest idea of what we were going to do when we got there. We did know that we were at last pushing into the frontier and that we would not see town again for a long time.

The trip through the Chilcotin to Tatla Lake took two days. Although the road was muddy in spots, and steep in others, still we considered it to be a good bush road. The country through which we passed varied considerably. At Riske Creek we traveled through a wide open prairie. The grass was grazed down close—too close—for the good of the range and the cows that would have to live off it the following year.

"Grazed off as bad as most open range in the States," commented Pan.

We rattled through a jackpine timber belt, then a partially open piece of grazing land. Stunted jackpine and bullpine replaced the poplars and firs of the lower Cariboo. Log ranchhouses and barns, many miles apart, indicated that the axe was playing a vital role in the building of this frontier.

East of Alexis Creek, the road wound and twisted through the lower contours of grassy rolling foothills, bordering a long lush meadow. Later we found that this was part of one of the largest Indian reserves in British Columbia. Years before this area had been the central camping spot of the Chilcotin Indians. Fierce, warlike members of this tribe traveled far into the north to liquidate rival tribes of coastal Indians.

Not many years before, massacres of white adventurers in the district had been the order of the day. But now, outside of an odd murder, the Chilcotins, with headquarters at the Anahim Rancheree, were content to quarrel only among themselves and carried on a relatively successful cattle- and horse-ranching business. The Chilcotin is an interior Indian, and bears little resemblance to the oriental type of coast Indian, or fisheater.

Perched on a flat-topped bench, the Anahim Rancheree presented a fantastic spectacle, a sordid contrast to the surrounding scenery. An expanse of dust-gray log shacks in various stages of decay and collapse reared ugly heads above frightening piles of litter and rubbish. Hundreds of half-wild, half-starved dogs crawled like vermin around and amongst the debris, gnawing and rooting through the filth for food. Dirty ragged children threw sticks and bones at the dogs. A freshly painted church with spires and steeples stood forgivingly among the ruins.

Pan slowed the Bloater to a stop. We didn't pause for long. A horde of ragged women, children and wrinkled old men picked their way through the garbage to the car, no doubt thinking we were peddling goods of some kind. I doubt whether any of them could read well enough to conclude that we were supposed to be purveyors of bloaters and blood sausages and bologna. Pan stepped on the gas, and we chugged slowly on, leaving the babbling, giggling mob behind.

Twenty miles west of a log-cabin trading post at Alexis Creek, Pan stuck the Bloater in what appeared to be a bottomless mudhole. Luckily a rancher, driving four horses and a wagonload of jackpine fence poles arrived on the scene. He unhooked his horses and pulled the Bloater to safety on a dry patch of hardpan road.

He was a lean, weather-beaten man with a hungry look. His pants and the lower part of a faded shirt were held together with binder twine and a huge horse-blanket pin. He gave me the impression that he had fought a long losing battle with these backlands.

He told us that we were now in Redstone, B.C., often the coldest spot on the North American continent; that the previous winter the official thermometer at Redstone recorded seventy-four below zero. I told Pan to make a mental note of this, and no matter what happened, we wouldn't end up in this part of the country.

The rancher sadly shook his head when we asked him about the distant Anahim Lake country. He told us we were crazy to go in there into that dark jungle land, where groups of law-dodging, half-wild men chased wild horses and lived on moose meat and muskrats.

Pan thanked the rancher for pulling us out of the mudhole, and for tipping us off on the Anahim country. He put the car in low and we bounced on west.

That evening we camped on the timbered shore of Tatla Lake. Looking northwest across the water, we saw in the vague distance a jagged mountain range, reaching in jumbled profusion above a black world of jackpine. Pan unfolded our map and studied it—then snorted loudly and stood up. He pointed to the range.

"There's the country. Sure as hell those are the Itchas."

The blue lake mirrored the dullness of gray dusk; a star or two twinkled out of the darkening sky. Pan walked to the edge of the lake and I followed him. He lit a cigarette and blew out smoke.

"Country north—unexplored—unknown. Maybe grass country—maybe most anything beyond those mountains. Next spring those pinnacles will be south instead of north of us."

We sat on the rocky shore. Night settled down around us. Out of pale endless space faintly drifted a long sad wail; lonely, hollow, unreal. Across the lake the echo caught and flung the sound again.

"Listen, Pan—what the hell's that?"

A long quivering cry gradually rose higher and higher, reached its zenith, and faded into hollow depth and black night.

"Wolves," said Pan—"a whole pack of them."

Almost in tune, a long sad chorus, rising out of the north and the silence of empty lands, proclaimed the eternal grievance of hairy brutes with empty bellies.

A stick cracked in the black bush behind us. In one movement, Pan whirled and whipped out his Smith & Wesson 44.

"You can't tell." The Top Hand spoke in a subdued voice. "This here is new country; it's better to be ready."

Then we could hear the sound. Softly a horse's hoofs on hardpan and rock moved towards us.

"Ho there," sounded a voice. "Somebody around here?"

Pan's gun settled back into its holster. A shadow, then a horse, appeared.

I said, "Howdy—we're here all right."

The rider twisted in his saddle.

"Seen your car—was ridin' on to Tatla."

"Come in," said Pan. "We'll brighten up the light right pronto."

Blazing fire cracked the darkness. Ten-minute coffee, strong and black, threw its smell from the lard pail into the air.

The lanky, black-haired rider was from Bob Graham's Tatla Lake ranch, two miles up the lake. He told us that a wagon road carried on west of Tatla Lake, and admitted that he knew of an odd car that had made it over the trail some seventy-five miles into the Anahim Lake country.

During the previous seven years, about twelve single men, most of them Americans, and several Canadians with their wives and families had moved into the Anahim area.

"They're havin' a tough time back there," said the rider. "I don't know that you boys will find much but swamps, jackpines, snow-balls and wolves. The men back there spend most of their time chasin' wild horses or runnin' down coyotes in winter. They've got a few cattle and lots of horses.

"They're a wild-and-woolly bunch, that Anahim crew, roamin' about in the jungle—only comin' out here to civilization about once a year."

Two long days, plugging ahead through mud, windfalls and up steep rocky hills, saw the obstinate, mud-encased Bloater roll to a stop a short distance from some old, barely visible holes, resembling caved-in trenches. We found out later that the rectangular holes were trenches dug not so very many years before by the road crew, battling for their lives against a band of Chilcotin Indians. The eighteen road men fought off the Indians for days, but were finally killed, their bodies left for the wild animals to devour.

The car was stuck hard and fast many times during those two days. Luckily Pan knew how to work what is known as a Spanish windlass, a pole and rope rig that he had used to pull cows out of bog and quicksand. By using this system it was possible time and time again to help the Bloater through mudholes and up steep inclines.

Later that evening the Bloater came to its final resting grounds on a little knoll overlooking a narrow, mud-bottomed creek. Our map showed it to be the headwaters of the Dean River.

The road from here on was not for us. Only a wagon or a pack outfit could travel it.

We strung up the tent, drained the water out of the radiator, and lit a fire a short distance from the stream.

CHAPTER III

Moose-hided Men of Anahim

THAT NIGHT bitter cold crept through the walls of the tent and into my bed. I shivered through the long hours of darkness.

In the morning, heavy frost had changed the forest world around us to a sparkling fairyland of flashing white lace. I shiveringly fried bacon and eggs with numbed fingers, while Pan cut, limbed and dragged in several dry jackpine trees for firewood.

Now it was time for us to make a few decisions. We had succeeded in winning our first objective, for Wyoming lay southeast of camp some two thousand miles, but although the Itcha and Algak barrier was now only fifty-odd bush miles away from us, lack of time for preparation, and heavy snows in the high peaks and canyons of the range, postponed all thought of tackling them until spring.

By the feel of the air it was obvious that winter was about to descend. A careful check of our grub supply revealed that in less than two months we would run out of everything but coffee and sugar and salt. Horses would have to be bought to replace the Bloater, and hay for the horses.

Our first and most urgent need was for a cabin. This should be built before the ground froze too hard. We planned to throw on a dirt roof, and knew that a cabin built on frozen ground would heave and crack and settle in every direction after breakup in the spring.

We agreed to start construction the next morning. According to Pan we could easily erect the cabin in two days. He claimed that he had built several up in the mountains in Wyoming some place, and knew how to improve on his last work.

"First thing at daylight we'll take an axe a piece and fall the trees over there across that swamp," said Pan, pointing to some lodgepole pine fifty yards away. "We'll need fifty logs, I figure. Then we'll each pack one end of a log, and tote them over the swamp on our shoulders. We'll square off the ground for the foundation, and then fit and notch those base logs—so that the foundation will be constructed by noon."

I looked carefully at Pan and then across at the big trees.

"It sure won't be much work to do that in half a day." I grimaced. "What next, Panhandle?"

"Let's see—oh yeah—right after lunch we'll put up the walls, and cut out a place for the door. The gable ends won't take long. Matter of fact, just a few minutes to notch and roll up those ends and stringers. We'll have to cut about thirty small, four-inch trees for the roof, drag them over, and set down the punchin'."

Pan thought a moment, and then bent swiftly over the fire to grab the coffee pot. It was boiling over. He burned his fingers, but pretended nothing had happened.

Hot coffee stimulated Pan to further optimistic calculations.

"To hell with the gable ends," he said. "We'll lay on just a shanty roof. That's it. After the punchin's set proper, we'll throw on about a foot of dirt on top of that much grass. One of us can cut slough grass with the big huntin' knife.

"The second day we can make a stove, a bunk, windows and floor, and any kind of finishin' work that's necessary."

I stood up.

"Yes, Pan, that sounds much more easy to do than I figured. I always thought it would take two men longer than two days to make the material, and build a house, and make the fixtures. Why, man, the way you tell it, we may be able to clean up the job in a day."

Pan again filled his tin cup with coffee.

"It's easy, Rich, mighty easy. Everythin's easy. It's just when a man thinks a job is hard and won't try that it's tough. No, sir, all a man needs is a small amount of brains, and enough strength to carry them up off the ground. Nothin' to it, boy, nothin' to it at all."

By the time the sun was near the middle of the sky, I was an exhausted wreck. Actually the two of us had cut, limbed and packed fifty green logs averaging about ten feet in length, and seven inches in diameter, through to the building site.

I started a fire and threw lunch together. Pan notched four logs and laid them in the grooves. The foundation was completed. Size of building now under construction, seven feet by eight. No more, no less.

Late in the afternoon I was earnestly cutting down slough grass with a hunting knife, when, looking up from my crouched position, I was startled to see a man watching me silently from a saddle horse.

He wore a long-visored, black beagle cap, a yellow wool shirt and moose-hide chaps. Bushy, junglelike, black hair sprung out in every direction from beneath his cap. It covered his ears.

The stranger grinned, then bellowed at me in a loud voice, "You'll have to work fast to beat the snow—horses eat lots of that stuff when it's cut late in the season—haw—haw—haw."

I was annoyed at the newcomer's humor, and curtly told him to ride around the bend and yell for a cup of coffee. A minute later I heard his loud voice, and then Pan's muffled answer. I continued cutting away at grass blades.

At last the hay was piled and packed into a canvas tarp, and I lugged it into camp. Pan was shoveling the dirt off a patch of sod, and the stranger was busy around the fire. The Top Hand had put him to work cooking supper.

Our first visitor, hard, powerful, loud-laughing Bert Leaman, had migrated into this backland two years before from the State of Washington. He owned six horses, four cows and three calves. His cabin was built on Cahoose Flats, ten miles west of us.

Bert's close-knitted, five-foot-ten-inch, 195 pound carcass was as strong as a three-year-old bull's. He had a big heart, but he was such a good-natured fellow that it got on your nerves. His ear-splitting laugh and his bellowing voice rang like a cannon through the silent jackpine land.

Inside his log cabin, where I later visited him, Bert's thundering laugh was terrific. The log walls quivered under it, my eardrums ached, and dishes on the shelves rattled. After a day with Bert, I found myself unconsciously laughing back at him—but my voice sounded weak and puny, and always before my giggle finished, it was completely submerged by Bert's continuation of his. It was kind of a laughing contest, with Bert a consistent winner.

Within a day of Bert's roaring departure from our camp, Anahim's mysterious moccasin telegraph went into action.

One of the spookiest phenomena of British Columbia's remote interior is this strange grapevine system. No one has yet given me a logical explanation of how Indians and frontiersmen, living in their widely separated and often isolated hangouts in the far reaches of Anahim's vast empire, receive messages or hunches about important events taking place in the country. But since then Pan and I have seen it happen many times.

Within two days of our arrival, frontiersmen thirty miles away felt that something of importance was taking place near the head-waters of the Dean River, and as their habits were much like nomads of the past, any excuse, at any time, to hit the trail was enough, and they crawled their horses and rode.

And so it happened, much to our own, as well as our limited grub supply's, surprise, that Bert's visit was the front end of a line of curious, coffee-hungry, talk-hungry riders who drifted into our camp at all hours of the day and night from every direction.

Wearing homemade, moose-hide chaps, moose-hide gloves and coats, hats of every description, torn and patched bright-colored wool shirts, and riding big, leggy, part-blooded horses, these men spoke a language of their own. Words, phrases and expressions had developed through their contact with one another, and were born out of incidents and mutual experiences encountered in their segregated lives.

Sixty-year-old Jim Holt—tall, dark, lean—carried a Texas accent.

The usual drawl was drawled out longer, slower, than with the natives of his home State.

Shorty King—a strange little hunchback, four feet tall, with a biting tongue and a dry sense of humor—had a fetish for big saddle horses.

Tommy Holte (no relation of Jim Holt's)—eighteen-year-old blond, blue-eyed, square-jawed, shy—lived with his family forty miles back through the jungle.

New Englander Cyrus Lord Bryant—middle-sized, middle-aged, bald-headed, keen-eyed, interested in world affairs—was addicted to eight cups of black coffee at a sitting.

Ole Nucloe Localo—twenty-five-year-old, wide-shouldered, straight-featured half-breed—was good-natured, always laughing. Ole had never seen a town in his life.

Billy Dagg—twenty-five years old, big, dark and humorous—was foreman of the biggest cattle ranch in the Anahim area, the Christenson spread.

Claire Munn—logger by trade, angular, brown-haired, dissatisfied with conditions everywhere—didn't know why he was throwing his life away back here.

Mac MacEwen—dark, agile, tall—was happy about it all.

Eddie Collett—thirty-year-old bronc rider, born in Merritt, B.C., of a well-known ranching family—was starting up a ranch of his own after being partners with George Powers of Charlotte Lake, twenty-five miles southeast of us.

Pan, in charge of construction, said howdy to each rider as he approached camp, and told him to throw on the coffee pot. I would quickly add that we were beating out the first blizzard. Then Pan would bark at me to quit talking and get to work. This always brought a laugh from the mounted stranger.

Pan would yell at the newcomer, "Get on the coffee, man, we're near dead for coffee, but we can't quit this work."

I kept a two-pound tin of coffee and a bucket of water in plain view of the fire. The rider would dismount, tie up his horse, chop some kindling, and soon the three of us would be squatting around the fire, gurgling coffee, commenting dryly on the weather, the low price of cattle, and the lawmakers who were forcing the rancher out of business in the States through government control and stupidity.

The night after we finished the cabin, no less than eight Anahim men sprawled about the fire.

Thirty-five-year-old Lester Dorsey, hailing from the State of Washington, wearing a silk stocking with a long tassel for a hat, and a gray tweed coat, was with us. Lester, big, bony-faced, baby-eyed, was a natural comedian. A top bush cowboy, he built a new ranch every two years, then always found another meadow bigger than his present one, and moved again.

Ronald Waite, born in London, six-foot-two, good-looking, with a British accent, was son of a well-to-do Englishman, had learned ranching in the Chilcotin, and was now starting a spread of his own.

I have yet to hear of any frontier that touched this Anahim country for hospitality. To a man, the ranchers invited us to—

"Come, boys, and hole up with me for the winter. I got horses, and we can split the grub bill."

Pan and I refused the thoughtful invitations because we believed it would leave us with a freer hand to organize and scout out our Itcha Mountains objective if we were independent.

We proudly pointed out our luxurious new home to the visiting cowmen. They were visibly impressed—I'm not saying how.

The stove was our happiest accomplishment. We had cut the ends out of two five-gallon coal-oil tins with a can opener, then fitted the tins together. They sat on top of an apple box filled with dirt. I cut a hole in top of the rear tin and inserted some stovepipe. Not having enough pipe, Pan cut out the bottoms of several four-pound jam tins, and finished out the chimney.

We hoped later to put a window in the cabin. The cracks between the logs were wide, and the wind blowing through them kept the house well aired.

The tin on the new stove folded in often, even after it was braced. We never could understand why the smoke leaked out into the cabin so much, but later found that most of it floated down from a hole in the north side of the roof. This Anahim smoke would, to all appearances, make it safely out through the stovepipe and the tin cans to the roof of the house, where, out of sheer meanness, it crossed the roof and dropped down through any available opening into the house again.

At times we were compelled to lie flat on the pole floor where smoke wasn't too thick and we could breathe.

We suffered from the smoke, the cold and the hard bunk for two nights before Pan got a brilliant idea.

"Friend," he said, "we're not doin' this thing right. Trouble is, it's not cold enough yet. This here cabin is built for real cold weather. We'll move back out to the tent and cook over the camp-fire until it colds up some—then we can move back into the cabin."

He beamed from ear to ear.

"Nothin' to it at all, boy. Everythin's easy if you just stop and figure it out." He paused for these words of wisdom to take hold, then continued, "Ya see, we're never stuck. Back in here we crawl when it gets real cold."

I shivered where I stood, balancing on a rather high pole, one of many which didn't sit flush with the rest of the flooring.

It was now two below zero. We'd wait for it to get cold, before moving back in the cabin.

Pan was busy whistling and carrying junk out to the tent. I followed with our bedrolls.

On the second of November, the thermometer plunged to thirty below zero. Cooking in the dark over the fire (we had been frozen out of bed), I shiveringly asked Pan if he thought it was cold enough to move back in the cabin.

The Top Hand leaned against his usual tree. His teeth were chattering with cold.

"No, Rich—that's not the idea at all. We moved out here to harden ourselves up so we can take this here B.C. winter like men, not like shiverin' rats. Look at you now—why man, your face is frosted near white, and you're stutterin' with cold. I ain't too warm myself. No, friend, we ain't toughened ourselves up yet."

He paused for breath, then continued, "Soon both of us will be hard, can stand the cold. We'll be trained, and can walk in that there house like men, knowin' we can take it—and besides it's not colded up much anyway."

I thought this over. It was now apparent to me that Pan didn't like living in the smokehouse. I must have been soft all right. I still remember how cold I was that first week at Anahim.

We chinked the smokehouse by stuffing moss between the cracks against little, fitted poles. The mercury had climbed to zero and it was snowing hard. I had a hunch Pan was on the verge of giving in and was now thinking up an excuse to move back into the house, when we looked up to see Cyrus Lord Bryant riding into camp, leading five horses tied head to tail behind him.

We both yelled "howdy" at the same time; I started for the coffee pot, and Pan stepped forward to hold the loose halter shank of the lead horse while Bryant stepped down.

The bright-eyed rancher was very serious and acted as though he had something important on his mind. He tied his big black bald-faced horse to a tree and strode hurriedly to the cabin, followed by Pan. Bryant swung our sad-looking door open and took one sweeping glance around the cabin, and grunted,

"Thought so—yeah—just what I thought."

At the fire Cyrus Lord lifted off his Stetson and shook an inch of snow off the brim. He still didn't say anything, or respond very cheerfully to Pan's cracks about the weather.

I began to think that we might have offended the rancher in some way the last time he'd been in our camp; however, after thoughtfully drinking down two cups of coffee, he faced us and came immediately to the point.

"You two young idiots plan to live in that cabin this winter. Am I right?"

He looked at the Top Hand. Pan smiled.

"Oh sure, we'll move into that palace after it gets cold or the weather gets bad." He brushed the snow off his coat.

Cyrus Lord snorted.

"Now you boys pull yourselves together and listen to common sense. This isn't Wyoming. This is central British Columbia. We're near the Fifty-third Parallel at thirty-eight hundred feet elevation. The temperature may drop to sixty below zero, and hang between thirty and fifty below for days at a time.

"That little pile of poles can't hold heat for an hour. Now I'm telling you both the truth when I say that there will come a morning when you won't wake up, neither of you. You'll sleep all that day and the next. Boys, you'll be froze stiff in your beds, and I'll be damned if I'll start digging holes in frozen ground to bury you."

Bryant stopped for a moment while he poured himself another cup of coffee. Pan rubbed his hands together and held them over the fire. He watched the rancher, who stirred his coffee, poured it out into another cup, repeated the operation, then blew furiously at the still-steaming stuff. He stuck in his finger, grunted happily and swallowed the contents.

Burping slightly, Cyrus Lord continued, "I'm living five miles north of this flat. There's only my boy, Alfred, and myself there. The girls are out at Williams Lake with their mother getting civilized. Alfred and I like company, we've got all the horses that four men can ride, and a lot extra besides.

"You two sure aren't proving anything to anybody including yourselves by toughing it out. Now roll your beds, pack your grub, as much as these horses can handle on this trip, and come on home with me."

Cyrus Lord said no more. He walked over to the horses with the packsaddles and started to cinch them up tight. Pan scratched his head, looked after Bryant, and then at the Wyoming Flats cabin.

"Smart idea," I mumbled, and without giving Pan a chance to turn down the proposition, hopped over the fire, and dashed for the tent, where I quickly pulled up the pegs, allowing it to collapse.

Snow was falling thick, blanket-like, purring as it piled up over everything. Finally mounted and leading the pack horses behind, Pan called ahead to Bryant who had taken the lead.

"It sure looks like we had the right idea about building that cabin. If we'd had a few more days and a team, we'd have made a bigger shack, and a better-finished one, but we had a hunch about this here weather and figured we had to get it set up before a storm. We laid her up on time. It's a good shack—it'll always be there to come home to."

CHAPTER IV

Pioneers of the Wild Interior

THE ANAHIM LAKE COUNTRY, its sullen forests recently echoing the shots of explorers who had fought and died there, is a dark and forbidding land, jealously guarding its immense boundaries from men creeping north and west from the rim of civilization.

Here—locked away in the solitary regions of this continent's last great cattle front—families like the Bryants were enduring hardships, facing climatic conditions and fighting natural land barriers in many ways greater than those our pioneer ancestors encountered in opening up the western plains.

Cyrus Lord Bryant is one of that visionary, doggedly independent breed of men who have opened up our tougher frontiers. Twelve years earlier, with his wife and four children, he had driven a wagon and six horses nearly a thousand miles from southern Washington into the interior of British Columbia.

They were on the trail for months. It was a tough trip. Winter cracked down on them suddenly and without warning. A harsh blizzard swished down out of the northeast before the little family in the wagon had reached Alexis Creek. Cyrus' driving hand, his left one, froze almost solid inside of his inadequate leather glove.

It was growing dark when he swung his leaders around a narrow bend high up on the edge of a deep ravine east of Alexis Creek. The rear wheels of the wagon slipped on the icy road. The outfit slewed out so close to the edge of the precipice that one hind wheel dipped for an instant over space.

A gnawing wind stabbed the forty-below-zero weather into the huddled bodies of Mrs. Bryant and the children. They bunched together around a coal-oil lantern beneath the wagon tarp.

At last, when their limbs were almost past the hurting stage and a sleepy numb feeling was creeping in on them, Bryant hauled the horses to a stop near the log cabins of Alexis Creek. Mrs. Bryant and the children were rushed into a rancher's house for frost treatment, and Cyrus took care of the ice-caked, frost-covered horses. Bryant left the coal-oil lantern burning beneath the wagon to keep their food from freezing.

Inside that oversized wagon box were the family's precious and most priceless possessions: family portraits, oil paintings handed down through the family for generations, Mrs. Bryant's jewelry and music—she was a gifted pianist and singer—Cyrus' pocketbook with a considerable sum of money. Their life savings to be invested in their future ranch and stock were carefully wrapped in oil paper and locked in a little fishing box. There were rare old books, the family's winter clothes, their winter's provisions, tools, saddles and extra harness. All these things added together were to be the start, the foundation of their new home and new way of life.

In the dark fifty-below-zero dawn of the following day, Cyrus Lord kicked the black hissing ashes of what had once been that wagon box. He rooted out a fifty-cent iron wrecking bar, an axe head and a few well-tempered horseshoes. That was all.

The coal-oil lantern had touched off the load.

The Bryant family was in a position that was more than critical. Here—without money—in a strange country, with winter upon them, Cyrus, his wife and his four children pitched blindly into the toughest proposition of their lives.

A rancher advanced them grub and what clothing they could get by on. Cyrus cut and hauled logs out of the bush, and in a month's time had built a two-room cabin for the family. Later they moved on to Tatla Lake.

For years every member of the family worked from dawn to

dark. In the Chilcotin, Cyrus hired out with his well-broke teams for cash, cows, sheep or vegetables. Mrs. Bryant helped shear the sheep, cleaned, carded and spun wool garments for the family and the neighbors. Thirteen-year-old Alfred worked with an axe, a saddle horse and a rifle. The girls became as good as men at riding jobs and axe work.

After nearly four years of ceaseless privation and work, the family had once again outfitted themselves. With two wagons, a dozen cows and eighteen head of horses, they axed their way through the bush to a swamp meadow five miles from Anahim Lake.

Here, on the banks of a twisting mud creek named Corkscrew, the family threw their combined strength into the building up of a new home and their future ranch. They worked steadily and un-relentingly for two more years. The girls axed down trees, bucked up wood, made new clothes out of moose hide, and patched old ones with gunny sacks and binder twine, moose hide and rabbit fur.

Mrs. Bryant put everything she had into making a home for her family. She had little to cook with—the vegetable garden wouldn't grow in the new and sour land. Alfred eked out their supplies of coffee, spuds and flour by contracting and driving pack trains for his neighbors a hundred miles down a narrow trail through the bush to the tiny fishing village of Bella Coola on the coast, where he picked up their supplies brought in from Vancouver by boat.

In 1931 there was no money at all in the country. A big twelve-hundred-pound steer brought two and a half cents a pound at the Vancouver market. Freight and feed from Williams Lake to Van-couver absorbed any cash returns. There was no work on that frontier as there was nobody to work for, and no relief, for these staunch frontiersmen were not the type to accept it. There were only six other pioneer families at that time in an area as big as the State of Maine, but located over two hundred miles from the nearest town.

By the spring of 1934, the year of our arrival in the country, the Bryants had, through their courage, determination and terrific work, pulled themselves up and out of the almost bottomless hole into which the wagon fire had plunged them twelve years before.

Already their herd of whiteface cattle had increased to nearly a hundred head, and they ran nearly fifty head of saddle, work and pack horses. The Bryant women decided to spend a year out in civilization. They leased a cottage in Williams Lake and opened up a cake and pastry shop. Jane went south to study medicine and nursing. At the present time Alfred was driving a pack train to the coast for their neighbors, the Christensons.

We had ridden single file on a well-used pack trail through jackpines and lodgepole pine for about an hour and a half, when Cyrus reined in his bald-faced saddle horse on a wide snow-covered opening. He waited for us to ride up to him.

I could see the rancher was excited. He pointed to a narrow, obviously man-made ditch that cut in a straight line through the snow in front of us.

"There she is!" he said. "There's the ditch! That's what made this place. Drain ditches!"

He paused and, turning in his high-cantled saddle, pointed up the opening.

"Three quarters of a mile of her. Used to be a swamp. Couldn't ride a saddle horse out here without bogging. Now this land grows tons of the best wild redtop and bluejoint cattle feed in the county.

"Ditches—ditches—that's what's going to make this country. Thousands of acres of useless swamp and muskeg land and shallow lakes. Nearly all of it can be drained. That's Anahim's secret!"

Cyrus Lord paused for breath, lifted his hat and shook the snow off the brim.

"Three to four acres of this old lake bed or swamp bottom will carry one cow. Someday this backland will be a great stock country. You'll see!"

Bryant stopped talking as suddenly as he had started. He whirled his saddle horse towards the ditch, bucked his horse across it, and carried on across the opening.

We had traveled about a half mile on the snow-covered meadow when I saw, through the falling snow, a long, shake-roofed, log house standing on a spruce-covered knoll. The horses trotted up in a knotted bunch trying to crowd each other into a lope, and we held them back.

We splashed in a body across an open creek, and up into the

Bryants' log-fenced yard. A short distance away, a high hip-roofed barn nestled among a group of gigantic silver spruce. A log corral system spread from the barn down a slope to the creek. Everywhere about us sprouted the evidence of careful planning and hard work.

We caught, tied the horses to a twenty-five foot hitch rail in front of the long axe-hewn porch that ran the length of the house, and while Pan and I unpacked, Cyrus Lord started the fire, and put on the coffee pot.

Cyrus Lord didn't seem to be particularly impressed by the fine job he and his family had obviously made of house building, but as we sipped coffee from large white china mugs, around a big, broad-axed plank table near the stove, he carried on with his rapid-fire, short-sentenced eulogy on draining and developing the vast marginal lands of the Anahim country.

I looked about at the structure that was to be Pan's and my second British Columbia home. It was quite unlike our first one. The walls of huge peeled jackpine logs were thirty-eight feet long on one side and about twenty-eight feet wide on the other. Hand-hewn log partitions divided it into three rooms. The building was chinked with little peeled poles and moss. The floor had been made by splitting ten-inch logs through the middle, and hewing the split sides level with a broadaxe. They were laid flush with each other, the flat sides up, and to save nails, Cyrus Lord had pegged them to a row of log stringers, and then polished them with linseed oil. This floor was smooth enough to dance on.

The only evidence that showed that this log house was located more than 225 miles from shops and railroad was the complete lack of ornaments, upholstered furniture, spring beds and heavy equipment. Freighting-in bulky or heavy paraphernalia by pack horse or wagon is a frustrating and discouraging business. It is impossible to average more than fifteen miles a day on a 450 mile round trip. A load of two tons, which is plenty for a four-horse team to lug over the hills, rocks and mud flats of the interior, becomes a mighty valuable poundage, when finally landed at Anahim more than a month after the freighter started out.

Although the Bryants' terrific, unrelenting and well-directed

energy was evident everywhere about us, the earmarks of this remote and cashless frontier were easy to read.

The following day Cyrus assigned Pan and me our string of
three saddle horses apiece. He generously turned them over to us
to use as long as we needed them.

As soon as I saw the horses I recognized my top horse. He was
a tall, long-geared, white gelding, going by the name of Slats. Slats
had a gentle nature. He towered seventeen hands off the ground,
you needed an elevator to get up on his back, but in spite of his
height he was trim legged and active enough to buck over windfalls
and to cut out cattle. I fell for Slats as soon as I saw him. He was
slightly wall-eyed, and very serious-minded.

Pike, Pan's top horse, was a thousand-pound dark bay cayuse
with fair action. He looked as if he could run, had a fair sense of
humor, and was one of Slat's most intimate friends.

Cyrus Lord wanted us to meet Andy Christenson, one of Anahim's first pioneers, and its biggest cattle rancher. He particularly
wanted us to see the swamp land Christenson had drained.

It took us about forty-five minutes at a fast trot to reach the edge
of the Christenson opening some five miles west of Bryant's. The
Christenson buildings gave one the impression that they were
perched on the top of a high mesa, overlooking the parklike country and the jackpine hills which rolled away in three directions to
distant mountain ranges. It was kind of an optical illusion, for
actually the ranch was not over fifty feet above the surrounding
land.

To the south, the highest mountains in British Columbia, the
Mystery Mountains, the Waddington Group, rose to over thirteen
thousand feet elevation in a series of white spires. The Waddington
Group melted into a dreamy white range which swung northward
forming the impressive battlements and towers of the Coast Range,
walling in Anahim to the west.

I was almost overwhelmed by the magnitude of the distant world
of rock and snow. Pan and Bryant must have been affected in the
same way. We were about to ride into the Christenson yard, when
they reined their horses about and faced the awesome panorama
in silence.

To the north of us and reaching east, the towering walls of the

Algaks were overshadowed by the ominous crags and domes of the impregnable Itcha mountain range.

Andy Christenson met us at the door, and told us to put our horses in the barn, throw them some hay and come on in.

Andy ran a successful store business in Bella Coola, trailed beef from his ranch direct to his butcher shop there, traded clothes and supplies to the Indians for fur, and ran five hundred head of beef cattle. He maintained a twenty-horse pack train which was in almost constant motion on the Bella Coola trail.

Andy looked more like a bank manager than a rancher. An average-sized man, about forty years of age, fair-complexioned, with wide blue eyes that looked questioningly at you from behind gold-rimmed spectacles, he wore tweed suits, smoked cigars and played a winning game of poker.

Andy's attractive young wife Dorothy was slim and auburn-haired. Her finely chiseled features and quiet voice seemed out of place here in this rugged man's land. But Dorothy was the daughter of John Clayton, British Columbia's renowned factor, who had bought out the Hudson's Bay post at Bella Coola, and her pioneer heritage showed itself in her sparkling sense of humor, her versatility and the ease with which she ran a large household under frontier conditions.

It was a dark night towards the end of November, when, outside of Bryant's house, many hoofs pounding the hard snow urged us hurriedly out into the night with lanterns to help Alfred catch and unpack his train.

He had eight horses, packing over two hundred pounds apiece, and from the look of them, and of Alfred, I judged the round trip of 190 miles to and from Bella Coola had been a hard one. Silently we unloaded the horses and threw them hay. In the house we shook hands with the wide-built, black-haired packer who grinned when Cyrus Lord informed him we were two Wyoming society men, spending our winter vacation in their guest room.

We sat around the stove until after one o'clock, laughingly talking of range cows and tough trails, slough grass and swamp meadows, until at last, groaning with exhaustion, Alfred poured down his tenth cup of coffee, staggered apologetically to his bunk, removed his shoes and collapsed.

CHAPTER V

Moose—Hundreds of Them

IF YOU ASKED an Anahim frontiersman how he managed to stick it out during the lean years when he was building up his small herd of cattle, and had no other source of income except the beef he drove to market every other year, he would invariably answer you with one word—"moose."

The moose is about as important to the meat-eating, moose-hided pioneers at Anahim, as the caribou is to the caribou-hided Eskimo of the arctic.

A big, full-grown, interior bull moose will weigh between thirteen hundred and sixteen hundred pounds on the hoof. Nearly every pound of his carcass is used except his skull and hoofs. His bones are boiled into soup, his brains, tongue, liver and heart are considered delicacies by most settlers. They can, dry, smoke, and in winter, freeze every ounce of his coarse-grained meat.

Before rutting season in the fall, a fat bull moose carries from sixty to ninety-five pounds of tallow on his frame. This whitish grease is used as lard for cooking purposes, butter, sandwich spread, and as a basis for soap.

His sinew is strong and, when cured and treated properly, makes excellent sewing-material, string and harness thread. The possession of moose hide is a must among these isolated pioneers. Moccasins and other types of high-legginged footwear are shaped and sewed to order for its owner. Coats, vests, shirts, chaps, skirts, mattresses and bed coverings, are essentials that only the moose could provide.

For ten months out of the year, Anahim was one of the most densely populated moose areas on the continent.

The rugged sixty thousand square-mile chunk of swamp, pine, willow and mountain, stretching from the Fraser and Nechako rivers west to the Pacific Ocean, between the Fifty-second and Fifty-fourth parallels is ideal moose country. Near Anahim, vast interwebbing slough grass swamps, bounded by black willows, reach mysteriously back into a labyrinth of slow-moving sloughs and lagoons and dark spruce jungles. Scattered here and there among the willow brakes and spruce swamps, small, lily-padded, mud-bottomed lakes add to the ominous monotony of this dank spidery land.

For some unknown reason this made-to-order moose country was inhabited by caribou instead of moose up to 1914, when the first big flat-horned animals were seen browsing in a swamp near George Powers' Charlotte Lake ranch. Within a few years moose were migrating into the country by the thousands, and the caribou were vanishing equally as rapidly. In 1934, the only remaining caribou were reported by the Indians to be banded up in the mountain fastnesses of the Algak and Itcha mountains.

Moose had then become so numerous and so bold that ranchers were forced to pack guns on their hay sleds for protection when the animals were rutting in October; and in June, after the arrival of the calves, the settlers took care to avoid the dangerously maternal cow moose.

Coming in contact with moose almost daily for ten months of the year, the Anahim frontiersmen learned much about their habits.

They found that the moose preferred country inhabited by beaver; that wherever the little engineer and woodcutter went, the moose soon followed. Both animals eat almost identical food: willow tops, poplar bark and small limbs, buck brush and swamp birch. And moose, like beaver, prefer mud and water where they can remain submerged, all but their heads, away from flies and mosquitoes on hot days.

Early in the spring, moose sometimes browse on slough grass and wild redtop if the old bottom has been burned off.

Moose are near-sighted. They cannot see far or too well, but, in keeping with their long noses, have a specially sensitive sense of smell, and a good sense of hearing, and at certain times of the year absolutely no sense of humor.

Contrary to the generally accepted theory that moose don't herd up, but wander about singly, in pairs, or in small groups, the old-timers found that at certain times of the year the moose band up and migrate to special types of terrain at different altitudes. For instance, bulls are run out of the calving country at lower swamp levels late in May and early in June by the cows. The males then throw in together and drift back into the mountains where they stag it for most of the summer.

Early in September the stag party breaks up. Bulls leave the willow brush and grassy feeding grounds and hunt out solitary hideouts. The hiding grounds are generally located in inaccessible country, where down timber is piled high and the terrain checker-boarded with black stinking mud and deadly muskeg—a night-marish land, devoid of feed.

Here, isolated in desolate surroundings, the lonely bull moose goes through a strange transformation. Gradually the sleek black animal changes from a cautious, timid creature who trots off at man's approach, to a red-eyed maddened brute, ready to charge at any object that attracts his attention, a man, a horse or a freight train

It takes from seven to fourteen days of self-inflicted starvation before this Mr. Hyde-like giant reappears as a fly-bitten, half-starved Dr. Jekyll of a creature, his huge muscled chest and bulging shoulders tapering to a shrunken belly and sinewed hindquarters.

Heavy frosts and cold nights bring the bull moose out into the open to test out his changed body on windfalls and trees which he smashes down with his horns. He sharpens his hoofs to razor-like edges on rocks; then, chanting his frightening but monotonous call, he roars down the mountains in search of the cow herds, pre-pared to battle anything that crosses his trail.

It is at this stage of the game that young bulls are the most dangerous. Equally unpredictable and dangerous is the rogue bull, a frustrated old warrior who has been decisively whipped by younger animals and has been driven by them out of the cow herds. The lone rogue goes off by himself to some little-traveled spot, and lies in wait for any two- or four-legged animal that may pass by.

Late in the fall—generally after the first heavy snow—the moose invariably vanished. Where they went, nobody knew. In tough winters, if several feet of snow covered the ground, they would reappear in great numbers and dig into the ranchers' haystacks.

This was one of those light-snow winters when the moose had migrated out of the country and hadn't come back.

The situation had become serious. Several Indian and white families had become dangerously hungry without their basic moose-meat diet, and everyone had been without meat for a month and a half. Your system needs meat and fat to fight the cold and carry on with the heavy work required to survive in this country.

A council was held at Cyrus Lord Bryant's house. The older heads agreed that something had to be done immediately. A hunting party was organized. Alfred Bryant, Bert Leaman, hunchback Shorty King, Pan and myself were instructed to take a pack train in search of moose and not return to Anahim until we had loaded our pack string with meat and hides.

The day before our hunting party hit the trail, Pan rode to Cahoose Flats to help Bert Leaman drive his cattle and horses to Bryant's where Cyrus would feed and take care of them during Bert's absence. Lester Dorsey was looking after Shorty's few head of stock.

Old-timers agreed that the most logical country to look for the moose was either in the Algak Range or the Itchas. The boys had decided on the Itchas as our first objective. If we found no moose in these mountains, the idea was to manoeuvre the outfit through the upper swamp levels west into the Algaks.

Alfred was elected guide since he had hunted further back towards the Itchas than other Anahim men. Even the Indians seemed to draw a blank when it came to information on the breath-taking billowy white world that sprawled high across the sky on Anahim's northern horizon.

Alfred, Shorty and I started throwing the trail outfit together. Our grub consisted of mixed flour and baking powder for bannock, rice, sugar, coffee and salt. We lined up packsaddles and rigging for fifteen horses.

Horse feed would be our biggest problem. Snow would be deep on the mountains, and horses would have little chance to fill their bellies during the few hours' rest, by pawing through the snow for grass.

Because of Anahim's isolation, and the terrific cost of freight, grain was a seldom-used luxury. Thirteen of the pack horses would have to transport on their backs as much hay as its bulk would permit.

Alfred harnessed up a team, hitched it to a nine-by-eighteen-foot hayrack, and with ninety empty gunny sacks, a three-cornered sack needle and a roll of moose-hide sinew, drove Cyrus Lord, Shorty and myself over to the Bryants' best stack of green redtop hay.

The idea was to crowd as much hay into each gunny sack as it would hold. The first few sacks were ridiculously light, and certainly contained little hay. Then Alfred had an idea.

He stood up from a half-filled sack and, looking at Cyrus and myself, said, "What the hell's the matter with us? Here we've got this peewee Shorty King, and we're not using him to advantage."

"The devil you're not," snapped Shorty from the haystack. "I'm doin' all the hard work—I'm throwin' the hay down."

"Come on down here," Alfred snapped at him. "Dad can do that."

"You bet your life," said Shorty. He stuck the pitchfork in the side of the stack, and using it for a handhold, swung down to the snow.

"Grab him," said Alfred. "We're gonna use him as a tamper in each gunny sack."

Alfred and I grabbed hold of Shorty and stuffed his wiggling miniature frame feet first into the sack.

"Hold on to our shoulders now," said Alfred.

Shorty complied, and Alfred and I lifted and shook the sack with Shorty in it until the hay was packed down into the bottom in a hard mass. Cyrus pitched down more hay. We refilled the sack.

It took a few hours of using Shorty as a movable piledriver to stuff ninety gunny sacks.

We were up long before daylight the following morning. Each man had his respective job to do. Alfred wrangled the horses, Cyrus cooked the usual bannock, boiled rice and coffee for breakfast, and the rest of us laid out the packs.

With baling wire we squeezed two gunny sacks together, making a bundle. By using extremely long lash ropes we were able to diamond hitch an average of three-and-a-half bundles on a horse. Ready for the trail, each animal looked as if he were toting a small tarp-covered mountain.

We were a bulky and weird-looking outfit as we strung north out of Anahim towards the distant Itchas with Alfred in the lead.

Most of the first day was spent axing out a trail wide enough to get the packs through. On the second day we bucked the pack horses over great piles of windfalls to a frozen muskeg that stretched to the base of the mountains.

Alfred rode his horse cautiously along its edge with the train strung out behind him. We slid and skidded across a frozen creek, bypassed a spruce jungle, and came out on what looked like a huge open meadow. Grass protruded a foot above the snow in spots.

We made camp that night at the far end of the opening. This was a break for us and the horses. We saved one night's hay. It was good pawing and the cayuses got a bellyful of grass.

The following day we pushed the train through to what is known in this country as the second swamp level—a long series of slough grass swamps that web together on south-tilted benches at an elevation of about 4,200 feet above sea level.

Along the western side of this continent, one of nature's well-patterned phenomena is the way the timberline drops to lower elevations as it slants northward. In California's High Sierras, near the Thirty-sixth Parallel, gnarled wind-blown trees cease to exist above 11,500 feet. Further north in Wyoming's wind-swept Tetons at the Forty-second Parallel, timber doesn't creep much above the 10,500 foot level. Here in the Itchas at the Fifty-third Parallel, the line of timber clings to the five thousand foot contour.

If you can get a pack train up the south slope of a range to the second swamp level, the thousand foot elevation between it and timberline can usually be negotiated without too much windfall- and timber-dodging.

For hours Alfred twisted and wound back and forth between the willow-fringed swamps towards the main mountain range, with the long line of horses and moose-jacketed men weaving in and out behind him. Late in the evening we skirted a narrow burned-over ridge where a close-knitted, barkless mass of fire-killed trees, almost identical in size, stretched east across the snow like a vast line of gigantic matchsticks.

Just before dark that night we came to the first moose signs—and they were not pleasant ones. The bones, bloody hair and skulls of a cow moose and her calf were strewn about a much-trampled and disorderly circle.

Wolf tracks, some of them the size of small plates, had trampled the snow down to a hard-packed mass around the dead bodies. Several snow brush trees were torn up and smashed down. All signs confirmed the short one-sided battle that had taken place.

We kept the pack train moving.

"The same old story!" Bert yelled. "Those big black northern wolves workin' on the game. More wolves every year—less game. Give 'em time and they'll be cleanin' out our cattle."

Shorty King spoke bitterly, "They killed two of my best cows this fall—hamstrung 'em and left 'em there, kicking."

The following day we rode out onto a high plateau near timberline. Alfred turned in his saddle and yelled back to us.

"We've trailed them down—they were here only a few days ago. Look at the tracks."

Old moose sign and tracks crisscrossed the crusted snow.

We made camp under some stunted spruce in a narrow draw, protected from the wind. There was an hour of daylight left. Shorty King, horse wrangler, kicked the horses above camp where he would let them paw through the foot of snow for grass until dark.

Pan spread our old map on a canvas before the fire and we bent over it. The nearest surveyed areas shown on the map were the few sections of land around the Christenson ranch at Anahim Lake. Alfred figured we were camped near the headwaters of Corkscrew Creek. There was an arrow on a fine line pointing south from the southwest face of Itcha Cairn, a triangulation point, with Corkscrew Creek written along the line. There were three or four named peaks. Nearly all the rest of the map showed a blank space.

The next day we split in two bunches. Alfred and I rode east along the open stretches of the south face of the range, the other boys rode west. None of us got a glimpse of a moose that day, and all tracks proved to be several days old. At our common camp that night Alfred said that the moose must be banded north of us some place. Pan agreed with him.

"They sure ain't took wings and flown away," he said. "So boys, those moose are sure as hell north of where we're sittin'!"

We were blessed with a good run of weather. The next morning the pale sky was tinged with red streaks, and the world of rock and snow above timberline turned to pink blood as the distant sun broke over the green carpet of timber far below us.

We swung in two groups in wide arcs towards the north and the peaks of the Itchas. As we rode out of camp our saddle horses suddenly tensed, their ears stood erect. Alfred's horse began to dance.

From far to the north of us drifted a strange lonely wail, rising in bell-like clearness to a high quivering note, and fell off gradually into the silence. We tried to hold our spooked horses down to a walk as the air suddenly vibrated with the combined chorus of a vast pack of northern wolves. The strange wails stopped as suddenly as they had started.

"There's where the moose are," grunted Alfred. "Just follow the wolf packs."

Now the going was rough and steep. Alfred and I took turns breaking trail up the face of a high ridge. I was riding Slats. Alfred rode Coyote, a bald-faced bucking horse whose color seemed to change with the variation of the landscape. Today it was hard to place him either as mouse-colored or roan.

Alfred finally took the lead and kept it, so as to give Coyote something to think about other than downing his head and plunging into a series of high-crooked pitches, with which stunt he had just about unseated the packer twice in two miles.

This range was deceiving. Every time we thought we were about to climb over the last summit, we found another higher one ahead of us. Finally we skirted a mass of high peaks and cliffs to the west, and for the first time paused on a slope which appeared to be on the north rim. Coyote had gained about twenty-five yards on

Slats, and Alfred swung him in a half circle and stopped, facing northeast.

I finally got up the incline and pulled up alongside of the packer who remained solemnly gazing down into a valley below. He said nothing. I looked down and gasped. My heart pounded.

"Good Lord— Look! It's unbelievable."

Alfred smiled easily,

"There they are, boy—just the tail end of them."

We were on a long bare ridge about a half mile above the first of a series of valleys running east and west, parallel with the summits of the Itchas. The lower side of each valley fell off into the next, forming a gigantic staircase, each white-carpeted step dropping at least five hundred feet on the lower side into the next valley. At the west end of the valley series, they all ended at the base of a titanic gray tower of solid granite, rising in a sheer cliff at least two thousand feet towards the sky, where its miles of perpendicular face stopped abruptly at the base of a perfect cone-shaped spire.

Halfway up the cone, a thin line of tiny black specks, like the points on a fine hacksaw blade, moved across its face so slowly that, unless watched closely, it hardly appeared to have changed position.

"Caribou," said Alfred. "That's the way they graze through the snow, in a thin line, one behind the other. Then they'll come together and maybe move forward in fan shape or like a V with the leader at the point."

With my field glasses we got a better look at them.

But it was the bottom of the basin that interested us most. At least three thousand feet below the thin line of moving caribou on the cone, in the floor of the basin, and moving about much like tiny black ants in the bottom of a shining white bathtub, were vast herds of moose. I had never heard or read of hundreds of moose being banded up together like this.

Visible to the naked eye were fifty-four animals in the upper end of the first valley, the one directly below us. Off to the east, tiny pinpoints on the white surface of the snow could barely be made out where the herds vanished into snowy distance.

We could not see down into the other valleys from this point, but later witnessed group after group of the brisket-belled, antlerless bull moose scattered along the banks and upper edges of the second valley.

I had a camera along and took pictures. If the animals had shown up more clearly, there would have appeared herds of caribou and herds of moose, each grazing or resting in its own peculiar native habit, all in the same photograph.

Alfred grunted with satisfaction and, with his hackamore, neck-reined Coyote about, facing me.

"Well—there walks meat for Anahim. The rest is easy."

He paused for a moment while he found his tobacco and papers. I watched him slip out a cigarette paper and, holding it directly above his head, let it go. It floated straight downward for a moment, then with a vague fluttering settled ten feet north of the horse and a bit to the west.

"That's plain enough," I said. "We're working on the wrong side of the valley."

Alfred looked down at the moose again.

"It's best to angle down towards the foot of the cliff, then swing across the floor of the valley, and once we get the wind in our favor, if we don't first scare them out of the country, we can stalk up close enough for a cinch-bet shot. I don't like to see these dudes or smart Indians taking these three hundred yard shots, unless there's no other way out. These long shots cripple two animals to every one killed.

"No sir, I like to get up close, maybe a hundred yards, then I know there's going to be meat. I could eat the tail end out of a skunk right now," he added.

We started angling down the slope, gradually working west towards the base of the granite cliff. Alfred in the lead spoke back to me over his shoulder.

"I guess this is going to be your first moose, Rich."

"If I get one, it's my first," I answered.

"Well—I'll tell you, you are in for a lot of fun. This moose hunting on a horse in the snow is real big sport. Just wait, you'll see. How does that 30-06 Winchester carbine please you?"

"I take a half bead in this buckhorn sight," I answered, "and to me it's the best gun I've ever used. I like a bolt action myself, but everybody's different."

Alfred reached across his saddle with his right hand towards the butt of his 250-3000 Savage take-down model. I guess he was going to show me a trick way of cross-drawing a gun from the saddle, but his hand never quite reached the butt of his gun.

With one quick spring to the right, Coyote seemed to gather his close-knit body in a ball, and when his feet hit the ground, he pitched high and crooked, snapping his hind legs above his head which had gone out of sight between his front legs.

There was no rider, being caught off balance to start with, who could have stayed that sudden vicious twisting plunge. Alfred seemed to be suspended in air a long moment before he disappeared in the snow. Coyote swung completely about and bucked straight up the hill with the stirrups flying high above the saddle.

I glanced in Alfred's direction, and saw him moving up out of the snowbank. There was no time to be lost. Slats just outran Coyote enough to cut off direction. The roan made a mistake. He swung up towards the shoulder of the mountain, and in doing so stepped on the dragging hackamore rope. I had him.

By the time we reached the valley floor, all the moose that had been in sight on the upper part had disappeared like magic. We dipped down between several low draws, and crossed to the far ridge. Here I suddenly got my first close glimpse of moose in a herd.

Seventeen of the animals, caught unawares by our downwind approach, and at first thinking no doubt we were also moose, suddenly sprang up out of a wash, and fanned out in front of us. They moved jerkily ahead at a kind of long high trot, covering ground at a remarkable speed. I was tugging at my gun when Alfred cautioned me.

"Don't get in a hurry, Rich. We weren't ready for that bunch. You'd only get them in the hindquarters. Just wait a little while until we get over the ridge to that bunch of snow brush. We'll tie up these cayuses and get around the wind towards the base of the granite. That's where we'll get our meat."

We had pulled up to a stop, and watched the moose disappear over a ridge. A short time later we reached a patch of giant snow brush. This bush had the appearance of a bunch of juniper trees coming out of a single root. Here we tied up Coyote and Slats, and cautiously began working our way along low spots towards the bottom of the cliff. Alfred's knee and his hip gave him some trouble. The spill from Coyote had shaken him up pretty badly, but he didn't complain.

"All part of being a damn fool," he whispered, when he stopped to unlimber his knee. "I'm used to it—all in a day's riding."

We crawled over a low rise, and Alfred motioned me down flat on my belly. Slowly he led the way on all fours. My leather mitts filled with snow, and so did my rubbers, but it made little difference. This was the day. "I'm about to shoot my first moose," I thought.

Suddenly Alfred stiffened and lay rigid. Slowly turning on his side, he wiggled one finger at me. I crawled to his side; and then my breath nearly stopped.

Nine bull moose, swinging their dangling brisket bells and followed by two cows and a calf, were walking slowly towards us. As they moved up out of a swale, I noticed how velvety black they were. The leader nibbled at a little brush clump not over eighty yards from our almost-hidden position.

Close up the bulls took on the look of prehistoric monsters.

"A minute longer," whispered Alfred in my ear, so low I could hardly hear him. Then he said, "You take first shot. Shoot the second from the leader behind the shoulder. I'll take the one behind him. They're both fat."

I waited no longer. Raising up slowly on my elbow, I aimed and fired. The herd threw up their heads, stunned, unbelieving.

Nothing happened. The leader spotted us against the snow. I groaned. I swore. Pumped in another shell.

"Try her again." said Alfred.

The moose whirled as one animal. I stood up. I was breathing hard. My gun barrel wobbled around in a circle.

"Easy," cautioned Alfred. "Take it easy, boy."

I pulled the trigger. The big black bull swung around. A front leg dangled at the knee joint. The rest of the moose were racing madly away towards another bunch of brisket-belled animals, scared by the shots, who suddenly trotted out of the dip to the south of us.

Alfred's gun barked twice. One animal went down. Got up. Went down again. I ran forward towards my wounded animal.

Alfred yelled to stop. The moose snorted and bawled. Somehow he leapt ahead on three legs, and in my direction. I shot again, aiming for the middle of his brisket. He went down hard this time.

Two bulls down.

"Meat," I yelled.

"Yours isn't dead yet," said Alfred, when we were twenty feet away from my bull.

The animal suddenly towered above the ground, with long ears laid back on his wicked beaked head, tiny rattlesnake eyes gleaming dangerously. The hair along the back of his neck stood straight up. Mine did too.

"Quick—between the eyes," cried Alfred.

Now I was cooled off. My gun steadied. The monster crow-hopped forward three paces. I looked up at him through a half bead in the buckhorn sight, and with the thunder of the report, he slid to within five paces of us, with Alfred still holding back his shot to give me my first moose.

We sat down, smoked, laughed, kidded—then cut two throats, and skinned and gutted two animals.

That night in camp five men had five moose, about a ton and a half of meat and hides. The few white families, the half-dozen Indian families, the bachelor population soon had meat in Anahim.

CHAPTER VI

Trail Drive into a Frozen World

Soon after we returned from the Itcha Mountain moose hunt, Andy Christenson gave Alfred a contract to drive a few head of beef to Bella Coola, and return with a pack-train load of flour, sugar, beans, rice, dried fruit, ammunition, clothes and a radio.

Alfred asked me if I wanted to make the trip with him, and explained that he'd have to hire someone if I didn't go along. It was a big opportunity for me to learn about driving beef and horses in one bunch through the snow and bush, and to look over the country. I eagerly accepted.

Alfred's safari was made up of twelve shod pack horses, our two saddle horses, Coyote and Slats, six steers, a milk cow, sixty gunny sacks of hay, our bedrolls, axes, camp outfit and grub. One horse packed the grub and equipment. This animal is called the kitchen horse or chuck wagon.

We had to feed hay to the stock the first two nights out of Anahim, and we left hay bundles at Camp 1 and Camp 2 for the horses on the return trip.

It was clear and sunny the day we left, and we had no premonition of what was going to happen. The first morning on the trail we crawled out of our soogans in a white shimmering world. Lakes and timber thundered and boomed beneath a cold half light, with the temperature at sixty below zero. By eight o'clock our frosted shivering outfit, almost obscured in a blanket of rising blue steam, moved methodically west towards a gap in the Coast Range and distant Bella Coola.

This was the kind of a trip that any man with normal intelligence would have steered away from. January was just about the worst month to trail stock and camp out in, particularly on the glare ice of the precipitous Bella Coola trail. However, it was just the kind of trip to trail-break a man on. On future trips, when the going was tough and most everything had gone wrong and I was about ready to collapse with fatigue, or freeze solid with cold, I would compare the existing conditions with my first mixed cattle and horse drive to Bella Coola. The thought of those ten days would give me enough mental uplift to carry on, and I always made it through somehow.

I shall never forget the second night out. Both of us were sleepy—a bad sign. We dragged windfalls and down timber into camp with our saddle horses at first, but the cold became so unbearable that we were forced to keep moving on our feet to keep from freezing; and from then on and during the entire night, one of us constantly dragged in windfalls and roots by hand to the fires.

We kept two fires burning about thirty feet apart, and between them we kept the horses tied to trees. The man that wasn't dragging in windfalls kept himself and the horses alive by leading alternately two horses at a time up and down the trail. This kept the blood circulating. We couldn't turn the horses loose, for they were ready to break back for home.

The cattle walked steadily all night around bundles of hay, their hoofs making a brittle cracking sound on the crusted snow. These suffering animals wouldn't stop long at a bundle of hay, but would snatch a mouthful or two and continue to walk. I think this is nature's way of keeping these animals from freezing solid. Their instinct is to keep moving. Coyote and Slats were left with their saddles on, the cinchas loose, and Alfred's only two horse blankets covering saddle and animal.

Here—in this camp—with death hovering close, no little detail of survival could be overlooked. It was necessary to be constantly alert. We took every precaution that Alfred, experienced in this game, was wise to. Later we learned that on this night thermometers in the Anahim district had dipped to sixty-six below zero, and at Redstone in the Chilcotin to seventy-four below.

My first impressions of sixty-six below were startling. What I had read and pictured in my mind was reversed in actuality. Since this first experience I have learned that forests, lakes and sky react differently and in accordance with the speed of the falling of the mercury, the length of the cold wave and the humidity of the atmosphere.

For instance, I had heard and visualized, and have since witnessed, a silent land gripped in intense cold, but during this almost-record cold snap, the thermometer had dropped from ten above zero, with probably a fairly high degree of humidity, to sixty-six below zero in about fourteen hours. The sudden expansion of the trees, rocks, lakes and atmosphere produced a weird and fantastic effect.

On this day, instead of traversing a silent brilliant land, we found ourselves in the midst of a volley of explosions and gunlike reports. The lakes, woods and rocks, suddenly being forced to freezing point, and filled as they were with a certain amount of moisture, simply were all bursting at once. The air was alive with a very fine frost, and although the sun shone out of a clear sky, it threw a strange dulled yellowish light over the land.

On our return from the coast we met Pan around January fifteenth at Bryant's. He helped Alfred and me take care of the horses, then told us we had taken such a long time on the trail that it must have been a nice vacation for us instead of a pack trip.

Alfred retorted that it had been a cold and terrible trip. At Bella Coola we had weathered the coldest spell in the country's history, and we had only taken off two days there. The other day had been spent on business.

Pan told him not to apologize, that it wasn't necessary to do any more explaining as long as Alfred now produced the bottle of rum he owed him on a poker debt. Alfred was damn mad. For an instant I thought he was going to explode, but he seemed to catch on to the Top Hand's special type of humor, straightened himself out, and took a hand in the game himself.

He explained in great detail how the two of us had extinguished Pan's bottle with two young ladies at Tommy Walker's lodge at Atnarko. I cut in then and told Alfred to explain to Pan how the girls had mixed the drinks. Pan turned, and although a grin crept across his face, I saw a certain telltale expression soften his lips and a worried look come into his eyes. But he said:

"I sure am glad to hear you fellows had some fun out of my bottle, because that sixty-six below night when you boys were on the trail, Christenson gave a little supper party which Cyrus and I attended. I remember little about the supper, but lots about the drinks. You put a large teaspoon of honey in a big glass, pour in hot water, add a cup of thirty overproof rum, a shake of cinnamon, a squeeze of lemon. Repeat every twenty minutes until cooked."

This was too much for Alfred. He said, "You win, Pan, you bastard."

He reached into the kitchen box and produced the bottle in question. We sat in front of the living room heater, sipping hot rums with a honey base, telling lies until Cyrus Lord arrived.

Two days later Pan and I rode east ten miles to Bert Leaman's. As we walked our horses down the trail through the jackpines, I told Pan the story of the trip and explained to him that Bella Coola was really a garden spot.

"It was a bit cold when we were there," I said, "but the old-timers had extra beds and lots of horse feed, timothy it was, and nobody was fooling when they told about the beautiful Norwegian girls down there. There were dozens of them. Strange thing: all the young fellows raised in the valley move away to the city when they grow up, but the girls stay on. Mrs. Drainey's old lumber hotel was just like home."

"Where did you see all the girls?" asked Pan. He slowed his horse down. It was outwalking mine.

"We went to a couple of parties," I said. "I was careful to play the whole field, seeing as how it was my first trip to town—no favoritism. But there was one really cute mite of a kid there. She wasn't quite five feet tall, and was a real nifty. Some of the girls there had the nerve to start telling me about a Wild Horse Pan-handle who had just come into the interior from the States, was supposed to be some great kind of a guy."

"Ha ha," laughed Pan. "These women can smell a real horseman a hundred miles downwind."

"They sure can," I admitted. "Those gals wanted to hear all about you when Alfred told them I was your sidekick. It made me damn mad when right in front of them stood a real man who can cut the mustard when it comes to looks."

Pan grinned. "I guess you forgot and took your hat off. Always keep that hat on when you're around the ladies; you don't want them to see that bald head. Tell me some more about the cute little girl," Pan said happily. "What's her name?"

"Shorty," I answered.

"Shorty, hell," said Pan. "That's not a girl's name."

"Well, that's what they called her down there."

Pan bent forward in the saddle.

"I'm not interested in women at all, no interest in them whatsoever."

I laughed. "Sure, I know that, Pan, so I kind of straightened them out about you. So don't worry, they won't bother you when you go to Bella Coola. You've got me to thank, boy, for saving you from being rimrocked by a bunch of females in that town."

"Just what in the name of hell did you tell them about me? Ya don't have to spoil my name every place ya go. What did ya tell that little—that—uh—Shorty?"

"I just told her about you being married once, and that you had two sons growing up in Wyoming."

"What else did you tell her, you helpful wolverine?" asked Pan.

"I just told her the truth. That you chased wild horses so much that finally your wife gave you two choices, her or the wild horses. But I didn't tell her that when you went to Lander the next time and the boys told you your gentle bunch had broke from the holding grounds, your wife never would believe that those three days you didn't get home, you were hunting your own tame horses, and not breaking your promise and chasing wild ones.

"So, anyway, I told Shorty your wife had grounds for desertion or something, and so here you are a divorced man with two kids nearly as big as she is."

Pan looked crookedly at me from his horse.

"You damn fool," he said. "That won't discourage a smart young lady. It ain't no crime to be divorced. That might kind of add what your New York friends call glamour. If I meet the little girl I won't have to tell her how I got divorced. They never believe the story when I tell it myself. Thanks pal—ya done did me a favur."

"Learn to talk like a white man," I advised him. "This Shorty is a schoolteacher, and 'done did' won't sit very well with her. Don't say 'you done did me a favur.' That sounds like hell. Say 'you done me a favor.' Leave out the 'did.'"

CHAPTER VII

The Arctic Blizzard

A<small>N INTERESTING CUSTOM</small> of this isolated and far-flung country was the way the frontiersmen eased their thirst for talk and company by throwing in to help each other out, when the circumstances necessitated it. In this land where there was no such thing as hired help, neighborliness was taken for granted.

With the slightest provocation or with the frailest kind of excuse, a rancher would saddle up a half-broke colt or one of his snappiest horses and start to ride. His destination would be some particular friend's cabin; any distance up to fifty miles was not considered unusual.

What usually happened was that after two or three days of talk—during which the visitor helped his neighbor with the work—the two men would think of some other friend to visit, and off both of them would go to the next place. Most visits turned into a kind of progressive party, which gained size and momentum, until as many as seven or eight men would come trotting into the last victim's yard, intending to leave after one meal; but generally, being put to work, they would stay three or four days.

Pan and I, wanting to learn as much about the country and the people as possible, took advantage of this nomadic custom to move around to different ranches to take up the slack wherever an extra man was needed.

Andy Christenson loaned Pan and me his Behind Meadows cabin and corrals to use as a horse camp.

The Behind Meadows layout was located some four and a half miles north of Christenson's main ranch on a wide sweep of meadow land, dotted here and there with small jackpine islands. This was an excellent location for a holding ground to break out our horses and line up the outfit for the spring push into the mountains. We planned to move into the Behind layout as soon as our horse-buying program got under way.

In the meantime, Pan and I made several reconnaissance trips through the bush towards the base of the Algaks, looking out a future pack-horse route through the tangle.

Returning from one of these forays, we laid over at the Behind cabin. I was cooking supper and Pan was taking care of the horses, when I heard the well-measured thuds of a saddle horse being ridden to the house.

I looked through the window and saw a black-haired, dark-skinned Indian, wearing a black Stetson hat and a red silk neckerchief. He was moose-hided from his red scarf down, including his trousers and chaps, a big, square-built fellow who made a neat and colorful figure astride a tall, trim-legged buckskin horse, whose coloring matched the clothes the man wore.

I opened the door as the Indian dismounted, and then I recognized him. He was Thomas Squinas, the youngest son of the chief of the Anahim Lake Indians.

"Howdy, Domas," I said. "Domas" was the way you pronounced Thomas in Anahim vernacular. "Take care of your horse. Come in and eat."

"I been my father's trapline," replied Thomas. "I see 'em big bunch black wolf."

He pulled off his moose-hide mitten and stuck out his hand. We shook hands.

Pan appeared from behind the house and stopped by Thomas' saddle horse. He looked the cayuse over and turned to the Indian.

"You ride damn good horse, Domas—but what's a matter you

don't fix 'em up that ringbone? Pretty soon that cayuse he go lame on you."

Thomas' mouth fell open. He said, "Ugh?"

"Ringbone," said Pan.

"No ringbone," said Thomas.

"Look," replied Pan. He pointed down at a very sound-looking coronet above a well-shaped hoof.

Now I knew what was going on. Pan had taken a fancy to the buckskin and was getting the Indian softened up for a thorough fleecing.

"Dinner's ready, you knotheads," I said. "Throw that spavined, ringboned wreck some hay and come and get it."

I walked into the house as the horse talk continued.

That evening Pan and I heard about Nimpo for the first time.

Nimpo is the ugly little black range horse with the dished face, whose story is so closely interwoven with the opening of this new frontier that it is a part of the saga of the country itself.

He was to be my first British Columbia horse, and his amazing tracks were to leave such a lasting imprint across this back country that even today, along the trails and around the campfires of northern British Columbia, wherever ranchers and cowhands meet and the inevitable horse talk begins, someone is sure to tell a new one about Nimpo.

Nimpo's story goes back to the fierce winter of 1929. That was the winter when most of the wild horses west of the Chilcotin district were wiped out.

It was one of those rare winters when deep snows were melted by chinook winds and in turn frozen by terrific cold. In February, when the grass on the range was covered by a series of ice and snow layers nearly two feet deep, the air and sky suddenly crackled and popped with the temperature at seventy below zero.

Out on lonely icebound meadows, and along glassy slopes of shimmering mountains, wild horses made their last desperate attempt to survive.

The strongest mares and stallions worked close together in semi-circles in the front of the bands. They used their front feet like sledge hammers and cracked at the great ice blocks in front of them. Of what little grass they finally uncovered, these animals would nibble but a mouthful or two, then carry on with their terrific work, leaving what remained for the colts and the weak and dying horses behind them.

The stronger animals, with their feet and ankles cut to ribbons by the sharp ice, succumbed first, and it was only a matter of time before the weaker ones followed.

On the lower slopes of a mountain called Sugarloaf, a few miles east of Anahim, a yellowish sky threw an incandescent light on the bloodstained snow, and on the scattered bodies of a wild band.

Nimpo, then a tiny, mouse-colored sucking colt, staggered dejectedly beside the withered body of a black mare. He had survived only because of his mother's rich milk which she had produced for him almost to the moment of her death. He lowered his head, and with his ice-caked nostrils touched her frozen body.

A few paces away, his little half brother, a bay yearling with white-stockinged legs, pawed feebly at a patch of frozen ground.

In the distance, lakes expanding with the frost thundered and roared, and the cannon-like reports of bursting trees echoed and re-echoed across the frozen land. Slowly and insidiously the terrible cold crept into the gaunt bodies of the two little colts.

Thomas Squinas was camped with a group of relations at his trapline cabin on a wild hay meadow a few miles west of Sugarloaf. He was examining a trap on an open knoll at the base of the main range when his well-trained eyes picked up an unnatural blur on the distant snow.

He commandeered the other Indians, and long after dark his sleigh pulled into camp with the two little survivors.

Thomas was a good horseman. He watched the gradual development of the two colts with unusual interest. He was certain that their sire had been a well-bred Arabian stallion that had broken from a ranch in the Chilcotin district a hundred miles east of there, and had run for two years with the Sugarloaf wild band, for each of them was short one vertebra, an Arabian characteristic.

As they grew up the two animals formed a strong attachment for each other. Unlike other horses of their age, they were business-like and sober. Even as two-year-olds the inseparable pair did little prancing or playing.

They were turned loose with the Squinas remuda when the black was a coming three-year-old, and for two years their whereabouts remained a mystery. Early in the winter of 1934, riders picked up fresh horse tracks near a hidden and seldom-visited lake called Nimpo. Later they found the two horses feeding in the high slough grass along the shoreline of the lake. The wary animals were harder to corral than wild horses.

Sitting before our cook stove, the Indian chief's son described the hard rides and the trouble he and his friends had encountered corralling the two colts. His dark, square-cut face twisted into a crooked grin when he told us about the black.

"That cayuse he don't like any kind of man. Can't get close to him. I feed him lots—but he won't make friends. Now I have a hell of a time to break him to lead. He fight all the time—won't give in. He got funny look in the eye, not a mean eye—but he look at you hard and cold."

Pan and I rode from Behind Meadows to Bryant's, and were just unsaddling when Bert Leaman rode up and asked us if we could help him for a few days on a new barn he was going to build. Cyrus told us to go ahead and help Bert. We resaddled, threw our bedrolls on a pack horse, and trotted over with Bert to his Cahoose Flats cabin and corrals.

I couldn't get the Squinas' black Nimpo horse out of my mind, and one day walked over to the Squinas village to have a look at him.

He was tied by an inch hackamore rope to a corral post. Before Thomas and I got to him, he suddenly shifted his feet, bunched himself into a knot, and sprang back hard against the rope. He fought for a moment, and then straightened up and looked suspiciously in our direction.

I could see what Thomas had meant by his cold eyes. They glinted with a strange unfathomable hardness, and seemed to say, "I expect no favors from man, and I will give none."

Thomas pointed a finger at the black.

"Gonna be lots of work to break that Nimpo Lake cayuse, but I don't think he's gonna buck."

I studied the shape of the horse's head, his deep girth, and the weird look in his eyes, and knew he had something. I pulled out my pocketbook, stripped off three ten dollar bills, and shoved them at Thomas who quickly relieved me of them.

"That includes a good skookum hackamore," I said.

Thomas grinned happily and nodded his head. I had the feeling that one of the ten dollar bills would have swung the deal, and noticed too late that the black had one crooked front foot.

I had arrived at the village on foot. There was only one thing to do. Ride Nimpo back.

After some trouble we manoeuvred him around so that he stood lengthwise to a panel of the corral, and about three feet away. I had made a kind of looped bridle rein with the long hackamore shank. I tucked the loose end of the rope in my belt, and holding the loop reins in my left hand, eased down onto his back from the corral fence.

Nimpo was running before I was set. I caught a blurred glimpse of Thomas, as he threw open the gate and jumped to the side, saw the Squinas village flashing by. Several Indian children and two old women flung themselves behind the Chief's long, single-storey log cabin as we charged past them.

With my left hand I pulled up hard on my hackamore shank, grabbed a handful of black mane and leaned forward as we pounded into the jackpines.

It was a runaway. There was only one thing to do—stay on his back and let him run himself out—preferably in the direction of Bert Leaman's.

Bert's place lay due east some eight miles from the Squinas village. We were traveling north just as fast as Nimpo could run. A gnarled jackpine limb suddenly loomed ahead of me. There was room for Nimpo to squeeze underneath it, but none left for me.

I was far from being a trick rider, and not proud of my ability at bareback riding, but as the tree limb reached out for me, I scissor-gripped the black's neck with my legs, pulled myself in hard with my mane hold, and slid over on his right side.

A green bushy jackpine branch gave me a whiplike cut across the face. The big limb tore at the back of my shirt.

Another half mile of timber that seemed like ten faded behind us. The ten inches of snow on the ground began to take its toll. The cayuse was breathing hard, my hands were wet with his sweat.

I could feel the dampness soaking through my pants and underwear.

Ahead of us a narrow wagon road sprang into view. It was running at right angles to our head-on charge. Nimpo was slowing down.

We came out onto the road. I leaned forward and with my left hand pushed the black's nose hard in the opposite direction. It turned him. He slowed to a lope, then to a trot. An hour later I rode in to Bert Leaman's yard. Pan was helping Bert roll up the foundation logs and squaring them off with a broadaxe.

As soon as Bert saw me come prancing sideways into the yard on the lathered Nimpo, he dropped his axe and came roaring towards us. This was what I was afraid of. I jumped clear of the black, signaled unsuccessfully for Bert to take it easy, then dug my heels into the crusted snow and sat back hard on the hackamore shank.

"Hooray—ha—ha—haw," yelled Bert as he ran forward.

Nimpo was panicked. He plunged wildly away, dragging me through the snow. Bert ran to cut him off, and Nimpo nearly went over on top of him. But my first B.C. horse didn't quite get away from me this time. Bert cut off his advance, and I yelled at the woodsman for the God's sake to shut up until we got the colt in the corral.

I couldn't drag the black through the corral gate until Bert cleared out of there, but once behind the horse, Bert let out a jarring laugh, and Nimpo sprang for his life into the enclosure.

I had planned some time to visit frontiersman George Powers. George ranched twenty-five miles east of Cahoose Flats on a twenty-mile-long, rockbound lake called Charlotte. At the east end of the lake George wintered around eighty head of heavy-boned whiteface cattle on a black loam flat, and he was experimenting with various types of tame grass seeds new to the country. This should be valuable information for our own future activities.

Neither Pan nor I had met George or been to his ranch, but through what we all thought was a mutual acquaintance in the States, messages had been sent back and forth between us.

The day after my explosive arrival on Nimpo, morning broke in a strange gray darkness with the temperature at twenty below zero, and a fine arctic snow was sifting in from the east. If I had used any common sense at all, I would have postponed my visit to George Powers.

Pan tried to talk me out of my bullheaded decision, but Bert kept roaring with laughter, and I couldn't hear what Pan was saying. Finally Pan yelled, "Bert and I will help you saddle up, and I'll see ya down the trail a ways until that bronc blows some of the snuff out of his frame."

I had on heavy wool underwear, a wool shirt and an eight-pound raw-wool sweater. On my feet I wore two pairs of wool socks, moccasins and moccasin rubbers with felt inner soles. I snapped on my latigo leather chaps, but I didn't realize that my clothes were more suited to a Wyoming winter than what was to turn into an arctic blizzard.

I tried to get up to Nimpo with a bridle, but he met me with a loud snort and both front feet. Then Pan shook his lariat out on the ground and, with a quick flip of the wrist, snapped the loop at Nimpo's front feet, jerked up the slack, and the cayuse lit on his back. I grabbed his head between my hands, and knelt with one knee on his neck. Pan hog-tied him and then slipped my bridle over his head and got the bit in his mouth.

In order not to hurt Nimpo's mouth, I had swapped my curb for a snaffle bit.

This was to be Nimpo's first experience with a bit and saddle. I figured that the fifty-mile round trip to George Powers' would get him pretty well used to them, and that when I arrived back I'd have a horse with the rough edges off and broke enough to handle easily—and here again I was wrong.

I eased into the saddle before Nimpo got to his feet. He ran sideways around the corral trying to scrape me off on the logs, made a poor job of crow-hopping, then stopped in his tracks and looked about him.

We were ready to start. Pan crawled up on Pike, and riding up to the gate, reached down, pulled the latch and swung it open.

Nimpo sprang like a tiger through the opening. Pan spurred Pike in ahead of him at a hard run. Nimpo followed. We pounded out onto the road. Pan kept the lead position, looking back over his shoulder every few seconds.

For several miles Nimpo followed close on Pike's heels, but when Pan pulled up, he was willing enough to stop.

I had on a silk stocking under my Stetson hat, but the fine snow stung my neck and face. The horses were covered with frost and little icicles hung like a white beard from the fine hair on Nimpo's chin.

Pan said, "Yer crazy, man, to ride an unbroke cayuse into a snow-storm and a new country. Use some common horse sense and turn yourself around. It's too cold to do any work on Bert's barn today so we'll go over to Bryant's and do some powwowing and coffee drinking. We'll be there in a couple of hours."

But I was too inexperienced and boneheaded to listen to Pan.

For a few minutes after he and Pike vanished into the blowing snow, Nimpo trotted jerkily ahead—then all at once he realized he was alone.

He stopped in his tracks and refused to go one step further. My spurs only made him jump in the air and try and twist around into the back trail. Finally after a lot of trouble, I broke off a jackpine branch and quirted him up the road.

The miles dragged slowly by. I trotted and then walked Nimpo, and occasionally broke him into a lope. About an hour before dark I swung him south onto the narrow seldom-used wagon trail that reached some fifteen miles to Charlotte Lake.

I was in new country now. It was about three in the afternoon and almost dark. The snow was piling up. In places Nimpo had to plow through it above his knees.

The sweat I had worked up during the fast beginning of the journey had turned the inside of my underwear damp and clammish. A cold chill ran like an icicle down my spine. My feet began to hurt.

The wind moaned through the tall jackpines, and the fine sharp snow made a hissing undertone as it swished in great gusts through the trees. The cold bit like a million stinging bees through my sweater.

Now Nimpo plodded methodically, resignedly, on through the

drifting snow with his head down. Black night seemed suddenly upon us. Visibility became almost nil.

The storm now increased to a deep roar. Great white blankets of snow swirled out of the timber, throwing Nimpo off balance. One blast followed another.

It seemed to me that it was much colder than when I had left Bert's. I remembered Bert's bellowing laughter. Even that seemed like something pleasant, far in the past. If I'd only listened to Pan, I'd now be warmly and safely at Bryant's, drinking hot coffee and yarning with the boys around the heater.

In between the wild blasts of wind and snow, I noticed that the timber had become more park-like. The trees were further apart, but last summer's ruts in the road were drifted over—hard to follow in the dark and the swirling snow.

For some time Nimpo had been following what looked suspiciously like fresh horse tracks, not over half an hour old, or they would have been filled with snow. "Some rider going into George Powers'," I thought.

Suddenly Nimpo stopped. I looked down at the barely visible holes in the snow. They ended abruptly at the edge of a willow thicket.

Nimpo snorted wildly—jumped fast to one side.

In front of us—not twenty feet away—loomed an immense black object. It made a grunting sound like a hog. The great shadowy bulk vanished in the willows. Nimpo was trembling. I realized at once that we had been following a moose.

The moose had not been following the road.

I was lost.

I turned Nimpo around. He didn't want to follow our back trail. The sickening truth suddenly swept over me. Nimpo would not lead me homeward on those tracks. He didn't consider Thomas Squinas' village or Bert Leaman's corral his home.

Instinctively he was sensing his way towards the slough grass shores of his old range—the distant Nimpo Lake or Sugarloaf Mountain.

My feet were numb. There was no feeling in them when I thought I was wiggling my toes. One mittened hand was almost numb, and I was chilled to the bone. If I got off Nimpo's back tracks, or they filled with snow before we got out to where I'd recognize the road, I would never survive this night.

I gripped the cheek strap of Nimpo's headstall with my left hand, pulled his head around to me, then stiffly jumped into the snow. Nimpo pulled back, but I held onto him.

I tied him to the nearest tree and stumbled over a submerged log. I figured I had possibly one chance in two of getting out of this mess alive. I must not get panicky, and I'd have to thaw out my feet.

Ten feet beyond me Nimpo whinnied. I couldn't see him, but I heard sticks cracking and his heavy breathing, as he circled the tree he was tied to.

I pounded my arms crisscross back and forth across my chest, sat down on the log, and removing one of my rubbers and moccasins, beat them hard against my socked foot. It sounded like a hammer hitting a wet board.

Circulation began to come, and with it a fierce pain. Ten minutes of this and my feet felt hot. I put my moccasins and rubbers back on and stood up.

After some difficulty I rolled and lit a cigarette. It gave me a strangely realistic sense of security. I took several long drags on it, then groped through the dark to Nimpo's tree, and our fast-vanishing tracks.

My mind was made up. I'd follow the back tracks on foot leading Nimpo. Those tracks were the big thing—once off them and I was done.

I thought of the great forest space that reached around me in every direction. Charlotte Lake was a pinpoint in a wilderness of mountain ranges that ran without a break some four hundred miles south towards Vancouver. Williams Lake and the Cariboo country lay more than two hundred jungle-miles east of me. The Pacific coast lay behind the glacial rim of the Coast Range, more than a hundred miles to the west, and the Itcha Mountain country stretched endlessly into the north.

Now, for the first time since our arrival in British Columbia, the terrifying isolation of this back country impressed itself upon me.

The snow was above my knees. It was hard going, and Nimpo

pulled back on the bridle reins, but the wind was now at our backs, and I began to warm up.

Nimpo's back trail was beginning to fill up, and I had to stoop over with my head nearly in the snow to keep them in sight.

I thought of our reconnaissance map of the area—a few unnamed lakes—and the fine winding lines of an occasional stream; but I remembered Charlotte Lake, and the dotted trail that ran from the Anahim road almost due south to its eastern shore. It suddenly dawned on me the wind was pounding on my back. I had faced into the east wind all day on the Anahim wagon road. The driving east wind at my back meant that the moose tracks had veered almost at right angles from the Charlotte Lake wagon trail, and that I was completely turned around.

I had to adjust my mind to this change. When at last the wind struck me on the side of my face, I knew we were once again on the George Powers' road.

I found a deep blaze on a jackpine tree, and then another one. Nearly every other tree on each side of what must be the road was blazed. I knew that these blazes meant life and death to me; that was why frontiersmen blazed their main trails and roads so carefully.

I plowed through the snow from one tree to another—often feeling the smooth axe marks with my mittens when I couldn't see them.

By now I had no idea of time or distance. The panicky moments of uncertainty, the vague dread, and then the final and overwhelming realization that I was lost and fast freezing to death which had gripped me at the end of the blind moose trail, was now replaced by the torture of exhaustion, and the knowledge that I had to stagger, plunge and shove on and on—that I could never stop, that if I sat down to rest I would fall asleep and freeze to death.

I had no idea how far I had come and how many blazes ahead lay the end of the trail.

I stumbled over a submerged stump of a tree—fell heavily into a drift. For a moment I lay there, death gripping the bridle reins. It would be a terrible effort now to get back to my feet. I tried desperately to think clearly. My energy was used up, my strength gone. I wanted just to lie there in the snow drift and sleep.

I knew now that my only chance of survival lay with Nimpo. Someway, somehow, I would have to get up there into that saddle again and ride from blaze to blaze.

Would Nimpo stand long enough for me to crawl into my hull? Was I too stiff and exhausted to pull myself up into the saddle without stampeding the bronc? Ominous thoughts flashed across my mind as reality and roaring wind and snow began fading in distance.

I wondered if my rubber would slide too far into the stirrup and Nimpo would plunge away from me, and in wild panic drag me to death. If I didn't make it into the saddle on the first try, and slipped or stumbled and excited him, I knew he'd plunge away from me, and from then on it would be doubtful whether he'd let me get close enough to him to get on.

I noticed a faint light around me. I could see trees ten feet away. "Daylight must be coming," I thought.

With a great effort I pulled myself together and struggled out of the drift. I stepped slowly and awkwardly to Nimpo's side, gently slapped the saddle fenders. A dull snort rose out of his nose and he edged slightly away from me.

I saw his eyes. They glared icily at me. Now I walked forward and led him a few steps to the next blazed tree. I rubbed and slapped the fenders again. I repeated this performance four times. The black accepted my fifth approach as routine.

Now the big moment had come. I stood in the snow on a high strip of ground, and prepared to mount. I rubbed the saddle skirt, slapped the fenders again, was conscious of the horse's hard merciless eyes upon me, the blowing snow, the darkness, the snow-covered saddle.

I made a silent prayer, reached slowly for Nimpo's headstall, bent his neck around to me. He didn't move. I lifted my foot to the stirrup, got a death grip on the horn, then swung hard into the saddle.

I could feel the vibrations of life throbbing through the cold, snow-caked saddle between my legs as Nimpo stood motionless beneath me.

He shook himself, and then with some effort plowed through the snow towards the next blazed tree.

It was around noon when Nimpo bucked through a deep drift into a gate. A few minutes later we emerged out of a great white swirl into a wide, log enclosure. Thirty feet away, the shaked roof of a tall building suddenly appeared through a hole in the blowing snow. Nimpo had carried me through to George Powers'.

George Powers looked more like a dignified science professor than the adventurous, hard-hitting frontiersman that he was.

He walked out of the barn and greeted me in a soft mellow voice. A six-foot tall, trim-built, neatly dressed man, wearing tortoise-shell glasses, a medium-sized Stetson hat over a silk skull cap that was pulled down over his ears. It was obvious that his plain form-fitting, softly tanned, moose-hide shirt and jacket were tailored. His carefully knotted, brilliantly colored bucking-horse scarf was unusual.

George knew who I was before I got off my horse. He took one look at me, and leaving the frost-covered Nimpo where he stood, rushed me through the barnyard and into the house.

"You're frosted-up bad, boy," he said. "We've got to thaw you out right now."

The heat of the house felt like a blast from a furnace. I felt unsteady, and started to clump across the kitchen floor to the stove, but George caught me by the arm and steered me over to a wide homemade armchair in a far corner of the room.

"You've got to stay away from that stove, Rich, until we've got the frost out." He grinned reassuringly.

"Jessie," he called, "Rich has just rode in out of the snowdrift."

At one side of the massive log-walled kitchen, a narrow hallway ran back to other rooms. I could see a big, lodgelike living room through the wide doorway on the other side of the kitchen.

Suddenly, through this opening, stepped lithely and gracefully, the most strikingly beautiful Indian woman I had ever seen. I stood up from my chair, and George presented me to his wife.

She had the grave stoical face of an interior Indian, but underneath its smooth, symmetrical lines I saw a controlled vivaciousness, and a certain sensitiveness poured from her wide, soft, almond-shaped black eyes.

I had heard the amazing story of how, more than thirty-five years before, eighteen-year-old George Powers had ridden into the unsettled, hostile Indian country of the Chilcotins, and after a series of the most hair-raising adventures with the Indians, had fallen madly in love with sixteen-year-old Indian Princess Jessie, the daughter of the great Chilcotin chieftain, Bob. How he and the beautiful Jessie had pleaded with her father and the witch doctor to marry them, had been refused, and George threatened with his life. How the two youngsters had defied the order-in-council of the braves, stolen horses and, during the night, ridden for their lives into the dark, uninhabited forests west of the Chilcotin with the Indians in close pursuit.

Now, as I looked at the smartly dressed and extremely young and attractive-looking Jessie, and realized that she was over fifty years of age, it was easy for me to understand how George Powers had risked his life to run away with her.

George hurried out into the storm to feed and take care of Nimpo. Jessie brought in a can of coal oil, and took charge of thawing out my frosted spots.

My lips were frozen, and later the skin dropped off them. The tip of my nose and the groove between nose and lips were white and marblelike, as were both cheekbones. One tip of my left ear, already slightly cauliflowered, wasn't improved by the frostbite.

But my feet were in pretty bad shape. Coal oil when applied to a frostbitten portion of the anatomy is extremely painful, but it is a great frost extractor. Jessie poured coal oil out in a pan, and I dunked in my feet.

If I'd shoved them in a stove or heater of any kind, I would have lost the flesh to the bone. As it was the only aftereffects I suffered were the loss of my toenails, and a few small chunks of flesh. But after that exposure and to this day, my feet freeze up very easily, and grow calluses which I have to trim down more often than I get my hair cut.

George and Jessie were a grand host and hostess. I enjoyed their hospitality for a week.

George hailed from a ranching family in the State of Washington, which, as a sideline, ran a saddle and harness-making shop. As a boy, George had been fascinated by this work, and before he headed north into the new frontier, he had become an expert in leather-work.

Every summer after the cattle were turned loose on their Charlotte Lake range, he and Jessie loaded a month's grub, a stitching horse, and all of his leather-repair equipment in a wagon, and drove towards Anahim. They combined business with pleasure at the Anahim ranches, repairing harness, saddles, and delivering the homemade leather and moose-hide chaps, moose-hide coats, vests and shirts that the frontiersmen had ordered from George the year before.

Before I left the Powerses' ranch, Jessie presented me with a long-fringed, tailored moose-hide coat.

"Now you put this on," she said. "It will fit over your big sweater. You won't get so cold any more."

George rebuilt the swell on my saddle, leather-wrapped the dilapidated horn and inserted new wang leather strings.

One of George's many accomplishments was whip-breaking obstinate, rump-turning and kicking horses. Very few horsebreakers have the patience or the know-how to whip-break, and others don't believe in it.

The trick is performed with a long bull whip. When the cayuse turns his back to you, walks away, or lets fly with his hind feet, the whip-breaker pops the lash at his ankles. Usually three or four whip snaps do the deed. The horse catches on faster than you'd think. When he hears the whip or even a halter shank pop, and a man's commanding voice, he swings hurriedly around to shield his legs, and faces the whip man.

This system works on ninety-nine out of a hundred stubborn, back-turning cayuses, but it didn't go with Nimpo. He just whirled around in the corral, snorting and kicking at us. Once he put George and me over the fence.

"I never saw a horse quite like that before," said George. "If I had plenty of time, maybe it would work on him."

And so it was that I finally and reluctantly rode away from George Powers' layout, carrying at least ten pounds of new flesh, a dandy moose-hide coat which I still wear, a built-to-order saddle, a more useful and experienced saddle horse—and much more respect for the storms and arctic blizzards of British Columbia's interior.

CHAPTER VIII

Social Life on the Frontier

WHEN I RETURNED FROM GEORGE POWERS', I found that Pan and Bert had the barn well under control. I picked up my bedroll and rode on back to Bryant's.

Nobody had seen or heard of Jim Holt for a long time. Pan dropped into Bryant's one day and suggested that we ride over to the Three Circle and check up on him.

We found that the lantern-jawed, mystic, black-eyed Texan was in a jam. He was worried. He drawled his story to us slowly, emphasizing important parts of the narrative by raising his low voice to a high whining pitch that sounded like a jet plane taking off, or lowering it to a deep throaty purr like a cat with her first batch of kittens.

Pan and I balanced uncomfortably on wobbly log stools, whose uneven butts rested on the hard dirt floor. We stared down at the ancient stove, hats on the back of our heads, and sipped black coffee out of cracked enamel cups, listening without comment.

"Ya see, boys, this ain't my or'nary spread; my layout done flew away in a poker game long ago; but this here land and cows belongs to Austin Hallows, who never come back after the beef drive in October.

"I give my word to Austin to take care of the place till he got back. My job as foreman of Duke Martin's spread in the Chilcotin, with fifteen hundred head of cows, was due to begin November fifteen. Duke expected me November fifteen, and jobs like that just don't sit around waitin' for a man.

"Well, here it is February, nary a word from Austin. He wanted to pay me my back wages when he left, but I told him I wouldn't need 'em till I rolled my bed.

"I've been out of grub here for a long time, just that leg o' moose, some coffee, beans and a sack of flour, that's what I'm livin' on fer a month. I ain't got any money left atall. Can't leave here to get to the Christensons' for grub and tell them about Austin not gettin' back. I'm just tied here.

"The crik's dried up solid, and I got to trail a hundred head of critters two damn miles to water 'em—then drive 'em back to feed. The fences is all down. Austin left this layout in a hell of a shape.

"I got to ride till dark bringin' in the critters. There's a pack of wolves hangin' around. They done killed a yearlin' steer, then worked over a big cow that was heavy in calf, so I can't leave this herd fer two hours without maybe losin' a bunch."

Jim paused for a moment and spat through a crack in the wall where the cow manure chinking had fallen out.

"I'm meltin' snow to water the stud horse, the team and meself. And all this time Duke and fifteen hundred head waitin' down in Chilcotin with no word from me.

"Boys, it's just one hell of a fix. Now I'm half loco. What's gonna be done?"

This was a long speech especially for the Texan. As a rule he didn't have much to say. He sucked in his breath and looked at Pan and then at me.

"Can one of you ornery siwashes throw in with me until we get grub in and word out aboot Hallows? There's somethin' happened to that Englishman sure. He ain't alive today. Austin Hallows is dead some place between Anahim and Vancouver."

Jim was right. There has been no trace of Austin since then. His assets, including a bank account and the Three Circle Ranch were finally taken over by his uncle who later died there.

It was decided that I stay on with Jim until further notice, Pan ride to Christenson's and report Austin's disappearance, then on to help Bert Leaman who was also in a bad fix.

Bert's cabin had burned down, and Pan was helping him build a new one. In the meantime Pan and Bert were sleeping with the horses and a milk cow in the half-constructed barn.

Bert had to haul hay five miles while he waited for his recently drained swamp to produce. Hauling hay for his small bunch of stock wasn't too inconvenient when everything was going right, but now his water hole had dried up. This was serious as the nearest creek was miles away in the bush. The boys kept stoves going all day with washtubs and coal-oil tins full of snow, constantly replenished. By this method Bert's stock could lap up enough water to get by on.

Pan's face lighted up while we were talking and he grinned.

"You fellows should have heard Bert when he and I come ridin' in there and looked at that smoking pile of charcoal. Well sir, Bert starts to laugh—you could have heard him a mile upwind.

"'Look,' he yells, pointing at the ruins, 'We haven't finished the barn yet—the water hole's froze up—and look what happens—the cabin burns down. Haw—haw—haw—hooray. What a country!'"

Before Pan left for Christenson's, he said to me, "Friend, if we ever spot a piece of ground to throw our ropes down on, she's got to be settin' on the edge of a river that won't never dry up or freeze to the bottom. This cold wave froze a lot of little criks and springs solid for the first time that these men know of. But there sure ain't gonna be no first time for our layout."

Two provincial police constables arrived at Jim Holt's early in March to check on Austin Hallows' disappearance. It had taken them twelve days to make the 225 mile trip from Williams Lake with a team of horses and a sleigh.

They told me they were also looking for some bad Indians. Reports had it that a man named Seymour and another half-breed, both wanted for murders in the Chilcotin, were now holed up somewhere in our vicinity. The murderers were taking no chances, and would shoot on sight anyone they encountered in the bush.

The next day the police left their team with us and snowshoed off into the bush on their hunt for the criminals.

Jim Holt watched them out of sight, then turned from the window to me with an owlish grin on his face.

"Wal, boy, your chance has come. Either you've got to plug those confidence men when they're out in the willows, or else creep over the mountain so they can't find ya. Those boys are also lookin' for sixty-five head of nice fat whiteface cows with calves that was rustled out of West Chilcotin Range last fall. It's the second raid on that range. They're doin' a leetle investigatin' back here.

"Ya know, kid," Jim continued, "this here Anahim country 'pears to be goin' a leetle western; maybe we better start movin' our rags before she's plumb plain whoopin' western. Let's go back to some peaceful land like old Texas used to be."

The Texan was pleased no end with the livening-up of the neighborhood. Now that the work was caught up on the Three Circle, I decided to saddle up Nimpo and ride over to Bert Leaman's to tell Pan the latest news. Thus the moccasin telegraph system was soon in motion.

At Bert's, Pan joined me, and together we trotted over to Bryant's. Riding abreast into the yard we met Bronco Alfred pulling out on Coyote.

"Hey, boys," he beamed, "I was just pulling up for Jim's and Bert's to round you up—lots of fun coming up."

"Yeah," answered Pan. "We've got a bit of disquietin' news ourselves, Bronco, but let's hear your lies first."

"That so?" laughed Alfred. "Mine is real good news. Shorty King and Lester Dorsey have sent out invitations via moccasin telegraph to the members of the Anahim Lake Men's Club. Both you fellows are invited to attend as prospective new members."

Pan's face had reverted to its usual solemn and thoughtful look, the only contradiction being the deep twinkling eyes.

"Who all's in this exclusive club?" he asked.

"All members of Anahim Lake country who have passed the initiation and the essential tests."

I asked what these tests were, and Alfred replied that they were mainly a man's capacity to drink the famous Itcha Mountain fog. He said that a few other points were taken into consideration. A member must be able to handle at least the required amount of the firewater without going berserk, and he must be able to conduct himself during the process with no arguments, fights or bragging. Alfred concluded that talk of meadow hunting, exploration, new country, horses and cows was the order of the day.

These meetings took place about every four months, and lasted from two to four days. The first day was spent in a general celebration. On the second day liquor was imbibed within reason, and community ideas, ranching plans and business of the area were discussed; any decisions made were jotted down by the treasurer of the outfit, Shorty King. And if anyone was around the third day, there were three old milk cows the boys saddled up and took turns getting bucked off of. The Anahim men also did their horse and equipment trading at the meetings.

As we rode down the trail Pan told Alfred about the murderers being at large, and that the newly arrived police were planning, among other things, to clean up this bad man's hideout once and for all.

As we came in sight of Shorty's cabin, Pan leaned forward in his saddle. He turned towards Alfred, "That Shorty King has somethin' besides a hump on his back. He seems to have a hankerin' for the real joys of life—that's a man after my own heart."

The arrival of a newcomer at Shorty King's was the sign for the population of the log cabin to scramble out of the house to meet man and horse. The whole bunch walked forward, calling "howdy," wisecracking, and immediately reported that the liquor had all been consumed. Some of the boys relieved us of our horses and led them to the barn and green hay, while the rest laughingly hurried us to the house.

The outstanding feature of the party was the cabin decoration, which stood out like the lone limb on a jackpine tree. In the middle of the axe-hewn floor, a heavy log table supported a thirty-gallon barrel with a spigot attached.

The interesting liquid inside was made of twenty pounds of black figs, soaked for three months in a gallon of brandy in a battle-scarred charcoal barrel. Added were twenty-five pounds of sugar, fifteen gallons of water and ten pounds of raisins. The works were then drained off, the mash and sediment removed, and the liquid returned to the barrel and allowed to age for another month. The result was an amber-colored liquid, slightly effervescent, with much the same taste as brandy, but not quite so strong.

The effect produced was a happy one, and the aftermath could be weathered by a strong constitution and a never-say-die will power.

The club members gathered together for this quarterly meeting and celebration were Ronald Waite; Lester Dorsey, who had recently been married to a Bella Coola girl; Billy Dagg, the Christenson foreman; Tommy Holte, who was also working for Christenson's; Ole Nucloe, just back from a prolonged wild horse foray; Eddie Collet; Mac MacEwen; Alfred; Pan and myself.

The bunch of us sat on the uneven, wide-cracked floor of the cabin, drinking the Itcha Mountain fog out of large tin mugs. A general hum of voices, broken occasionally by Pan's snorts, filled the room, until I got on the subject of the Chilcotin murderers who were holed-up in the Anahim country.

Blond-headed, blue-eyed, Tommy Holte told the gathering that he had seen strange horse tracks, spruce-bough beds and campfire ashes on the old Ulgatcho Indian trail. He had wondered who the riders were and had followed their tracks several miles north to where they had swung in towards the Algaks.

Ronald Waite swallowed his cup of fog and, rising to refill it, told us that the Squinas storehouse had been broken into, a sack of flour, several pounds of coffee and bacon, and a box of 30-30 shells had been stolen. He said that Thomas was convinced that there had been wild men in the country for several weeks.

The final conclusion of the group was that from now on every one of us would pack guns and, for reasons of self-protection, the shoot-first-and-talk-later custom would be adopted.

Most of the boys returned to their ranches and jobs the second afternoon. By night only Pan, Alfred, Ole, Shorty and I remained.

This little gathering was soon a whirlwind of swaps and trades. I broke the ice by trading saddles straight across to Shorty. The other boys gave me a big razzing over this, saying that I was a lousy trader and had got beat. Next I traded socks, shirt, an old pocketknife and some safety pins to Shorty for an old pair of misshapen cow-hide pack boxes, and again got the horse laugh.

Shorty then started working around towards Pan's old coonskin cap.

"I need this cap," said Pan.

"Oh hell, wear your Stetson." said Shorty.

"My ears get cold," said Pan.

"All right," said Shorty, "I'll tell you what I'll do. I'll trade you a silk headstall that will keep your ears warm—it's a good hat—plus a gold watch which I've got here now." He crawled across the floor, and showed it to the Top Hand who grunted disgustedly, and shoved watch and hand away from him.

"Now wait," purred Shorty, "I haven't finished yet. I'll trade you like I said, this gold watch, the headpiece, *and* that hackamore over on the wall, hand-braided, every bit of it."

Pan snorted loudly. "Who ever heard of a hackamore that wasn't handmade?"

"Okay," said Shorty, "I'm still talking. The knife Rich just traded me, a new latigo strap, a six-foot canvas tarp (it's laying right over there), that buckskin coat hanging on the wall (it's too big for me and worth ten bucks) and my new Rich Hobson saddle for your Porter low association saddle and coonskin cap. Ya can't turn that down."

They traded after much fussing and hemming and hawing.

"You damn fool," I frothed at the Top Hand. "That's the best saddle you'll ever get that you just traded off."

"Where's the hat?" said Pan, as Shorty lifted the coonskin from Pan's to his head.

Shorty stepped to a coal-oil box and reached into it. He shuffled to Pan and handed him a silk stocking. The Top Hand stared hard at the relic, and gingerly fitted it over his head. The foot end of the stocking dangled on his shoulder. His long hawklike face stood out like the Indian head on a buffalo nickel. He grinned.

"She's a dandy, Shorty—a real dandy hat. What the hell do ya want to trade me now, Shorty, for Rich's solid gold pocketknife, that tarp there with the rips and holes underneath the folded part that you just traded me, and that mouse-eaten latigo strap. That's all good stuff, Shorty, good goods—what ya got to trade?"

Shorty pondered a minute, then shook his head.

"I hate to do it, but if you throw in that silk scarf and that zipper jacket, I'll trade you a darn good horse—sight unseen."

"Leave out the jacket, Shorty—I'll trade ya this real high-class zipper tobacco pouch instead of the jacket."

"Who cares about a zipper?"

"Zipper pouches are all the style down in New York and Wyoming, ain't they, Rich?"

"They're stylish as hell," I said. "Anybody can see that."

"Can a guy get as far as Bryant's on the bone model ya want to trade, Shorty?"

"The horse ain't showing a rib," said the hunchback. "You want a horse for the works then—a poor deal for me."

"Horse has to be delivered to the cabin door," said Pan.

Shorty hurriedly went through the door, and Alfred turned to Ole. "What cayuses has Shorty got in?"

"He's gonna get rid of Old Scabby White," said Ole. "He's got one half-Arabian, a wild horse, in the pasture, but he wouldn't trade him for a hundred dollars."

Ole turned to Pan.

"Scabby White—he's okay, but must be twenty-five years old. Everybody knows Scabby long time."

Pan was standing at the door. He spoke over his shoulder.

"Panhandle Phillips has got himself a horse—and a good one." He stepped out the door. "A real top cow horse," drawled the Top Hand.

We followed him out. The sound of hoofs thudding the ground announced the arrival of the new member of the Bloater crew.

Shorty neck-reined a long-built, long-necked, slab-sided white gelding awkwardly around in a circle. He jumped off and handed the reins to Pan. Pan grinned and winked at me. He hopped on Scabby and forced him into a belabored trot, then he proudly rode on to the water hole below the house, where Scabby sniffed first at the water, and then at his new master. I saw the Top Hand spit on his right hand, and then rub it into Scabby's mouth. Without further ado, he led his new-found friend to the barn, where sounds of rustling hay issued forth.

Shorty yelled, "Hey, Pan, what the hell are you doing? Bedding down that old crowbait in my good redtop hay? That don't go on the deal. Just a horse, not a half a ton of hay too."

And so it was that our ranch took a stride forward towards ultimate operation. This was to be the beginning of a life in which the Top Hand and I took second place, while various other beings such as Nimpo and Old Scabby White stepped to the front of the stage.

Before we pulled out the following day, Shorty rode with us around his pasture and showed us his ranch layout. In a narrow slough we rode up on four horses, who snorted and whirled back towards Shorty's east wing. By doing a fast quarter we were able to run the wild horses into the corral.

There were two bays and two browns. One of the browns was a mare which Shorty deftly roped. As soon as the rope lit on her neck, she trotted up to the hunchback, throwing her head up and down.

"Whip-broke," said Pan. "You can tell 'em every time."

"She's broke," said Shorty, "and whip-broke too. George Powers did a good job."

The mare whinnied softly as Shorty rubbed her nose.

"She's worth a whole herd of horses," said Shorty.

Pan was not paying any attention to Shorty. He was looking at a trim-legged bay horse that pranced around the far end of the corral with its head and tail in the air. The white-stockinged bay occasionally snorted. His eyes had the look of a wild animal in a trap. My eyes, like the Top Hand's, became glued to this magnificent specimen of horse. The shiny, short-backed bay danced and whirled back and forth in front of us, looking for a way under or over the seven-foot corral fence. It was just a bit too high for him.

Alfred turned to Shorty.

"That bay ball-of-fire is going to be just a little too much for you, Shorty. What will you take for him as he stands?"

"Ole is going to take his rough edges off for me. There's nobody in this country will deal me out of that Sugarloaf Arabian."

"He sure has the earmarks of an Arab," said Pan, "all but his forehead. It ain't got quite enough dish in it. But then he's got something else in him too. Must have."

Shorty turned to me.

"That bay there is the partner of that Nimpo Lake cayuse you're riding. He's the other colt that Domas saved when the Sugarloaf wild band was wiped out. I helped run them in and dealt Domas out of him. He's the best-looking horse I've seen out of a show ring."

"What show ring, Shorty?" Alfred asked. "Where did you ever see a show ring outside of some cattle-loading pen."

"That's all right," returned Shorty. "I'm not telling you uneducated bunch of farmers where I've been and what I've seen before I got rimrocked back here. That's my secret."

Back at the house, as we were preparing to leave, Pan asked Shorty to name a price on the bay gelding. Shorty said, "No price."

We rode away towards Bryant's.

I made up my mind I was going to get that horse. I didn't know how it would be done for our budget allowed us only thirty dollars for top saddle horses.

Pan, wearing the long dangling silk stocking pulled tightly over his ears, rode Old Scabby White ahead, while Alfred and I snickered to ourselves behind.

I yelled, "Old Scabby Pan and Old Scabby White."

Then Alfred chimed in:

> "Old Scabby White and Scabby Pan
> Proudly rode towards Anaham."

We kept up the razzing until we crossed the creek near Bryant's. Then Pan, who had paid no attention to us whatsoever, called over his shoulder, "Ride up here you gigglin' diaper-changers, and listen to a man talk real horse sense."

We rode our horses up on either side of Pan and Scabby.

"You two boneheads better learn how to make a trade," said Pan.

"Yeah—you sure are a smart guy, giving away a Porter saddle that can't be bought in Canada, and is only three years old. You look like the bonehead to Alfred and me."

"Just look at me now," said Pan easily. "I've got a buckskin coat worth ten dollars, a saddle that's good enough for any man—and all I give away was useless junk. Not worth seven dollars. I figure Scabby here cost me six dollars, and Scabby is going to be just like a colt when I get through with him."

He patted the neck of Old Scabby who kept stoically plodding ahead.

"You're wearing a nice-looking hat," said Alfred. "Your neck's going to get frosted. I don't see anything to protect it from the wind."

"I'm ridin' home a horse," said Pan, "and he's got a saddle on him—that's what counts. What have you guys got to show? Too bad, boys, but always give boot when ya trade, little stuff, piled up high to look good—and walk out with the prize!"

CHAPTER IX

The Snuffy Arabian

Early in March, a hot dry wind whipped across the snowbound Anahim country, breaking up ice-choked lakes and streams, and peeling off the crust from the snow.

It was a real chinook wind, and that same day of the chinook I rode happily out of Shorty King's yard on Nimpo, leading behind me the snappiest thousand pounds of horseflesh I had ever seen.

Nimpo was just as happy as I was to be reunited with his old pal. They both whistled and blew through their nostrils, and pranced and danced on springlike pasterns beside each other on the road.

It was Cyrus Lord, our first real Anahim friend and our much-respected adviser, who had suggested to me that I trade my rifle and a few smaller items to Shorty for the bay horse if I wanted him so badly. Cyrus told me that Shorty had spoken to him several times about the old 250-3000 Savage take-down model that I never used.

Cyrus' tip had proved good. When I had added fifteen dollars to the rifle and a pile of junk, Shorty gave in.

After I showed the bay to Cyrus, I carried on to the Three Circle, where I was helping Jim Holt put a floor in the cabin and repair fence. It was there that I was finally put on the spot and had to ride the bay.

Billy Dagg had dropped in for coffee on his way to help Eddie Collet and Tim Drainey finish a drift fence. He whistled through his teeth when he got a look at the stocking-legged bay.

"Have ya topped him out yet?" asked Billy, eyeing the horse and then me.

"No, he ain't," drawled the Texan. "We sacked him out yesterday, and now we're gonna slip a blindfold over his head, and the boy here is gonna crawl his frame. He's not gonna stall it off any longer."

Billy, a top bronc rider, shook his head.

"You're gonna have a real nice little ride, boy."

By this time my knees were shaking so hard I was afraid the two men would notice it. Most of the Anahim men could ride and break out their own colts, but they knew nothing of my past riding experiences, taking it for granted, mostly because of Pan's obvious horse savvy, that I had done a fair amount of bronc twisting. This was the way any young rancher would want it, and I made up my mind that someway, and with the help of God, I would ride this horse.

I knew that if he bucked me off the first time, it would be near impossible for me to ride him a second time. A sure way to spoil a good horse is to let him pitch something or somebody off the first time. The next time he bucks harder and higher than before, determined to feel again that object on his back unloosened and piled off.

I figured that as long as I had to ride the horse, I might as well act like an old-time bronc fighter. I turned to Jim.

"I'll bring out my chaps and spurs. If you guys want to watch a show without putting up any dough, you've got to earn your admission tickets. Throw down that cayuse and cinch my scab down good and hard on him, and I'll be out."

"I'll haze for ya, Rich," said Billy. "You'll need some hazin' to keep ya off that one strip of fence over there, and out of the jungle."

I walked over to the cabin and lay down on a bunk a minute to get my muscles completely relaxed. I heard hoofs pounding, and men grunting. I could hear the Texan say, "I got him." Then Billy: "Where the hell is his saddle? I can't let go his head."

When I figured the horse was saddled and ready, I buckled on my chaps, fitted on my short-shanked bronc spurs, and walked towards the corral.

The bay was standing rigid and trembling, his legs wide apart. A gunny sack, used for a blindfold was tucked through the hackamore headstall. Jim had taken a long end of the hackamore rope and made a joined set of rope reins. The left-over loose end he had half-hitched around and around the chin side of the noseband until it fitted tight.

When a man rides out a colt with a hackamore, the animal has the best of it until his chin gets sore. The pressure of the noseband, if low on the horse's nose, partially shuts off his wind; and when his chin gets sore, the rider, by exerting pressure on the shank rope, is able to twist the horse around in a circle or hold him in. Thus he can gradually teach a horse to neck rein.

The first few times a green, high-lifed colt is ridden, his mouth can be ruined by fighting against a steel bit. That is one reason why a rough string rider often uses a hackamore instead of a bridle.

Now Billy prepared for action. He loosened up his lariat rope, put it back in the rope strap, tested his cinch, and crawled up on Basilo, his tall, half-thoroughbred, half-Percheron mixture, by record one of the fastest horses in the country.

Jim handed me my hackamore rope and stepped back quietly. I pushed my hat down hard on my head, then moved in cautiously towards the point of the bay's shoulder, carefully tested the cinch. It was tight.

The Arabian stood motionless. I caught and twisted a handful of mane in my left hand, fitted the tip of the toe into the stirrup, took a deep breath, prayed, and swung up into the saddle.

The blind fell away from the horse's head before my right foot caught the off stirrup. He sprang into action.

I was off to a damn poor start. I remember being completely unseated that first jump. The gelding's twisted body shot me up three feet above the saddle. I reached desperately for leather with my hands and spurs, but missed completely. I could hear Jim yelling something, and saw Billy and his horse cutting in in front of us.

I came down with a crash in back of the cantle; then lit forward on the horn. I lost both my stirrups—and my legs flew high in the air as I was again pitched clear. But the horse miraculously lit back under me again.

"What a hell of an exhibition I'm making of myself," I thought.

Somehow I got both feet back in the stirrups, and for a moment was sitting down tight in the saddle. The bay quit pitching and crow-hopping ahead—now it seemed that there was nothing to it. I thought I had him and let out a whoop—but before either Billy or I realized what he was up to, the horse changed direction, and leapt high over the fence, and ran in the direction of Sugarloaf Mountain.

Limbs and sticks slashed by my face; bark and tree trunks pounded my chaps unmercifully. I thought, "Kick clear, you fool— this is death coming at you like a battering ram."

I had no control over the bay who raced low to the ground at a dangerous speed.

We shot out onto an opening. I could see deep holes filled with rocks scattered across its surface. The horse bucked and ran between the holes, whirled to one side, and pitched along the edge of the opening.

By this time I had just about had it. A dull misty haze settled down around me. Would this horse never quit? Every bone and muscle in my body ached. My nose started to bleed. A kind of high-tension humming sound rang in my ears.

Suddenly Billy Dagg charged out of the sticks. He caught the horse by the headstall, gathered the loose end of the hackamore shank, and snubbing us up, led us back to the Three Circle, where Jim Holt met us yelling, "Coffee for the buckaroos."

He grinned as he drawled, "I never see'd a man get throwed so damn far so many times, and still get back in the saddle. Boy, you're either a great trick rider—or an awful lucky guy!"

I didn't tell him which of the two I was.

(An interesting side note. After Jim Holt at the age of sixty-six made a spectacular ride in the Williams Lake Stampede, investigators found that James Guy Holt is listed as one of the ten great American bronc riders of all time.)

Those days in March were bronc riding, bucking practice days for me. The bay horse I named Stuyve, after an old friend of mine in the East. Every day I saddled Stuyve, slipped into the saddle and rode out eight or ten crooked pitches. The only trouble was that he seemed to be getting higher, more crooked and consistently better at his bucking, and I wasn't improving fast enough with my riding to keep up with him.

Nimpo was still hard to saddle and extremely touchy around the head and ears. I had to squeeze him in between a gate and the corral to get his saddle on. Often, when he was ready for a bit and bridle, I had to spill him on his back to adjust his headstall.

Bert Leaman's barn and house were finally completed, and Pan rode over to Jim's on Scabby White. He watched me get nearly unloaded on Stuyve, and struggle a long time with Nimpo. He rolled and lit a cigarette, looked thoughtfully at my two saddle horses, and turned to me.

"Now, friend, as I see it, you've got to give those cayuses some exercise. That's all they need—plenty of trail behind them. I want to drop in on Eddie Collet and see that new set of corrals he's built, then ride on to George Powers'.

"We can plan on four days of long trail rides, and then you'll have saddle horses you can use. I'll ride one colt, and you ride the other. Today fifteen miles to Eddie's. Tomorrow twenty miles to Powers'. One day riding around George's, and the fourth day thirty-five miles back.

"After that we'll have to start buying horses and get our outfit ready to crack those Itcha Mountains by May first. I bought that small stack of good green hay at Behind Meadows from Andy. We can harden up our ponies on it. Behind Meadows is our new headquarters.

"By the first of May this here outfit is gonna hit the trail around the western base of the Algaks. I've found we can follow the Ulgatcho Indian trail to within a few miles of Andy Holte's, before we swing northeast into the bush. We're all set to go into action. Go in and tell Jim you've got to roll your bed. The big push is on."

CHAPTER X

Horses for the Long Trek

Behind meadows was an ideal horse camp. We turned our newly purchased horses loose in a 160-acre log-fenced pasture. Inside the enclosure, green grass two inches high mingled with the dry stubble of the previous year. Slough grass grew high and rank in little gullies and swales, and when the horses really wanted a bellyful before picking at the tender shoots of new highland grass, the low spots were where they got it.

Nimpo and Stuyve never left each other's sides. They grazed close together and completely ignored Old Scabby White. The two of them acted suspiciously as if they considered their social background far superior to that of Scabby's. Although Scabby tried to be nonchalant about the whole thing, occasionally I could see a wistful lonely look come over his sad face.

Then Pan traded Cyrus Lord out of Old Joe for what he claimed was less than six dollars' worth of useless junk. Old Joe was a dirty brown-colored, sway-backed wasp of a horse, who stood a little above a tall Indian's waist. His ears were as long as a donkey's, and moved like signal flags back and forth on his head.

When Cyrus got wind of Pan's brag that he had got Joe for six dollars, Cyrus started the rumor that Old Joe was at least twenty-five years old. Besides his burro-like appearance, the old cayuse had another claim to fame. He was a natural running walker. He could walk hurriedly away from the fastest flat-footed walker in Anahim.

Pan was ecstatic about his outstanding saddle string—Old Joe and Old Scabby White. He curried them up, trimmed their tails and shaggy foretops, massaged their pasterns and shod them. Each night he fed them the best hay.

When Pan turned Old Joe loose in the pasture, the waspy little brown burned a rag across the opening towards Old Scabby who stood by himself, ears alerted, expectantly watching his approach.

Scabby stepped forward and greeted the newcomer with a high happy whinny. Old Joe whinnied back. They came together, stood shoulder to shoulder, and with their old worn-down teeth started scratching each other's manes.

The next morning I noticed that Joe and Scabby deliberately turned their backs on Nimpo and Stuyve. They had formed their own little club.

Alfred Bryant joined us in our real horse-buying expedition. The trip to the Chilcotin took us two weeks, and our horses burned up about four hundred miles of trail. We used the Bloater as our chuck wagon. I was driver and cook. Pan and Alfred pushed the horses down the road behind Bloater.

We had quite a time getting the Old Bloater started. Fortunately Pan had removed the battery when we moved to Cyrus Lord's in the fall, so that after it was cleaned up, it still showed a faint spark. Alfred hooked on to the front axle with a snuffy four-horse team. Pan gripped the wheel, threw the old car out of gear—the horses smashed into their traces, and away they went.

The high-strung horses, sensing the car rolling behind them, and hearing the crunching noise of the gears when Pan threw them in, nearly got away with the outfit. But Alfred swung the leaders into a jackknife and stopped the runaway.

The horses finally got used to the car and quietened down. They had to pull it some two miles down the road before the engine began to heave and sputter.

On the return trip we stopped at Pete McCormick's Kleena Kleene ranch. Pete was a tall, sunburned, slow-talking Montanan, who took out hunting parties, trapped and played with a small bunch of good horses. Pete had been the official guide for Sir Norman Watson on his ascent of Mount Waddington.

While Pete and I were up in the Kleena Kleene hills pounding leather in back of Pete's string of horses, Pan and Alfred were busy taking the rough edges off the unbroke stuff we'd picked up at the rancheree near Alexis Creek.

That day the boys halter-broke five of the six head and topped out two horses apiece, and sacked out the works of them. It was a good day's work for two men, particularly as Pete's corral system wasn't the handiest place to work in, what with collapsing log fences, and the ground covered with a generous sprinkling of stumps.

The expression—"taking the rough edges off"—is a cowboy colloquialism meaning the "topping off" or riding of an unbroke horse for the first time. It can also mean riding a snuffy horse that hasn't been used for a long time. Further, the expression includes the use of a saddle. You simply don't take the rough edges off a cayuse bareback.

"Sacking out" is an expression used to cover the method of rubbing a gunny sack, a saddle blanket or any soft material over, around and under an unbroke horse to accustom the animal to the feel of objects touching his body, and to show him that physical contacts with man are not going to hurt him.

Pan traded Pete the faithful Old Bloater for an unbroke two-year-old stallion, two unbroke bay geldings, Eddie and Crop Ear, the Bear, a coal-black five-year-old, and Piledriver, a big, half-standard-bred black colt with a bald face. Pan also beat Pete out of six pack-saddles, assorted ropes and cinchas, some latigo leather, several moose-hair saddle blankets, and raw-hide pack boxes, or alforkases.

At Pete's, Pan looked between the corral logs at our bunch of horses. Turning to Alfred and me, he squinted, and in his twangy nasal voice said, "Did you two boneheads ever figure out what we've got to do to those cayuses before we leave this place?"

I said nothing but waited for Alfred to stick his foot in it.

"Sure," said Alfred. "We'll trim up their tails and their hoofs, then throw on their packs."

The Top Hand studied Alfred closely, shook his head sadly at him, then turned to me.

"Look here, cowboy," he drawled, "you're supposed to have

strength enough to carry your brains off the ground, and I'll bet you ain't got a real thought stirrin' in that bald head under your hat."

I cut in before he could get any further.

"Sure—it's the usual way of big-headed Pan Phillips. He's just now thought of some little trick that we've overlooked, and he's going to rub it in on us because he's thought of it first."

The Top Hand snorted through his long nose. The noise sounded like a disgusted moose.

"Boys," said he, "nobody's thought about registerin' a brand with the B.C. government, and if any of these horses get loose on us, we ain't got any claim on them at all. Here's fifteen horses, including the five head we traded Pete out of, our Anahim Lake bunch, and the rancharee colts. They all belong to us, yet we've got no way of provin' it."

"Ain't you smart?" said Alfred. "You must have lots of brains back of that big beak of yours."

The Top Hand continued. "Now you fellows figure we're stuck, but let me tell you a real stick man's never stuck. I've talked it over with Pete in there, and it's okay with him. We're gonna slap Pete's brand on all our stuff. That's good enough for us for the time being and until we get a brand registered with the government. So, boys, tomorrow on goes Pete's MK Bar brand on the left hip, and I'm alterin' the stud horse. He's too small and fine-built for any stud we want. Nothin' to it, boys. One man with brains is all any outfit needs."

Back at Behind Meadows, eighteen head of broke and unbroke cayuses bucked and played about the pasture. As younger horses were added to the string Nimpo had taken charge.

He was a terrific fighter. No group of horses was too many, and no horse was too big for him to handle. His sinister approach to a strange horse was terrifying. He would approach a newcomer with bared teeth, his body low to the ground, writhing and twisting more like a snake than a horse. Horses seldom waited to find out what Nimpo's intentions were.

After watching his short but rough encounter with Andy Christenson's big, supposedly mean, eighteen-hundred-pound, half-Clyde stallion, I was convinced that Nimpo was the quickest, shiftiest and most vicious thousand pounds of fighting horse I had ever seen. The clumsy Clyde lasted about ten unhappy seconds. Nimpo leapt in and out with front and hind feet so fast that the stunned beast was on the run before he knew what had hit him.

After Nimpo had undeniably established himself as the leader of the cavvy, new arrivals must have been warned by the old-timers that the serious-minded, blazed-faced black meant business. They left him strictly alone, and seemed to be content to be herded by him to any part of the pasture.

But now, strangely enough, Nimpo allowed Scabby White and Old Joe to feed fairly close to him and Stuyve. Although he paid little attention to the two old cayuses, he never bothered them, nor did he allow other horses to get mean or ornery with them.

All the while Stuyve lived the life of Riley. Nimpo would find a new two-inch growth of lush redtop, drive the other horses away, and he and Stuyve would move happily on to it.

Pan and I were shoeing horses in one of the corrals, and Alfred was pounding out shoes on a homemade anvil, when he called to us, "Hey fellows—there's George and Mary Ann Turner and some stranger looking over our horses. Wonder what's on their minds."

I remembered meeting George Turner when we had been in Williams Lake the fall before. I also remembered that the Turner ranch ran a bunch of horses on the same range as Pete. I had seen the Turner brand on several groups of stick-cracking cayuses when Pete and I had rounded up his horses—and the Montanan had told me about Mary Ann.

"Just as tough as a man," Pete had said. "Chases wild horses bareback in the jungles. Can outride most men."

Now the trio came trotting up to the corral. George Turner yelled "hello" at Pan and me, and he and his thin-faced friend rode on over to Alfred, where they dismounted and began to talk.

The girl pulled her horse up sharp at the corral and looked down at Pan and myself. I noticed she was trim-waisted, narrow-eyed, dark and very good-looking. She had thin lips and extremely white teeth. She wore a wide-brimmed Stetson, a red scarf, tight-fitting rider's pants, and wide-tailed bat-wing chaps. A shell-studded gun belt with a leather holstered six-shooter hung from her right hip.

I said "hello" in unison with Pan, and noticed, just in time to avoid hazarding further pleasantries, that she was angry. I quickly picked up Eddie's front foot and started rasping it off.

I heard Pan say, "Nice day." Then a moment's silence. Then the girl:

"Mister, that's my horse you've ruined. My half-blooded stallion. First I want an explanation, and then I'm turning the rest over to the law."

Pan spoke low and with a nasal drawl, "Lady, I'm afraid I don't savvy your talk."

I knew Pan was getting his wits together, and was stalling for time.

The girl cut in: "You'll savvy a lot in a hurry, mister. You've not only put Pete McCormick's brand on a horse that's neither Pete's nor yours, but you've ruined a valuable animal."

I realized immediately what had happened. Pete had picked up Mary Ann's stud by mistake, traded him to us, and Pan had altered him from a stallion to a gelding.

This was dynamite. I reached for Eddie's shoe, placed it in position on his hoof, and without looking up, began tapping in the horseshoe nails.

"Well, well," said Pan. "Now that sure is tough going. You've done lost a horse, lady? Is that what you're tellin' me? I'm sorry to hear about that. As fer this outfit, we ain't lost no horses, 'cause we've got a brand on each and every one of them."

By the slow easy swing of Pan's words, I knew he had now figured something out and was working towards the climax.

"I'll say you have," shrilled the girl. "You've got Pete's brand on my horse."

Pan cut in quickly.

"Easy there, lady—easy now. There's no use to get yourself all excited. If us boys can help ya find your hoss we'll do it."

"He's right there," screamed the girl, and pointed at the gelding who now nibbled at grass blades.

I let go Eddie's foot and stood up to see the last and final round. Pan looked around at the animal.

"That horse there?" he asked.

"Yes," the girl said, "that horse there."

"That horse there has a brand in plain sight, miss—MK Bar.

That's Pete McCormick's brand. Ya better not tangle yourself with the law, miss, 'cause that's the only brand he's wearin', and the law says the branded horse belongs to the owner of that brand. It's in the brand book in every country."

The Top Hand paused a moment. He looked speculatively at Mary Ann, a mischievous grin spreading slowly across his face.

"These here horses all belong to Pete McCormick by law, and it's up to Pete hisself to lay charges agin me for stealin' his cayuses. You can tell Pete that you've done caught up with his stolen herd, and that his herd has growed, 'cause there's eighteen swamp-eaters now carryin' his card."

George Turner, Alfred and the thin-faced stranger walked to the corral leading their horses. George snapped into the saddle. He turned in his hull and looked sharply at his sister.

"What's all the argument, Mary Ann?" he asked. "That's your Pet alright. There's no question about it. But it's not the fault of these boys. Pete made the mistake. He's got slick two-year-olds that look a lot like your horse. Come on now—we've got a long ride ahead of us, and we'll see Pete when we get back to Kleena Kleene."

George waved at Pan and me and turned his saddle horse towards the road.

The girl looked at the horse. Slow tears crept to the corners of her eyes. Pan glanced sharply at her as she swung her cayuse around.

"Hold on a minute, lady," said the Top Hand. "Go put your halter on that prize horse and lead him to Pete's. Anybody can make a mistake." Pan paused a moment, "Tell Pete if he's done made the mistake, to send me back a cayuse a hundred pounds heavier than that one, and one that ain't over six years old."

Pete had made a mistake all right, and to show his sportsmanship, he gave us the famous black pack horse Nigger to replace the Turner horse. After Nigger had helped us on several pack trips, we gave him back to Pete in exchange for a chunky bay cayuse. Later the little Turner horse turned into one of the best cutting horses in the country.

I was amazed at the ease with which this horse mix-up was settled. In most stock countries an event of this kind would have resulted in the arrival of the law, a lot of name calling, and bad feelings. Instead of neighbors taking sides, and stupid grudges resulting, this Anahim frontier straightened out such incidents with understanding tolerance and good humor, and the involved parties generally led the kidding and joking which invariably resulted.

The other day, when I reminded George Turner of this particular incident, the black-haired rider, who is now punching cows for me at my Rimrock Ranch, grinned, "I was mighty grateful to Pan to go to all the work of alterin' that stud," he said. "It saved me the trouble."

Alfred could not go with us on the push. He had his own cattle and horses to attend to, and a packing contract with Andy Christenson; but he told us he'd be ready for action after July.

Eighteen-year-old Tommy Holte joined us the last week at Behind Meadows, and offered to throw in with us. He had just returned from his first trip to town. His 450 mile round trip, saddle-horse expedition had been to Williams Lake, where, with soapsuds in his eyes and on his hands, he had nearly drowned in a bathtub, and later been run over by a bicycle. When he was escorted out of a beer parlor for being under age, Tommy rode away vowing that this was the first and last "city" he would ever visit.

"Now," said Tommy, "I want to get back in the bush as far as I can from this here civilization."

A few days after our return from the horse-buying expedition, Pan and I purchased the necessary grub and equipment for the Algak-Itcha push from Andy Christenson. We then went over our finances. Between us our cash had dwindled to a low of eighteen dollars, but I had two premium renewal checks, commissions from insurance policies I had sold in New York four years before. The checks together amounted to sixty-eight dollars.

"I don't know how in the hell we're going to finance grub, machinery and equipment purchases, if we find anything behind those mountains," I said to Pan. "We're in so deep now that we couldn't buy a return ticket back to Wyoming."

Pan snorted loudly. Then he looked down his long nose at me and snorted again.

His snorts were beginning to irritate me, but I had to admit they were rapidly developing character. They had a horsy undertone to them—and there was now little difference between Pan's routine snorts, and those made by a wide-nostriled wild horse trapped in a rodeo shute.

"Friend," he said, "ya never want to worry about that long green. There ain't no place to spend it back there behind those Itchas. When the time comes, and we need a little cash, we'll figure out a way to get hold of some. We're doin' fine. We got eighteen horses, a summer's grub and all the ictus we need for the time being."

It was on the tenth of May, the day before our pack train's departure into the no-know land, that Behind Meadows horse camp broke into wild confusion.

Pan, Tommy and I were pack-breaking horses in the corral, when out of the jungle came a loud blast of voices and yells. Looking up we beheld a body of moose-hided horsemen coming towards us on the gallop.

This group was the advance guard of a fast-moving buckboard, pulled by four leggy bay horses, and driven by Alfred Bryant. On the buckboard, and lashed firmly in place, stood a barrel of Itcha Mountain fog.

In accordance with the custom of these backlands, the men had ridden miles from their distant homes on saddle horses to see their friends off on what they knew would be a long and hard trip. These frontiersmen knew what we would be up against during the following months of complete isolation from the world, and, despite the rapid evaporation of the Itcha Mountain fog, I soon noticed that the gang had come for another purpose.

At the saddle shed I surprised George Powers, who was mending and repairing packsaddle rigging and latigos. He was working with his mug of fog and his opened tool kit in front of him. Young Tim Drainey worked in silence beside him. George looked up as I stepped through the door. He was embarrassed, and grinned at me sheepishly.

"Thought I'd give your rigging the once over before you pulled," he said simply. "Figured you boys might not have the right tools in case something busted on the trail." Tim didn't look up from the job Powers had assigned him.

Out at the corrals, Lester Dorsey, Billy Dagg and Eddie Collet helped Pan finish the heavy job of shoeing and rockpacking the broncs we were going to pack. Alfred and Cyrus Lord helped me sort out, weigh and balance the food and equipment into separate pack units of two hundred pounds or less each.

We had rigging for eleven pack horses. Most of the units consisted of three-quarter, double-rigged packsaddles, with the name of the horse the saddle fitted written in red letters along the side boards, a breast strap, set of heavy britching, a good rig to hold the saddle in place in steep going. Along with each rigged saddle were two side boxes, a twenty-foot length of three-eighths-inch rope to be used as a sling rope holding the pack in an even position, and a thirty-six foot half-inch lash rope with bone hook. This rope is used for the diamond hitch that is tightly lashed about the complete pack over the top of a twelve-ounce, six-foot-square canvas tarp called a pack mantle.

The metallic clanging of an iron bar on a washtub up at the cabin brought us all on a run for a big meal which Andy Christenson and Bert Smith had been busy cooking.

Before dark we were completely organized, and the men, sitting on the floor around the heater, gave bits of advice. Every one of them studied my grub and equipment list to be sure we had forgotten nothing.

Strangely enough, one terrifically important item was overlooked by every one of us—mosquito dope and mosquito netting—and Pan, Tommy and myself were later to pay mightily for this omission.

CHAPTER XI

The Carefree Horseman

THE COWBOYS SPENT THE NIGHT in the hayshed and on the floor of the cabin, and early in the morning helped us pack. They waved and yelled, "Good luck—good riding!" and rode off into the jackpines.

Riding one of his own horses, a short-backed, short-legged bay gelding, Tommy took the lead. Pan and I rode abreast behind the string. It was my job to stay at the rear of the main bunch of horses in the drag and hold them on the trail behind Tommy.

Pan was bush popper. His was a hard and dangerous job, particularly when moving a band of half-wild horses through heavy bush and stick country. When animals crashed off the trail into the jungle in an effort to escape, it was up to the bush popper, not only to charge his horse in after them, but also to outrun and manoeuvre them back onto the trail.

As could be expected we had some trouble at first, when the whole herd stampeded out of Behind Meadows, and forced Tommy into a hard gallop to hold the lead position. Some of the pack horses started to buck, and I expected to see our grub and equipment scattered through the brush.

Two hundred yards up the trail, the four unbroke, unpacked colts whirled off into the timber. Pan, leaning low in the saddle, reined his saddle horse into the jungle behind them. The running horses didn't get far before the big crop-eared horse dashed in front of them, cutting off their forward rush. Pan snapped them unmercifully in their rumps with the knotted end of a rope. They ran back into the main bunch.

We were lucky. No packs were turned under bellies. Finally Tommy slowed the leaders to a trot, and then forced them back into a walk.

To the north of us, the Rainbow Mountains and the Algak Range were split by the Dean River that flows out of Anahim Lake and finally empties into the Pacific Ocean after following a twisted and devious route of some hundred and fifty miles. The Algak Range reaches eastward from the Dean River split to merge with the Itcha Mountains somewhere along their rocky summits. Just where the two mountain ranges merge, we have never been able to ascertain.

The only maps available of the unsurveyed region to the north had been compiled from the notes of a party of B.C. Lands surveyors, who in 1912 used one of the highest peaks in the Itchas as a triangulation point, named it the Itcha Cairn, and established its elevation at 7,998 feet.

On their epic mountaintop-to-mountaintop triangulations, to establish known points for the overall mapping of British Columbia's gigantic forest empire, the pioneer surveyors jotted down in their notebooks distant lakes, watersheds and any contour information they could obtain from these high points. But the so-called detail maps of the unexplored country sported few details. The empty white blank space glared up significantly at us; its only marks being a few lines with arrows indicating watersheds and, here and there, a lake. North of the Itchas, and extending east at the mountains' base, small arrowed lines converged to a bigger one, and marked the headwaters of the Blackwater River.

It was our plan to follow the Dean River north for the first twenty-five miles using the old Ulgatcho Indian trail. Then to swing east to Andy Holte's swamps. Andy is Tommy Holte's father and his homestead is the northernmost in the Anahim country. From there we hoped to move the train north under the foot of the Algaks, and later, if possible, swing up onto high land, where we could map out the country immediately beyond the mountains. From that point on Pan and I had made no plans.

Several hours before dark, Pan yelled at Tommy to halt. The pack train was on the edge of a slough grass swamp meadow rimmed by clumps of red willows and jackpines.

"A good place to camp," explained Pan. "Lots of feed and water, and we've made a good ten miles. Enough for soft pack horses. I don't want to see any sore backs or cinch galls at the beginning of the trip."

Tommy and I didn't object, but jumped down from our saddle horses, and tying our lariat ropes together, strung them around a group of jackpine trees. Into the rope corral Pan drove the horses. We roped them out one by one. Pan was trail boss. Now he told us to tie each horse up after taking the pack off.

"Get a couple of buckets out of the kitchen and start packin' me water," he said. "I'm gonna pour a bucket of cold water over each cayuse's back before we turn 'em loose."

Tommy and I began dipping buckets into a little creek on the edge of the meadow, and toting them over to the Top Hand. He used a gunny sack, and despite the flinching horses, rubbed the icy water over the middle of their backs where the pack saddles had rested during the day. The Top Hand explained to us the great importance of avoiding sore backs on a trip of this kind. A pack-saddle sore can be made in an hour, and yet take a month to heal, he told us.

"Once a cayuse gets a sore, a packer might as well figure he's dead flesh for the time being. This cold water and a good rubbing down at the end of each day cuts down the sore-back danger maybe fifty per cent, and not only hardens their backs, but stops any swelling."

Since then I have noticed that Pan has less sore backs in his string than many old-time packers.

After letting the horses roll, we staked three saddle horses out on good feed near camp, then belled a half dozen of the others, and turned them loose. The grass was good, and we didn't think there was a chance of any of them pulling out.

I cooked up a supper of frying-pan bannock, ham, rice and coffee.

We were dog-tired, and so crawled under a spruce tree into our sleeping bags soon after eating. We slept.

I opened my eyes. It was pitch-black. Pan was shaking me.

"Quick. Roll out and get a fire started. The horses must have pulled. Not a bell ringin'."

I rose up to a sitting position, cursed loudly, and groped about for my pants and boots.

Tommy had been looking for his pants, and I could see him moving about in his underwear. He kept saying, "I left them right here by the head of my bed."

I shivered when the cold air hit my underwear, and after some confusion got into my pants and started a fire. Finally Tommy found his pants, right where he had left them—by the head of his bed. Soon I had coffee boiling, and after swallowing down cupfuls of the brew, the two men rode off along the edge of the meadow under the pale yellow light of dawn.

Pan called back, "Have that cowman's breakfast for us. We'll be back in an hour."

I could hear their horses' hoofs cracking across the frosted ground; then intense silence closed over the camp. A vague breeze rustled the willow leaves. Far off in the direction of the Algaks I thought I heard the tinkle of a horse bell.

After a breakfast of oatmeal porridge, bacon and baking powder hotcakes, I grabbed up a double-bitted axe and cut down a small dead jackpine oozing with pitch. I chopped it into small blocks, then split the blocks into kindling and, sitting near the fire, whittled pitch shavings.

At ten o'clock there was still no sign of the boys. The disturbing thought crossed my mind that some of the horses might have struck out for their home range, more than a hundred and fifty miles away.

Later I became convinced that this was exactly what had happened. I realized only too well that horses will pull out for their home range early in the spring, even if their feed is good. It was possible that the remainder of the spring we would be riding behind tracks.

In the afternoon I threw my saddle on my staked horse, Stuyve, and rode along the edge of the swamp towards the mountains.

Stuyve was nervous and irritable. He didn't like being deserted by his pal Nimpo. He shied at birds and squirrels, and finally tried to down his head. I didn't want to take any chances of being bucked off or maybe hung up in a stirrup with no help around. I jumped quickly off his back and led him back to camp.

All afternoon I listened for bells. Occasionally I thought I could hear distant clanging, and then again I wasn't sure. The "hearing horse bells" illusion is a disease very common among riders who are hunting belled horses. The more you want to, the easier it is to hear them.

At dark I watered Stuyve in the little swamp creek, and restaked him by the left front foot on fresh grass. I made sure that the single leather hobble about his ankle was secure, and that the stake was solid. Then I strung up the rope corral in case the boys arrived during the night.

My dinner of dried moose meat, soaked in a pot of water during the day, and now fried in bacon grease with sliced onions didn't tempt me. I'd lost my appetite.

A fine haze rose into the darkness above the swamps. The staccato bark of a coyote broke the stillness, and out of the hushed silence drifted the watery gurgle of a northern bittern. I threw a couple of sticks on the fire. Sparks flared up into the dark. A night bird fluttered through the willow leaves above, and cackled as it came to rest on a limb.

I heard the distant whirring sound of a flock of ducks winging north through the sky—and finally all sounds in the swamps ceased. I crawled into bed under the spruce tree, and there spent a restless, rolling, uneasy night.

And then, all at once, the ground shook and trembled with pounding hoofs. Hoarse shouts rose above clanging bells. I rolled over in my bed and sat up half-dazed. Dark plunging bodies crashed through camp about me towards the rope corral. Pan was yelling at Tommy. I struggled into my clothes and groped for the pitch shavings. A dull glow in the dark showed me the dying coals of the campfire, and soon a cheerful blaze and the smell of boiling coffee broke the spell of the night.

Pan and Tommy staggered wearily to the fire and sank heavily to the ground. I passed tin cups of coffee into their outstretched hands.

Finally Tommy passed his cup back to me for a refill, sighed deeply and said, "We got 'em all. It was a hell of a trip. Changed saddle horses at Bryant's. We corralled one bunch there. The rest of 'em with Nimpo in the lead went cross-country to Toutestan where we cut off their tracks."

I handed Tommy back his cup, and glanced over to the rope corral where the horses stood dejectedly and without movement.

"You fellows have rode a long ways," I said.

Pan fumbled in his pocket for tobacco and papers, then carefully rolled a smoke. Reaching into the fire he picked up a burning stick and held it to his cigarette, then blew out smoke through his nose.

"We've rode seventy miles for them ornery cayuses," he said. "Old Buck, Big George, Little Roanie and the Piledriver were still on a trot behind Nimpo when we corralled 'em at Toutestan."

I looked at him and noticed that his long darkly tanned face was lined and haggard. His hard gray-green eyes were sunken in their sockets, and added to the impression that he was ten years older than his twenty-six years. The faces of both men were crisscrossed with scratches and cuts. Tree limbs and bushes and snags had left their marks. A long cut slanted upward from Tommy's cheekbone into his bushy blond hair, but I could see that the trip hadn't told on him as it had on Pan. I knew the Top Hand had been worrying as well as riding.

Pan had an annoying habit of never admitting he had made a mistake. No matter what happened, the Top Hand was usually able to think up some reason why a mix-up had been a good thing. The irritating part of it was that nine times out of ten he was able to vindicate the happening.

Now I wondered how he would manage to prove to us that this near-collapse of the expedition was a good thing. I winked at Tommy and said, "How about a few words of wisdom from the Top Hand? This is one crazy mistake that all three of us made, and this is also one time when Pan here is stumped. He can't think up a single reason why it was lucky the horses pulled out on us."

Tommy laughed.

Pan turned to him, "Rich here has got a blood clot on the head for sure. He doesn't realize that the best damn thing that ever happened to a trail outfit has just now happened to this one."

He paused for this opening blast to sink in.

"Maybe," said Tommy; "but I sure am tired, and so are the two horses I rode."

Pan snorted.

"Boys," he said, "we've learned a real big lesson—and we learned it at the start of the push. You fellows can figure out what could have happened if we hadn't had this wakin' up now, and stayed careless, and the cayuses had pulled out on us maybe a hundred miles or so back in no-man's land. They could have split in bunches of two or three head, each bunch pickin' a different way back over the mountains.

"Now—just figure that one out. We could easily have been left afoot, and never seen half the cayuses again. What's more, that run has taken the sharp edge off every last one of those ground-eaters. They'll be easy to handle from now on."

I grunted. "You win Panhandle—pick up the marbles!"

Pan continued, "From now on we either split the night into three shifts and ride herd on the horses, or else make up rope hobbles for every one of 'em. We're off to a good start and we won't get fooled agin."

After eating Pan struggled to his feet and started for his lariat rope.

I said, "You boys better rest today."

Reaching the rope corral, Pan called over his shoulder, "Nothin' doin'. We're gonna make Andy Holte's today—and I'm gonna break a horse to ride. Croppie's had too much trail already."

So saying, the exhausted Top Hand dabbed his loop on Big George, a five-year-old unbroke black horse with a blazed face from George Powers' remuda. Big George weighed about thirteen hundred pounds, and although he had a gentle eye and an easy disposition, still I thought Pan was taking a big chance riding him out in his exhausted and sleepless condition. I told him so.

Pan led the trembling black out of the rope corral, and Tommy and I started to snake out horses and throw on their packs. Pan tied his bronc to a tree, and joined us in the packing. In less than an hour we were ready for the trail. The horses had been easy to catch and pack.

Now Pan picked up his saddle and stepped cautiously over to Big George.

Tommy spoke up. "You're a fool, Pan, to take a chance of gettin' crippled up on the start of the trip. You sure ain't in no shape to ride today."

Pan paid no attention. Tommy looked at me and sadly shook his head.

"Get me a gunny sack," said Pan, "for a blindfold."

We saddled our own mounts for the day, and turned to watch Pan and the black. The Top Hand had worked the horse sideways to a group of trees, and was standing at the point of the animal's shoulder. He was talking softly to the bewildered horse as he ran his hand soothingly up and over his neck and behind his ears.

"You're just a big tired gentle fellow, ain't you, George? Just a sleepy tired horse. Sleepy and tired."

George's ears went from alert to relaxed. His eyes lost the frightened look. Pan said gently, "You're not even scared any more, are you, George? Most times you colts are just scared when we're breakin' you—you ain't mean like people think—and now you're too tired even to be scared."

Pan kept stroking and talking to him, and the animal's eyes began to flicker and his eyelids drooped. Then easily and without a single quick movement, Pan edged his saddle and pad onto Big George's back.

Tommy exclaimed to me, "The man's hypnotized the cayuse."

"You're right, Tommy," I said. "I always figure Pan hypnotizes a horse before he rides him."

Pan's eyes still stared straight into the half-shut eyes of the horse. He stroked him under the belly, and caught the dangling cinch.

"Get everything ready for the start," said Pan quietly—"the rope corral down, and the pack horses untied. We're gonna move out of here in a minute. Get me my bronc bridle, the one with the snaffle bit, and one of you boys pack my curb outfit on your saddle. I don't want to hurt this horse's mouth."

Five minutes later I swung up on Stuyve, and turning, saw Pan sitting on Big George's back. He tucked the blindfold under his belt and called, "Let her go."

Tommy and I started the train ahead up the trail. When they had strung out single file, Tommy dodged his horse into the bush and trotted into the lead position. Big George walked stoically along beside Stuyve in the drag.

"One more broke horse in the string when this trail gang hits into Holte's" said Pan. "There's nothin' that beats breakin' out a colt after he's got a lot of trail behind him."

Later Nimpo's pack turned under his belly, and he unloaded for a quarter of a mile. Tommy caught him by the halter. We were delayed an hour picking up tin cans and other paraphernalia.

Just before dark Tommy called back to us, "We'll be home in a few minutes. It's not more than a mile from here."

The train had left the heavy timber and we were skirting the edges of old beaver dams and willow patches. Grass and puddles of water spread before us. This looked like good country to me— and I wondered how much of it there was.

As I rode along, I thought about Tommy's father, Andy Holte.

Soon after their marriage, Andy and his fair-haired young wife left the security and comforts offered them by their well-to-do families on their rich gumbo land farms in Washington State, to drive a wagon north to the new frontier, west of the Fraser River.

In 1935, Andy held the unique distinction of running a cattle ranch further back from railroad and town than any white outfit in British Columbia, and as far as I know, in Canada or the United States. He had only trailed his beef out 260 miles to market twice since settling on his swamps seven years before, but each trail drive had taken nearly a month to reach Williams Lake.

Andy Holte is a real frontiersman. He is an extraordinary teamster whose deep-rutted wagon tracks are visible across this vast, uncharted, little-known country, through terrain where usually only a saddle or pack horse can follow.

Andy is one of the North's most colorful characters and his fame is legendary. He has an uncanny ability to sense a situation where a strong man and a fast horse are needed, and his sense of the ridiculous, love of strange contrasts and his desire to help his distant neighbors, leads him on a long trail of one adventure after another.

It is Andy who arrives on a fast horse in time to make a grueling ride for a plane or doctor to save some neighbor's life. It is Andy, on an errand, who happens to drop by in time to get a team out of a muskeg, or rope exhausted drowning cattle out of an ice-choked lake.

Andy is a hard-working and heady rancher, and a good provider, but he has one failing. He hasn't the slightest conception of time. Very seldom does he know what day of the month it is, or even what month. To him, winter and deep snow mean wild-horse-chasing time; spring and bad roads remind Andy that he has missed the short period when freighting is at its best, but he hooks up a six-horse outfit, and always manages to pound his wagonloads through. Summer is the season for exploring new country in search of bigger and better meadows where he can run more cattle—and any time is horse-trading time!

Young and attractive Mrs. Holte smiles when she says, "It's best to be tolerant and not scold Andrew when he does get home after one of his long absences, for when he's late I know it's because he's been helping some neighbor."

When I met Andy Holte for the first time, he came riding around a bend in the trail near Jim Holt's on a big short-coupled brown horse. I was startled by the man's close resemblance to one of my heroes, Will Rogers.

He rode straight up, but with a slight forward tilt in the saddle, a trim-built angular man in his early forties. Pale blue eyes looked shyly at me from a weather-beaten, slightly wrinkled, expressionless face.

An English tweed golf cap sat in the exact center of the stranger's head. He wore moose-hide chaps, a moose-hide shirt and vest, topped by a faded blue, satin-lapelled smoking jacket.

I couldn't help but notice his shoes. On one foot he wore an obviously expensive, high-heeled riding boot and a silver-mounted spur; on the other foot a worn congress boot, with a homemade, built-up heel and no spur.

He spoke in a twangy musical voice as he rode up alongside of me.

"You're ridin' a fine piece of flesh," he said, squinting at Nimpo.

"There's nothing wrong with him at all," I answered, "except he's hard to put a bridle on."

"Fights his head does he?" said the rider. "Well—there's only one thing to do. I'll trade ya horses straight across. My cayuse here will outrun and outwalk that black you're ridin'. This hard-grass ground-eater I'm toppin' will cut circles around that little swamp-bred saddler of yours."

I began to get mad.

"If that horse of yours is such a dandy, why don't you keep him?" I sputtered.

I didn't know that I was confronting Andy Holte, and that this was his customary approach—a horse-trade approach—that usually threw a stranger off balance, and always gave Andy an inkling of the other man's temper and his horse savvy.

Looking down at me he pushed his golf cap back on his head and scratched the fringe of blond hair over his ear. Then his face broke into an impish grin and he stuck out his hand.

"Shake hands, Rich," he said. "I've figured out which of the two new buckaroos you are. I'm Andy Holte."

I reached across my saddle horn to grasp a small, calloused, rope-burned hand that gripped like a vise on to my bigger one.

"I'm sure glad to know you, Andy," I said. "You're a long ways from home."

The Teamster grinned.

"Just on an errand," he said. "I'll ride along a ways with you, son. I want to hear all about what's going on down in the States. Tell me about this Roosevelt fellow; there's lots of news I've got to get caught up on."

He swung his horse about in the narrow trail.

Later Mrs. Holte told me the story of that particular trip of Andy's.

It was the end of February when Andy freighted a new cook-stove in to the Holte ranch. He couldn't find his monkey wrench to set it up. There was just one thing to do. That was to ride via saddle horse thirty-five miles to his nearest neighbors the Christensons, spend the night with them, borrow a wrench, and return the next day.

Andy hit the trail early. He trotted and loped his big brown gelding most of the way to Christenson's, but as fate would have it, Jim Holt had been down the day before, and borrowed the Christenson tool kit to work on a broken runner of his hay sleigh.

Andy wasn't daunted. He fed his horse hay and grain, spent the night at Christenson's, and early the next morning struck out for Jim Holt's—fifteen miles away. It was on this stretch of road that I had met him.

He laid over that night at Jim's. It was after dark when Gordon Wilson, a cowpuncher from the Tatla Lake country, rode in with big news. He had spotted a band of at least twenty wild horses, slicks, rimrocked by a heavy snowfall in a high valley beyond Tatla Lake. He said that the horses were big, flat-boned animals, many of them chestnuts and buckskins, and that there were a few pintos in the bunch.

Andy's eyes glittered. This was his failing—chasing wild horses. He looked at Gordon, and then dropped his eyes to the floor. He picked out a splinter from the Texan's woodbox, and taking out his jackknife began to whittle and to think.

He knew that the price he'd get for his bunch of beef in the fall would be no better than the two-cents-on-the-hoof he'd received the year before. At that time, in the 'thirties, Andy's financial position, like all other ranchers' in that discouraging period, looked grim. But he thought: "There's a market for horses of the type Gordon's describing. If I catch and halter-break ten head, and take the rough edges off 'em this spring, I can get seventy dollars apiece for them at railhead."

Andy had helped build the mile-long wings to the wild-horse corral near Tatla Lake. He asked Gordon how far the rimrocked horses were from the trap, and the cowpuncher replied that they were only about twenty miles back towards the mountain.

Andy knew that now was the time to corral the wild band. They would be half-starved and weak, and he figured the snow would be deep on the ridges. He would arrive home a week or so late, but with assets enough to cover the debt on the winter's grub and the new cookstove.

At daybreak Andy and Gordon rode east into a raging arctic blizzard. For two days the half-frozen men plunged their horses over the sixty miles of snow-choked trail to Bob Graham's Tatla Lake ranch.

Gordon and Andy had hard luck, for the wild horses had broken out of the valley and moved north onto a wind-swept plateau at the southern base of the Itcha Mountains.

The men followed tracks for days; once they had the thrill of jumping the band, and they gave their saddle horses a hard run for several miles at the flank of some of the mares and colts in the drag.

But Gordon's horse threw a shoe, but before he got lame both men realized the futility of pushing further, particularly as they were now on hard dry ground, where the snow had blown away, and the wild horses, having fed on bunch grass instead of snow-balls, were stronger than the tired saddle horses.

Back at Tatla Lake ranch, Andy found Bob Graham excited over samples of hard rock picked up some thirty miles southeast of Tatla Lake. He showed the chunks of quartz to Andy.

"Man, oh man," exclaimed Graham. "That vein's four feet wide and I'll bet it assays over a hundred dollars to the ton."

Andy was very serious. Practically his last dollar had gone for grain and grub for the horse run.

He had been away from home for nearly two weeks, and would arrive to face his family with the feeble excuse that he'd ridden more than three hundred miles, round trip, chasing a band of wild horses. Andy realized that this excuse wouldn't go far with Mrs. Holte and his daughters.

He listened carefully to Bob Graham's story, and closely examined the samples. Andy knew a little about rock, and what he saw set his blood to racing and his mind to working. Bob Graham studied Andy. He admired the carefree horseman. Graham rolled a chunk of quartz along the counter of his shop.

"Andy," he said, "I've got to get into that mine real sudden. It's not staked, and there's others are looking for it. I need a man who can pack and handle horses. How about coming in on it with me? We can stake all the best ground between the two of us."

Andy appeared to be thinking the proposition over as he carefully rolled a smoke. He lifted off his golf cap and laid it on the counter. Then he spoke.

"How long do you figure it will take us, Bob, to get in there and stake the country, and slide back out? Ya know, I left the missus and the kids back at the ranch a long time ago. Had to go to Christenson's to borrow a monkey wrench to set up our new cookstove."

Andy looked down at his congress boot. The built-up heel had come loose.

"I was just gonna be gone overnight," he said sadly. "Guess it's well into March now, ain't it, Bob?"

Graham thought a moment. He picked up the samples and dropped them in a sack. He spoke slowly.

"You know, Andy, strikes me that Mrs. Holte and the girls would be mighty pleased if you arrived home the part owner of a gold mine."

The next morning, as day broke over a bleak land of hard-crusted snow and frosted jackpines, Bob Graham and Andy Holte, leading two pack horses, rode southeast towards the headwaters of the Holmathko River. The riders covered the miles, and Andy's home grew still more distant.

At the end of March the two tired prospectors rode happily into the Graham ranch. They had staked the vein and the surrounding country in a legal manner.

Andy fed his horse grain, and immediately struck for home at a fast trot. He hadn't ridden far when his horse shied to the side of the road, and from the opposite direction came an Indian riding a black pony. Andy skidded to a stop as the Indian hailed him and explained in broken English that an elderly woman, whose husband had not returned from a freighting trip, was sick, and out of wood and water.

And so Andy, on his homeward journey, detoured thirty miles out of his way, and arrived at the old lady's homestead to find the place in really bad shape. The helpless woman was without wood, and her few head of stock had no hay or water.

For a week he labored and sweated, hauling hay to the feed racks, barrels of water to the house, timber from the bush. He later told me that the old homestead crosscut saw was in such shape that it took him over an hour to saw each log into stove-length blocks.

On April tenth, Andy rode timidly into the Holte ranch.

Mrs. Holte, after telling me the story, dryly commented, "It wouldn't have mattered so much being forty days late, but Andrew forgot the monkey wrench!"

Andy must have heard us yelling at the pack horses, for suddenly he came racing bareback out of a clump of jackpines on one of his daughter's cayuses, and confronting Pan for the first time, demanded that the Top Hand swap Big George for the little brindle pony he was riding.

He ranted and raved as he pointed his finger accusingly at Big George, insisting that the blaze-faced black was lumber-footed and petrified-boned. Pan, not knowing Andy's usual greeting to a stranger, was thrown completely off balance by the man's hard-hitting approach.

Tommy held up the horses, on his face a broad grin, and I doubled over my saddle horn. This was about the first time I had ever seen the Top Hand completely bewildered. He stared unbelievingly at the wildly gesticulating Teamster. Finally he pulled himself together enough to ask Andy what a lumber-footed, petrified-boned horse was.

Then Big George, who had had enough of this abuse, reared forward into Nimpo, who in turn ran into the horse in front of him. Andy yelled, and the whole herd of us pounded into the Holte yard with the Teamster bringing up the rear, his bald head shining, and his hat waving wildly over his head.

We found the wandering Teamster had been hard at work, making up for the six weeks he had recently lost. He was not only bucking up a year's supply of firewood, but was also blasting out a beaver dam which held water on over half of his home meadow. Where the frost had gone out of the ground, Andy was digging a deep drain ditch to carry the beaver dam water by and around the ranchhouse.

We lay over a day at the Holtes, repairing and reorganizing the pack outfit and resting the horses. Pan was correct when he claimed that the best thing that could have happened at the beginning of the trip was the break back and the subsequent miles of trail the horses had covered with little rest or feed. It was a subdued bunch of horses that now hungrily grazed within bell distance of the ranchhouse.

Andy helped us catch the horses and pack up. He insisted that he go along a short distance with us to see us safely down the trail. Catching up the brindle pony, and riding bareback with only a halter, he joined his son Tommy in the lead.

CHAPTER XII

Unexplored Territory

A WEIRD REDDISH LIGHT shone dully through a leaden sky on the long, snakelike line of horses, picking their way along the edge of an ugly expanse of dead gray muskeg, that dipped into space beyond the northern horizon.

Somewhere here—under the dark jungles of the unknown Algak Mountains, and on the southern edge of a fantastic world of muskeg and black stinking ooze—our bays, blacks, buckskins and grays passed into the big white blank space, shown on the map as "Unexplored Territory."

North of Anahim, the character of the land had changed so gradually that it wasn't until now, after we had trailed miles beyond the Holte meadows, that it suddenly dawned on me that this unexplored country we were penetrating resembled nothing I had ever seen or heard of.

A barren, grayish brown muskeg spread octopus-like before us; its huge body and tentacles vanished in dull dead space north and west of us.

Andy Holte knew muskeg country. Up ahead of the line of loose horses, Pan and I saw him pull his horse to a stop, and motion Tommy to drop back towards the middle of the string.

We saw him gaze a moment out at the great opening, then turn abruptly to study the wet, green, moss-hung spruce that rose abruptly from the muskeg edge to jut, sheer and impenetrable, hundreds of feet towards a misty haze, hanging low at the base of red rocky buttes, strangely incandescent and unreal.

The horses had all stopped. It seemed as though they waited in grave suspense for Andy's decision. Tommy's cayuse picked his way like a cat across a short piece of shaking surface to the center of the line.

"This bog sure looks bad to me," remarked Pan, without taking his eyes off the Teamster. "Look, he's took his cap off."

Looking from Pan to Andy, I saw Andy Holte, cap in hand, scratching the fringe of hair over his ear. This act usually denoted intense concentration on the part of the Teamster. It was as if he subconsciously thought the weight of the cap interfered with his thinking. Then he seemed to have made up his mind. He dropped the golf cap on the exact center of his head, swung the brindle about, and rode on into the north. He pressed his horse close into the trees and roots between the jungle and the ooze.

Andy's skill and judgment in picking safe crossings around and through floating, moss-covered arms of bottomless muck, his knowledge of the colors, the shape, the appearance of the muskeg, and what lay beneath its deadly surface, enabled him to lead the train without mishap for several miles over a terrain where ignorance or bad judgment would have resulted in horses and men dropping through the surface to possible death in the sucking mud.

The horses followed in Andy's tracks. Pan called to me over his shoulder, "This is the biggest break this trail outfit will ever get. I'm tellin' you, friend, not one of us savvies this bog country; and if you or me or Tommy'd been the lead, some of us would have swallowed mud by now."

"What about Mrs. Holte?" I called back. "She didn't even know Andy left the barn."

Pan grinned. "If I know Mrs. Holte, she'll never blame anyone, not even her Andrew for what he does. She probably figured Andy would miss his dinner anyway. We won't say a word to him about it. Let's see how long he stays with us."

Miles up the muskeg, Andy stopped the horses. Here, where a

narrow slough extended back into the mountains from the muskeg edge, green wide-bladed slough grass grew lush and rank.

"A good place to camp," said Pan. "You must be able to smell your way over the mud and moss, Andy." He dragged out his lariat, and jumped down off Big George. "Rope corral," he said.

I was the official camp cook. All I had to do was catch and unpack the kitchen horse, start the fire, find and haul a bucket of water, split the cooking firewood, and cook up the meal, and then set up the tent.

When it came to the trail duties of each man on a trip, the Top Hand was a perfectionist. He took each camp job seriously, particularly the cook's. Pan made an immaculate camp, and as I had unanimously elected him trail boss at the start of the trip, I had no kick coming when he barked at me and snorted down my back about some little detail I didn't think mattered.

It was our custom to relax and drink coffee for fifteen minutes before the fire immediately after the horses were disposed of. I had become a ten-minute-coffee expert. The Top Hand, who had given me inside tips, took a kind of personal pride out of the surprised look on the Teamster's face when, ten minutes or less from arrival time in camp, I yelled, "Coffee time, you tramps—come on the run, you miserable trailmongers, before I drink it down myself."

My system was as follows. Upon arrival in camp, I jumped off my horse, completely ignored the rest of the outfit and their routine camp-arrival conversation, caught and unpacked the kitchen horse —average time two and a half minutes. Now get this trick, you packers and campers, if you haven't already learned it. Here is where the big secret of ten-minute "coffee time, you tramps" comes in.

I reach into one pack box and produce two handfuls of finely cut pitch-pine shavings, and a few small pitchy sticks, cut the day before. Setting this incendiary material in a small pile within five feet of kitchen, I strike a match, and collect limbs from under near-by trees. By the time I run back to the fire with a lard pail full of water, the fire is going full blast. Average time for bringing java pail to boil—four to five minutes. Thus ten-minute coffee.

Unpacking ten horses, and bathing their backs, usually took the two packers two to three minutes per horse. I was usually able to let go my loud ugly blast before the boys were unpacked.

Tommy was wrangler. He kept two horses staked out close to camp. An hour before dark, he jumped on one of these camp horses and rode out bareback in the direction of horse bells to round up and drive the cayuses back to the rope corral. Here the Top Hand assisted in putting rope hobbles on all the horses, with the exception of the two animals kept at the end of the picket rope.

Usually I had the tent strung up, the firewood in, and the evening meal ready an hour and a half after reaching camp.

I repeat, "evening meal," for the benefit of minority groups who have unmercifully snubbed, and finally cowed me into inventing a new term for the nightly six-to-eight-o'clock repast. Friends of mine have taken definite sides on this dominant issue. I have been torn from one side to another, and often forget which team my immediate acquaintance is on.

Consequently I have been soundly reprimanded for blurting out "dinner," when I should have called it "supper," these friends insisting that only people who don't work use the expression "dinner" for the "evening meal." On the other hand, I know well-meaning people, many of them still lurking about the New York countryside, who appear to be badly shaken up when I've called the noon meal "dinner."

So there you are, you serious-minded friends of mine, not "lunch," not "dinner," not "supper," but "evening meal."

Andy was much impressed by our speedy and efficient camp routine. He squatted on his heels in front of the fire, and told us yarns of long trails, and horse trades, and horse runs. Never once did he bring up the fact that he'd forgotten to tell his wife about going along with us.

The dull dead sky had been gradually replaced by clear blue. After dinner, I filled my tobacco pouch, and while there was still light enough to see, struck out for a quick walk up the pothole. It was just about dark when I rounded a bend, and I was surprised to see the pothole widen to almost a valley that seemed to wind back into the heart of the Algaks. However, it was too dark to make sure of this.

I hurried back to camp, and standing before the fire, told my discovery to the relaxing bogtrotters.

Andy took off his golf cap. He fumbled for a minute with the bushy growth of blond hair over his ear, and then started to scratch it. The Top Hand looked at Andy and then at the campfire.

Andy replaced his cap and spoke in a high voice to Pan, "I'll tell you what I'll do with ya, Pan. I'll bet my ground-gainin' brindle saddler against your petrified-boned black hesitator that we find a trail startin' into the mountains from the end of this slough.

"I remember," continued Andy, "a Kluskus Indian called Alexis telling me about a swamp meadow running into the mountains from the edge of a big muskeg. He told me that, years ago, Ulgatcho Indians cut a trail into the mountains from the upper end of the meadow. They used to hunt the caribou herds between the Algaks and the Itchas and pack out meat in the fall. Chances are this is the route."

Before dawn Andy froze out of the saddle blanket we had given him and started a fire. As soon as it was light enough to see we had a cup of coffee, and Andy jumped on his horse and rode up the pothole to look for the trail.

It was a lucky day. Andy found an ancient trail that wound its way gradually up through the heavy jungle. Before sundown our horses broke out onto a parky grass land. From here on Andy picked the trail through the scattered bullpines, climbing always higher and higher towards the red buttes above us.

We began to get an occasional glimpse through the openings at the jungle we had outwitted, and the dead gray muskeg in the distance. The sun dipped behind fluffy white clouds on the horizon, throwing a pinkish light on the parklike land through which the pack train moved; and slowly, almost before we were fully aware of approaching night, darkness fell like a blanket around us.

On a high grass-covered bench Andy stopped his horse. I was sure that, had it still been daylight, we could have looked north into the unknown land we had traveled so far to reach. In the morning we would look down into the no-know land, and perhaps look upon our future home. We made camp. The flames bit into the darkness.

High up on the bench, at the base of the red cone-shaped buttes, dawn broke early. The mountain air was sharp and cold. A thin white lacing of frost covered the ground.

Sitting in front of the fire, Andy, Pan, Tommy and I drank steaming coffee, looked out into the north, and watched pale dawn lift like a magic curtain before us. Gradually distant shapes and shadows took form.

We gazed in awe down at the panorama of a silent, lonely jack-pine land, so vast, so immense in scope that its monotonous green boundary faded in hazy space at the base of a high, snow-capped mountain range that looked to be at least seventy-five miles north and east of us. Andy was sure that the distant snow mountains were the Fawnies.

I have seen great sweeps of arid desert wastes and burning bad-lands, and enormous stretches of prairie, but none of these sights affected me like this first view of the dull green jackpine world that stretches more than a thousand miles north from the Fifty-second Parallel into the arctic.

A strange hollow loneliness seemed to reach up out of the vast-ness of the jackpines, and caught me for the first time in its grip. An eerie, empty, lifeless land of monotonous sameness; uninspiring, unspectacular, colorless, exuding a sinister feeling of complete isola-tion from the living. A land that breathes no spirit of a past life, and gives little hope of a future one.

We caught up the horses, packed and herded the train east through the snow brush at the edge of timberline. As the day wore on, Andy led us higher and higher towards the Algak summits, and a great open gap in the country ahead, where a deep canyon split the range. The northern tip of the gray muskeg gradually be-came visible as we climbed higher. One arm swung around in front of our mountain range.

At this height we could see a scattering of small yellowish dots and lines, tiny, green-rimmed, pothole lakes, occasional brown splotches, and a few reddish-colored areas. These were the only marks that broke the monotony of the ten thousand-odd square miles of jackpine immediately visible to the naked eye.

As the day progressed, a thin mist rose up out of the bottoms and obscured any further view of what lay beneath the Algaks. For the rest of the day, as we traveled east, the ominous spell of the jackpines under the mist held us in its silence and gloom.

We made camp above timberline on the edge of a glacial lake surrounded by snow brush, alpine grass and rocks. It grew dark. The fire blazed up. Echoes of the horse bells clanged hollowly. Miles away, from down in the land of pines, floated a low moaning call, long-drawn-out and melancholy. I shuddered. Nobody commented.

Pan got to his feet and stepped out beyond the light of the fire. He reappeared a moment later dragging the scraggly roots of a dead snow brush tree and, after throwing it on the fire, walked to a pack box, and reappeared, this time tightly clutching a bottle of whiskey. He flourished it above his head. Andy stared up unbelievingly at the unopened bottle.

Pan said, "Men—it's country north—new country. A range beyond the stamping grounds of saner men. An empire where we can run stock without interference—and live our own lives."

He stopped for a moment. I wondered what was coming next. Pan lifted out the cork from the bottle, tilted it to his lips. The bottle gurgled for an instant. He replaced the cork, carried the bottle back to the pack box, then returned empty-handed to the fire.

He continued, "We've found our country—a green country as big as a quarter of the United States—a place that will be all our own—nobody else will want it. Nobody can get into it, and we're lucky if we can get out of it.

"Our neighbors will be the wolves. Our music the call of the loon. Our beds will be the earth. Our books and movie shows will be the look on the other guy's face. Our roads will be the muskegs. Our cars the cayuses. Our playmates will be the whiskey jacks and the squirrels—and, friends, our cattle feed will be the jackpines and the snowballs."

The Top Hand breathed a long sigh, looked sadly at the three of us sitting by the fire, and stepped to the pack box, lifted out the bottle, returned, took another long gurgle, shuddered, shook his head, and carried it back to its resting place. Pan resumed his eulogy on the country as he walked back to us.

"Gentlemen of the jackpines, this is sure one proud day of our lives. It's a moment for prayer and thanksgiving. After a year of careful exploration, my top-heavy, foot-heavy friend, Mr. R. Peterson Hoopson, and myself have found it. We are now noted explorers—noted for our discovery of a great jackpine cattle range."

Before he finished this, the Top Hand whirled on his heel and made two jumps towards the pack box. But before he got one gurgle, Andy had him by the legs, and I bowled him over. Tommy arrived late and sat on his head, while the Teamster put the cork back in the bottle, leaned it against a box and fumbled for a rope. The Top Hand offered no resistance as we half hitched his wrists and ankles, and dragged him over to the fire. I found the bottle and passed it to Andy, as Pan continued talking.

That evening in May near the summits of the Algaks might have been a sad and gloomy one for us all. Pan's disappointment at the sight of the jackpine waste country north, and his realization that our thoughts, dreams and efforts of the past year had been dashed to pieces in our first view of the unexplored country, was probably greater than mine. But Pan had a certain way about him, and so had Andy. They had a terrific sense of the ridiculous and, being born showmen, neither of them would show his keen disappointment by any outward sign.

Pan and Andy put on a regular show with Tommy and me as their audience. In accordance with the would-be civilized standards, we should have been a sad and broken-looking crew, but to all outward appearances, we were exactly the opposite.

We demolished the bottle of whiskey before the fire. Andy, leaning back against a rock, with his feet towards the fire, told us legends and stories and bits of history about the little known country below us.

He told us what he knew about the Ulgatcho Indians. They were the only inhabitants of the country, a wild, uncivilized, once-warlike tribe of Indians. Legend had it that they were part Sioux, that a band of forty buck Sioux had traveled west beyond the Rockies several generations before on a raiding trip. The band had kept coming until they reached the headwaters of the Blackwater at Ulgatcho Lake. There the Sioux were astonished to find a village whose only inhabitants were women, children and decrepit old men. All the young bucks had been ambushed and killed on a recent raiding trip by the warlike Chilcotins.

The original Ulgatchos were supposedly an isolated band of Carrier Indians, a widely scattered tribe, who still occupy a large section of country in the general vicinity of Stuart Lake in the northern interior of B.C.

The Sioux believed that the Great Spirit had guided them to this happy hunting land of Ulgatcho, and had ordered them to guard the country with their lives. They went through the Sioux marriage ceremony with the widowed Carrier women, and so the legends of the wild country have it that the Ulgatchos of today are the descendants of that strange mixture of adventurous and warlike Carriers and renegade Sioux.

Andy told us that there were supposed to be between three hundred and four hundred Ulgatchos wandering through the bush. Nine tenths of them had never seen a town, and the other tenth had only been to Bella Coola, where they journeyed in small groups during the fishing season in the summer. Some of the Indians had horses, a few owned a cow or two, and the rest were foot-traveling hunters and trappers.

"I've heard," said Andy, "that a white trader from Quesnel, a moose of a man named Paul Krestenuk, a real honest-to-God Russian frontiersman, travels more than two hundred miles into Ulgatcho once a year with a string of wagons, and trades the Indians grub and clothes for fur. So if that story is true, he must have cut some kind of a trail to Quesnel. That's a town at the end of steel on the Pacific Great Eastern Railroad, several hundred miles east of here. That would be a big help to you boys if ya moved into the country."

The Teamster rolled himself a smoke, chewed off the end of it, fumbled for his cigarette lighter, and then putting the mangled butt in his mouth, removed his cap and scratched his ear.

Pan reached into the fire, and pulled forth a burning log about three feet long which he handed over to Andy.

"A light for your smoke," explained Pan.

The Teamster gingerly gripped the non-burning end of the stick, and with some difficulty held it to his smoke. I thought for a moment I smelt burning hair, and saw Andy suddenly throw the log to the ground, bend over it an instant, and then straighten up with a satisfied grunt to blow a cloud of smoke in the air. I noticed one eyebrow was missing. The Teamster reached for his cap and placed it back on the center of his head and continued:

"Boys, before daylight tomorrow morning we're gonna have coffee, and then climb up that pinnacle to the highest point in the Algaks, and when daylight breaks, we'll see country no white man has looked at before, and we'll see the Itcha Mountains, and what lays at its bottom. I don't know, but I have a hunch there's a surprise in store. To bed, you night owls—we'll need sleep and strength to get up on that pinnacle."

Long before daylight Andy had us out of our beds and drinking our morning coffee. The air was cold. When it was just light enough to see, Pan took the lead, and we strung out behind him, climbing one behind the other up onto the cracked walls of the shadowy peak, giant of the Algak Range.

The pale sky turned to brilliant blue, and below us Ulgatcho Indian land unfolded. A few miles east of us, the snow-capped Itchas dropped abruptly some four thousand feet to a yellowish opening that stood out in bold contrast against the jackpine green. More yellow arms, necks and islands were scattered along the base of the mountains.

I had my father's set of high-powered Navy glasses strung over a shoulder. Andy borrowed them for a quick look. He held the binoculars to his eyes.

"Yellow patches down there are grass," he commented. "Highland meadow grass."

He swept the glasses in an arc to the east, held them there a moment, then continued the movement. Suddenly he stopped.

"Just a minute," he said.

Using his knees and elbows as a tripod, he squatted against a rock, and remained motionless for a minute, staring fixedly at a vague blur on the distant horizon—a blur that to the naked eye had a dirty yellowish appearance.

"Hurry up, Andy," I said. "Let loose of those glasses. You haven't the savvy to know what you're looking at, anyway."

"Hold on a minute," said Andy. "Wow!"

He sucked in his breath and took off his golf cap and laid it down on the rocks without taking his eyes away from the glasses.

Pan stared silently into the distance. Andy cleared his throat.

"I'll tell ya what I'll do with ya," he drawled. "I'll trade you boys ranches straight across—and I'll throw in the brindle pony—and what's more I'll throw in the halter he's wearin' and the set of number two horseshoes he's got on. It's a clear-cut swap," continued Andy. "I'll ride down onto your spread, and you boys ride back to mine. How about it? Ranches straight across."

Pan started across for Andy.

"Give me them oprey glasses—ya miserable hog!"

He grabbed the Teamster and the two of them rolled over onto the rocks. Pan came up with the glasses and began adjusting the focus to his eyes.

"Make it snappy!" I yelled at Pan. "One quarter minute and you've had it." Now I started for the Top Hand, who was still trying to adjust the glasses.

"How the hell do ya work these fancy things? I can't see as good with 'em at I can without 'em."

"Turn them around," Andy advised him. "You're lookin' through 'em backwards."

Pan snorted and hurriedly reversed the glasses. He pushed me away.

"Ranches straight across, Pan!" snapped Andy. "What say, Pan? Layout for layout. No questions asked."

Now Pan swung the glasses and I could tell when he saw the blur. His sweeping movement stopped abruptly. I watched him closely and saw him swallow. I could tell he was excited. He started to say something but stopped suddenly. Then he appeared to pull himself together.

Andy hissed at Pan, almost in his ear. "Ranches! Ranches! Shake hands!"

Pan answered slowly, "Andy, if ya throw in Andy Christenson's, Cyrus Bryant's, and Jim Holt's ranches to boot, I might be interested—but then that layout would be too cut up. I guess we'll have to ride down onto ours, and you backtrack to yours."

I touched the Top Hand on the back of his shoulder as I reached to get a neckhold on him. He swung around and shoved the glasses into my hands.

"Country north," he said simply. "The gold mine—we've found her"

Quickly I adjusted the glasses to my eyes. I was tense. I guess I was about as excited as an excitable person can get. I couldn't hold the glasses steady to my eyes. I sat down and rested my elbows on my knees the way Andy had done.

Pan was saying, "Nothin' to it. Nothin' to it at all. Any man, any boy can want to do somethin', and any one of them can do it if they want to bad enough. All they got to do is go ahead and do it. There's nothin' to it at all. And ya don't even need any brains. Just enough to keep ya in that straight line you've set your mind to."

"Shut up," I cracked at the Top Hand. "I can't concentrate with all that stupid babble going on."

Tommy laughed. This was the first noise that had come from him this day.

"Pan's all excited up!" said Tommy happily. "He's talkin' like he's makin' a speech."

What I saw through the field glasses was a wide open sweep of grass land. This opening was many miles north of the Algaks and the Itchas, but it was a whale of a big opening. Its northeastern boundary could not be seen, even through the glasses. It just kept going into the distance.

The main body of the opening was yellow. Andy knew that this yellow color was made by the old bottom, or last year's dead grass. He knew that, where the dead grass was heavy enough to over-shadow the new growth of green, it was a lush grass country. Brown arms and necks were scattered here and there, and reached into the jackpines from the main opening. Andy told us this was willow brush.

It was hard for me to realize what we, the first white men, gazed upon. A cattle-ranch proposition that could be the granddaddy of cattle ranches. An empire of grass, just sitting there waiting for some outfit to take over; an almost tax-free chunk of grassy acres that could eventually be surveyed and bought for from one dollar and fifty cents to two dollars and fifty cents per acre from the B.C. government. What a proposition this was! What an opportunity lay ahead of us now!

Pan brought my daydreaming to an end.

"Hand those glasses over to Tommy—ya self-centered society man—so he can have a look."

I knew the Top Hand wanted the glasses again himself; he'd talk Tommy out of them before the kid had had even one good look. I handed the glasses over to Tommy.

Back at camp, Andy caught his horse, and then turned to Pan.

"Jumping bullfrogs!" he said. "I forgot to tell the missus I wouldn't be back for dinner."

Tommy said, "Haw—haw!"

A sheepish grin spread slowly over the Teamster's face. He removed his cap and began scratching the hair over his ear. Pan began to choke.

"I just can't figure it out," explained Andy. "It seems like we just left the barn, and then again it's like a lifetime."

Pan was laughing so hard he had to sit down. I broke down myself, and Andy stood there holding his horse, his face split from ear to ear with that shy grin of his. Andy coughed and pointed at Tommy.

"Say, Tommy, just how long have we been gone? The hours have moved faster than I could keep up with them. I guess my dinner's got cold."

Tommy sadly shook his head at his father.

"Andy," he said, "we've been gone three long days and three short nights. Alice is goin' to be worried about her brindle pony you swiped on her."

"I've got to hurry," said the Teamster. "Time's movin' on. Can you guys spare me a little tobacco and a chunk of jerky?"

Pan got out a box of tobacco, some papers, and Andy filled his pocket, and then stuffed a chunk of dried moose meat in his hip pocket. The Teamster was now prepared to hit the back trail, but he squatted on his heels a moment to give us some advice—advice which we later wished we'd followed.

"Boys," he said, "you're all ready to go down there among the Ulgatchos, and throw your ropes on a grass country that has the earmarks of bein' a big layout and a good one; and I'm hopin' you bogtrotters lots of luck—but I'm gonna warn ya on a few points of what to do and what not to do.

"I've been meadow huntin' through these backlands for seven years, and have learned a few things. I don't claim to know very much about what goes on outside of the sticks, but in these mus- kegs and jungles I've learned a bit, and found out the hard way.

"You kids are pullin' north into a country so far back and so hard to get into, or out of, that ya don't have to make but a few of the same mistakes I made, and you won't come out. Nobody will drop into a country as big as the State of Washington to find out why you didn't come out for your winter's grub. Not this comin' winter. Ya can bet on that. Next spring some police boys with Indian guides might get into Ulgatcho. By then the coyotes will have picked your bones clean, and the wolves broke 'em up in pieces small enough to swallow.

"First, before ya leave this mountain, get yourselves out paper, and draw a map of what lays before you. Put down all landmarks you can, like the pinnacle we was up on. Spot your yellow openings on your map where there'll be feed for the cayuses, and where you can get far enough away from the trees to spot high landmarks.

"Never leave your camp without packin' a gun, whether you're afoot or horseback. That means each one of you knotheads. Pack your gun along whether it's trouble or not. When ya see a grizzly bear or a moose, stay a long way aways. If a cow moose or a bull takes after ya, shoot over their heads a couple of times. It may turn 'em, but don't potshot and wound one. If ya hit a bull in the horns ya might have a still better chance. A moose can't see very good. You can usually duck into the brush and crawl around out of view till ya get the wind blowin' from them to you. The front feet of a moose can reach out a long ways and slash a horse to ribbons."

The Teamster paused to reach into my pocket for my tobacco pouch. He was saving his own. Then he started to roll a smoke.

Pan was flat on his back pretending to be asleep. Loud plaintive snores issued from his throat. The Teamster picked up a chunk of charcoal from the fire, carefully aimed, and tossed it into his mouth. Pan sputtered and rose to a sitting position.

"You're petrified-boned like your black horse," snorted Andy, "and those wolves are going to make a meal of you, I'll bet."

"Whatcha talkin' about?" asked Pan, wiping the charcoal off his face with the back of his hand.

The Teamster ignored him and continued with his advice.

"When you boys meet up with Indians, it will usually be in your camp. Yell 'hello' at them and make them sit down and drink coffee with ya. If they want a little sugar or flour, give it to them—tell 'em it's a present. But don't give everything away. Pan here, he knows; he's got a pack-horse load of Indian stuff. Don't be mean or cheap, act real happy when you're around them, don't ever tell one of them a lie, and I don't have to tell ya, don't play around with their women. Remember they are your only neighbors closer than seventy-five muskeg-and-bush miles to our place. Talk on the same level with them, and pick out one or two good ones for friends.

"All three of you empty-headed walruses has got to know one thing, and know it right. That is that it's mighty easy to get turned around and lost down in those jackpines. When ya establish your headquarters, there will always be the loose horses around camp. Hobble or corral them when you leave camp. The cayuses you're ridin' will take ya back to that bunch of horses nine times out of ten. These swamp-eaters know where camp is and you guys don't. Remember, when the horse wants to go one way and you the other, ya want to let the feller have his head, and you'll land back with the other horses; and, boys, never cross a swamp or a muskeg even if you have to go miles around it. Take to the bush.

"That dinner is gettin' colder all the time, and Hard Grass here is gettin' jittery, so I'll just lope along down the mountain to the muskeg, up the muskeg and into the yard. So long, you mountain bums."

Andy rose to his feet, hopped onto the back of his brindle horse, and without saying another word, trotted off through the rocks on the back trail.

As he passed out of sight, I wondered if he'd make it back the long distance in one day—and if he'd get around the deadly muskeg without trouble.

What a country, I thought. There goes Andy, headed for home, riding over dangerous terrain. His wife and nobody else knows where he went in the first place, or how long he was planning to be gone. If his horse slipped into the muskeg, or stuck his foot in a hole, or got snagged in a windfall, there would be nobody out to look for him. The coyotes, wolves and grizzly bears would take charge of him so fast that after a couple of good rains, Andy's disappearance would remain a mystery for keeps

There were places in the muskeg where both he and his horse could drop out of sight, and the ooze close over the top of them to hide forever what had happened. The Ulgatcho Indians, disliking and distrusting the white man, who considered country beyond the Algaks a rightful Indian heritage, would think nothing of murdering Andy from the bush, should they find him alone along the trail. Spooky stories were rumored about the disappearance of certain white men who ventured alone beyond the Algaks and never returned.

Although Andy didn't mention it, I realized that, when he left home that day, he had only intended to see us a few miles safely on our way. Later when we came to the big muskeg, Andy stayed on with us to see the train safely through. It wasn't his nature to turn back at that point.

He had then stayed on with us until he saw the big opening where we were headed. Now he was trotting home satisfied that we would carry on okay from here, and that, now we had a definite piece of country in mind, somebody would know approximately where we were headed.

Good old Andy! This world doesn't produce many men with a heart of gold like that comical bald-headed Teamster.

CHAPTER XIII

Muskegs and Mosquitoes

Pᴀɴ ᴀɴᴅ I followed Andy's advice and made a series of maps, jotting down all the landmarks we could see from the mountains. A lone Bighorn sheep stood above us on a crag watching the procedure. In the distance we saw a herd of caribou, who stared incredulously at us, then whirled and disappeared behind the wall of a deep ravine.

We moved along the hogsback to the edge of a canyon that split the range. We believed it was the division of the Algaks and the Itchas. Far below us a creek twisted and turned along the floor of the gulch. The long gut between the mountains extended for miles in the direction of Anahim Lake, then came to an abrupt end at the base of a steep rocky slope, capped by a blue and white glacier.

"That's our future trail to Anahim down there," said Pan. "Just one mountain to climb at the upper end of the valley."

We crawled down the towering pile of rocks, drove the hobbled horses into camp, and found we were one head shy.

Nimpo had hopped, stepped and jumped off down the back trail during our brief absence from camp. Tommy saddled up and rode.

It was long after dark when we heard the hollow clattering sound of horses' hoofs on the hard glacial rock. Tommy rode into the firelight. He was riding Nimpo, whose ankles were raw and bleeding from scraping against his hobble leathers.

The little black looked disdainfully at Pan and me sprawling by the fire. Tommy dismounted and, dragging off his saddle, spoke tiredly.

"The son of a bitch must have loped most of the way. I never see such a cayuse—twenty miles—that's how far he got."

Sitting cross-legged before the fire, we made our plans for the expedition to the Big Blur. The idea was first to swing down towards the base of the mountains, then strike through the jackpines to the first series of yellow land openings. There establish Camp 1. Through the field glasses this first series of openings looked to be about forty miles west of the Blur.

We would cut a trail from Camp 1 through a narrow slit in the country, which appeared to be partially open, about ten miles to Camp 2. From Camp 2 cut through the slit to Camp 3. We had no idea how long it would take to slug through from Camp 3 to the Blur, for even with field glasses it was impossible to judge the type of country and the mileages from such a great distance.

We got away to an early start. Pan took the lead riding Little Roanie, a quick and sure-footed part-Kentucky. I rode Stuyve, and Tommy rode a brown horse of his own.

We hit good going for the first nine miles, as we zigzagged slowly downward through parklike timberline country towards the tip of the jungle. It was nearly noon when the train dipped down into the forests. Now we knew we had to break through at least four miles of heavy spruce to reach the foot of the mountain.

This was a long tough four miles. Although the packs were balanced as high as possible on the horses' backs to reduce their width, they still took up too much space between the trees. Finally, we could go no further, and Pan held the horses behind us while Tommy and I went ahead slashing out a trail wide enough to get the pack horses through. It was nearly dark when we broke out onto the jackpine flat at the base of the mountain.

There was no feed. Windfalls or down timber lay piled up between the trees.

It started to rain. A slow drizzle at first and finally a heavy gray cloud settled down around us and let go a splashing volley of water.

Soon we were soaked to the skin. Tommy and I now chopped out only the highest windfalls, and the horses jumped over the rest.

Soon we found ourselves on a mushy ground that grew softer as we advanced. Windfalls, big overturned roots, snags and scattered spruce and pine looked grotesque and unreal in the vague light of dusk. The situation didn't look good to me. I was sure the compass was wrong and we were traveling in the wrong direction; Tommy had no idea about it, and Pan thought we were on the right track.

It got dark. There was nothing we could do but catch and unpack the tired and hungry horses, and tie them to trees. We had trouble with Nimpo and a colt. They were not only hard to catch, but pulled back against their halter shanks so hard that the ropes broke. I got a fire going, and Tommy and Pan set up the tent and fly, and dipped me up a half bucket of dirty black swamp water for coffee.

Tommy lost his watch climbing over windfalls. It must have been past midnight before we crawled into our beds. The clouds belched out heavy spray steadily all night. It purred, then rattled, then pounded on the tent. The poor miserable horses stomped the ground and whinnied. We slept very little. After daylight Tommy and Pan packed the horses. I lashed on my six-shooter, and started afoot over the windfalls to look for a way through.

Heavy clouds still hung low over the land. The country all looked the same to me. I got lost. I crawled under a small, heavy-limbed spruce and fired a series of three shots in the air, spaced a half minute apart. I did this twice before hearing an answering shot. It was hard for me to realize that I was walking back towards camp instead of away from it, and had nearly completed a full circle.

The three of us cut steadily all day in a northerly direction, and moved the train a few miles ahead. We were soaking wet, worried about the condition of our grub and equipment. Water had seeped into the boxes and canvas alforkases despite our precautions.

Black dripping night reached down again. We tied the half-starved horses to trees. It would have been fatal to turn them loose. They would have vanished into the bush and windfalls in search of feed, and we would probably never have seen them again.

When a man lives with his horses, depends on them for his very existence, watches over them, works them, and finally knows each animal's individual personality, his good and bad points, his likes and dislikes, the horse gradually turns into a human-like personality. He becomes a friend and a companion, or a problem child.

Whether the horseman is a teamster, a cowboy, a packer or a jockey, when he lives with his animals, he suffers with them and rejoices with them. That night our horses were suffering, and we lay awake in our damp beds feeling the agony of our horseflesh friends.

We broke camp the next morning and moved east. Now we traveled through a burn. The top soil had been burned off to a jagged lava-like red and brown rock. It was hard on horses' hoofs, and by night we saw that we'd have to shoe up the four unpacked colts. The bark of the jackpine trees had fallen off, giving them the appearance of yellow matchsticks protruding above a dirty red base.

Herds of mosquitoes closed in on the pack outfit, and began to tear us apart. We had no mosquito dope and no mosquito netting. This was one business that we hadn't thought about.

The rain let up, and then a kind of low humming noise reverberated through the wet jungle air, the combined buzz from an endless cloud of mosquitoes. They got into our throats, were sucked in through our nostrils, and got into our eyes. None of us spoke. We just wiggled, and slapped, and grunted, and groaned. To axe and drag windfalls out of the trail was a torture, and shoeing the colts was a nightmare I shall never forget.

Never before had I seen Pan as gaunted, worried and beaten-up-looking as he was now. Actually our position was becoming more critical with each hour. It was quite possible that the wet, dripping, mosquito-filled jungle that swept endlessly to the north of us had sucked us into its green void. The exhaustion, the hopelessness of our situation, the knowledge that we could easily have missed the yellow land openings—and with spent, played-out horses, might be plunging still deeper into the dark horrifying tangle, whose green moss-hung immensity stretched uninterruptedly for hundreds of miles into the north—all this was terrifying.

The following day, a warm, stinking, mosquito-filled steam rose up from our slow-moving pack train. Once Pan was in the lead, and he turned and looked at us through a mat of mosquito and blood and gray beard stubble. He yelled, "I sure wish Dad was here instead of me, and I was safe back home."

Tommy grunted something, and savagely slashed his arms back and forth across his face and neck. You could hear the loud reports of the slaps as they landed.

The horses tried to roll with their packs on, kept up a constant swishing of their tails, rubbed into trees, whinnied and tried every method of circling around onto the back trail. Heavy clouds hung low over the burned treetops. The monotonous hum of the whining mosquitoes held the otherwise silent forest in a feverish pitch of sultry unrealness.

Where were the first yellow meadow openings—and where was Camp 1?

For days we'd been drinking swamp water. Now it hit us. Men as well as horses. Dysentery, chills and fever. Our faces and necks were swollen like boils. This was a sad-looking trail outfit.

Firewood was soggy and wet, but the smoke it produced helped solve the smudge problem. At noon, at night, and in the early morning, we kept a smoke cloud puffing. This was only a momentary relief from the savagely hungry mosquitoes.

It was about two-thirty or three o'clock the next morning, after a sleepless night, that Tommy came steaming up out of his wet blankets, and after a quick survey through the flap of the tent, announced in a loud voice that the horses had pulled, including the two on the pickets.

"They've pulled their pegs and hit for home," yelled Tommy, shaking us out of a sickly coma. "It's that god-damn Nimpo again."

Well—that was some day. The horses had split in two bunches. Pan and Tommy, following tracks down the back trail, got around the main bunch by afternoon. Nimpo was in the lead. Even with his hobbles on, and his ankles raw, blood-caked and flyblown, he was hard to catch.

I sneaked up on four head, led by Old Buck, who was still dragging his picket rope. The old boy stopped and looked resignedly at me through a haze of mosquitoes. He wasn't a buckskin any more. He was a dirty gray mosquito color. I wiped him off with my shirt tail.

"This whole damn thing has got to come to a stop," I said to Old Buck, "or the bunch of us, horses and men, will be standing on our heads in the mud—a bunch of raving maniacs."

About noon I got to the dismal camp and started a big smudge, then lay down. There was no use cooking anything up. None of us could eat.

The following day we received a hard blow. The train broke suddenly out on the edge of a muskeg arm. The muskeg here appeared to be about half a mile wide; its oozing, deathlike, gray surface gave off a nasty sulphuric stink that permeated the surrounding forests.

Tommy thought we should each go in a different direction afoot and return in a half hour to report our findings. We tied the horses to trees a little way back from the edge of the ooze.

When Pan returned he said that the muskeg still ran on east from where he had turned back. Tommy reported there was no place to cross where he had gone, and that the arm must have been at least two miles wide where he turned back. I had had no better luck.

We were now in a critical and dangerous position. It would be dark in a few hours. The horses couldn't hold up much longer without feed. There was only one thing to do—strike out east along Pan's tracks with axes, and cut a trail along the muskeg edge. I took charge of the horses and Pan and Tommy axed out a trail ahead.

In the late afternoon we came to a spot where the muskeg was split by a ridge several feet high, and about four feet wide. This little rise was an old beaver dam, and a scattering of willows grew along its sides. The clouds had lifted enough to let us see around. The beaver dam extended for three hundred yards through the middle of the muskeg to the opposite bank, where a small green slough grass pothole ran back into the jackpines and spruce.

"Horse feed over there!" Pan yelled.

Tommy and I yelled back, "Horse feed."

"I think we can cross here," I said. "Let's try it."

The boys agreed that we should tackle the beaver dam, and this was a bad mistake, for it was easy to see that soft places were scattered along through the willows, and in other spots the ridge was extremely narrow.

I took the lead, and the boys let a few head of pack horses follow single file behind me. It was lucky Pan held back most of the horses while he watched the progress of the first bunch.

On hard ground Stuyve was quick and sure-footed, but he always had trouble getting over soft spots. He wore a number o shoe, too small for a good mud horse, and he dug his feet straight down below him instead of laying them carefully out onto the ground in front of him, the way a good mud horse does. I couldn't lead Stuyve out onto the dam. He pulled back against the bridle reins, and no amount of urging or coaxing could make him budge. I had to ride him.

I leaned forward in the saddle as Stuyve stepped cautiously ahead. He jumped expertly across a narrow strip of muskeg, but sank to his knees in the opposite bank on the dam.

As he lunged ahead, Pan yelled, "Jump!" But I had waited too long.

Stuyve sank deeper on the next lunge. As I started to get clear of him, I saw Old Buck, overbalanced by his heavy pack, stagger for a moment, then fall sideways off the narrow dam into the muck.

Now Stuyve bogged. He tried to plow ahead. Halfway out of the saddle I was snapped loose-jointedly into the stinking muskeg. One of Stuyve's legs struck past my head. I kicked and fought my way free of his struggling body. Now we were off the bank and down in the ooze.

Pan and Tommy were yelling. I gasped for breath in the cold spray of mud, and wiggled and squirmed about trying to get the upper part of my body flat on the surface, but instead I sank deeper.

There seemed to be no bottom. The sensation was like being sucked down in quicksand. My arms and shoulders were still above the mud, and I could hear heavy bodies thrashing in the muck behind me. Snorts and grunts and groans filled the air.

I tried hard not to lose my head. Every second seemed like an hour. The muck smelled like dank vegetation and rotten eggs. It got in my nose and mouth. I could see the side of the beaver dam, it wasn't five feet away, but I couldn't reach it. It was impossible to move out of the suction that held me fast in the one spot, and drew me deeper with every struggle I made. An arm's length away from me, Stuyve's thrashing head and his horror-stricken eyes filled my vision.

For an instant I almost blacked out when I breathed in a mouthful of water; then something struck me hard in the chest, and I saw Pan above me on the dam.

He was screaming at me, "Grab that stick—grab that stick."

I gripped the jackpine he had shoved under the mud at me, tried to wrap my arms about it, but it was shoved down below my waist between my legs. Tommy was heaving on the jackpine with Pan.

I heard Pan snap, "Quick—get my rope—I'll try to hold him up—we can't get him out this way."

My head began to clear.

"Here comes the rope, get it under your arms," snapped Pan.

He threw the loop over my head. I let go my grip on the pole which was now directly beneath me, and tucked the coil of rope under my arms.

"Heave," yelled Pan, and he and Tommy pulled.

I was on the beaver dam. But four horses, held up mostly by their wide packs, still vainly struggled in the ooze; and only Stuyve's head was now visible.

Pan was tearing at Nimpo's pack. He yelled at Tommy, "Get the saddle off my horse—I'm throwin' it on Nimpo. If he can't pull Stuyve out of that muck, no other horse can."

Despite the monumental trouble, worry and loss of sleep Nimpo consistently caused us, he had become our best rope horse. He was brainy—and he was shifty. There was nothing on four legs that was too big for him to handle.

The boys made a lightning change, and by the time I had pulled myself together, Pan was leading Nimpo out onto the dam by the halter shank.

Pan called to me, "Cut some jackpine poles—as many and as fast as ya can cut 'em down. Three or four axe handles long. The axe is layin' on the bank over there."

I moved as fast as I could around the two boys and Nimpo, with the mud and water swishing in my boots and running down my face and clothes. I found the axe and began slashing down lodgepole pines, trimming them, and dragging them out on to the dam.

As I worked I could see the Top Hand and Tommy. They had manoeuvred the cagey Nimpo along the ridge, turned him around, and now Pan, balancing on a jackpine pole, was tying a bowline around Stuyve's neck. Tommy was shoving poles under the mud beneath Stuyve.

When the rope stretched from Stuyve's neck to Nimpo's saddle horn, Pan spoke in a commanding voice, "Git, Nimpo! Hit her boy!"

The thin little black leaned hard into the rope.

Nothing came—nothing gave an inch.

He backed up. The rope slacked. Pan, holding him by the halter shank, said low and harsh, "Ready, Nimpo—now hit her hard, boy."

Nimpo plunged and dug hard against the rope. I saw Stuyve's head come twisting up a foot above the muck.

"It's going to break his neck," I thought.

Again Nimpo fell back. This time to his haunches. He was breathing hard. Pan slacked up on the halter shank.

"Too much for any one horse!" Tommy exclaimed. "Too damn much. A big team is all that could get that bay out of the suction."

"God," I said. "We can't let Stuyve die that kind of a death."

"We'll try her again," said Pan.

Nimpo had swung around while we talked. I saw him stare down at Stuyve. He whinnied—and then his eyes took on an opaque look. He snorted—shook himself—then wheeled suddenly and fiercely into the rope.

"Look out!" yelled Pan. "Here he comes."

That blazed-faced, crooked-footed black plunged madly, wildly ahead. A red fiery light flashed out from the dark of his eyes—and there on that beaver dam we saw a miracle take place at the end of a rope.

The super-strength that lies dormant in horse as well as man had come suddenly to life in that little black—and we saw his partner come struggling up out of the depths of the stinking mud and a nightmarish death.

We all yelled at once. Nimpo stood with his head down, his body heaving, and his breath coming in great hollow gasps. Stuyve staggered groggily to his feet on the bank.

Pan snorted, "I knew he'd do it."

"The hell you did," said Tommy.

Tommy led the trembling, mud-covered horse along the dam to shore. Poor, tiny-footed Stuyve. He almost bogged again, but Tommy kept him coming, and tied him safely to a tree.

"Looks like Buck's about done," I yelled.

Dragging several poles with me, I ran out on the dam where Pan was shoving others under the buckskin. The horse's eyes were rolling and his head had a limp look. He had stopped struggling.

"Nimpo can't budge him with that pack on," said Pan. "I've got to get it off. Here, friend, hold this rope."

He quickly slipped a loose end around his chest and under his arms, tied it together with a non-slip knot, and handed me the loose end.

"You know what to do if I hit the mud," he said.

Pan jumped hard, and lit halfway up on Buck's wide pack, his feet in the mud. Balancing on top of the pack, the Top Hand slashed the diamond rope with his jackknife, pulled the canvas loose, cut the sling ropes, and pushed the pack boxes out into the mud. He took the rope off himself, tied it with a bowline around Buck's neck, and jumped for the bank. I took several fast turns with the rope around Nimpo's saddle horn and handed the halter shank to Pan.

The Top Hand, winded but still moving like greased lightning, started leading Nimpo down the bank.

When the rope came taut on Buck's neck, the old horse threw everything he had into a series of lunges and forward splashes. When he was out, he got to his feet like a cat. Nearly done? Why, that old buckskin had saved every bit of his energy for an emergency—and he hadn't considered this one. I'll swear, knowing horses fairly well, that Old Buck stood on the bank and grinned at us.

And so it was that horse after horse was snaked to safety by Nimpo, the fast-thinking, fast-moving Top Hand and Tommy and me who took up the loose ends where we could.

"Nothin' to it at all," wheezed Pan when it was all over. "Nothin' to it, boys—a good experience for us all. We'll know something about mud and beaver dams after this. Lucky thing this happened!"

Tommy looked disgustedly at Pan. I swore and flopped onto the ground.

Pan eased himself down against a tree.

"Who's got a smoke?" I asked.

Pan reached in his pocket.

"All wet," he said. "Tobacco and papers all wet."

Tommy went to one of the muddy pack boxes, and after fumbling about, brought out a half-pound tin of Ogden's tobacco and some papers.

We rolled our smokes. Dusk was creeping down on us again. It took a good deal of will power to clean off the horses and packs, tie cut ropes together, and get packed up again.

The horses staggered wearily and hopelessly behind Pan down the muskeg arm, which began to dip gradually to the east. A little further on a creek was flowing through its middle, and patches of grass grew here and there.

Rounding a bend, we saw through the gathering dusk an open meadow. The three of us hollered and yelled. Pan threw his hat in the air. The horses stopped in a body with their heads buried in the grass.

We unpacked on Camp 1.

CHAPTER XIV

The Lost Range

WE HAD NO WAY OF KNOWING it at the time, but several years later we found that the muskeg arm with the tiny creek flowing out of the meadow at its eastern end was the first gush of the remote headwaters of the Blackwater River that empties into British Columbia's great Fraser River near Quesnel, B.C.

Undoubtedly we were the first white men to bog down in its muskeg. From now on, we would stick closer to Andy's advice: "Don't cross a muskeg—go around it."

Tommy asked Pan how come we hit so far down the muskeg.

"I figure we got turned off center coming down off the mountain," said Pan. "And then we were too damn sure of ourselves."

I added that it was easy to miss the objective by a few miles when traveling through timber and windfalls, especially when a cloud bank is over the top of you.

"But we followed the compass," said Tommy. "That lousy compass must be wrong."

Pan flipped a smoke into his mouth, and asked for a match. "Rich had the compass," he said. "He wasn't glued to the needle. We moved in the general direction all right, and in the end we weren't many degrees off—but those few degrees threw us almost into the Fawnie Range. If we hadn't hit the muskeg that's where we would have wound up. Lost in the Fawnies with a bunch of played-out cayuses. So, boys, from now on we've got to remember it's near-impossible to hit dead center into objective."

Tommy stood up. He looked off into the sea of pines that encircled our camp, then turned to Pan who leaned against a high hummock, his feet towards the fire.

"We sure are in a big flat country now. It's gonna be some job to find that Blur."

The Top Hand blew smoke out of his nose.

"You bet. Our mileage, figurin' from the mountains, must be away off. It looks to me like that Blur may be any given distance from where we sit. Maybe forty miles—maybe sixty—but if it takes us all summer, us guys are gonna find that range. The lost range. That's what it is," he concluded.

Dawn was just breaking. It was nearly three A.M., on or about June first, when a whining, hungry horde of irritable mosquitoes drove us out of the tent, and into frenzied action. Amidst swishing tails, slapping hands and squirming bodies, we packed and left the meadow at a trot.

Underfoot the ground was hardening, and thin lodgepole pines grew far enough apart to let the pack horses through. The train made good mileage and good time this day. It was nearly evening when we rode suddenly out on a long narrow meadow, cut by a small river running in an easterly direction. This was the narrow split that more than ten days before we had figured out would be our Camp 2.

We followed along the steep banks of the slow-moving river for a mile or so, looking for a good crossing, and came suddenly to a group of old weather-grayed log shanties, and a large fish-smoking rack and pit.

We were astonished to see several bay and brown shaggy-haired ponies tied to jackpine trees in front of a long dirt-roofed log building that had collapsed at one end.

A pack of dogs, varying in size, breed and color, rushed out at us, nearly stampeding Nimpo and the lead colts.

It was now that we saw our first Ulgatcho Indians—a group of about fifteen dark-skinned, oriental-looking squaws, children and old men.

The children, dressed in moose hide and calico, and waving sticks over their heads, charged into the fallen-in hovels. The women backed shyly into the cabin doorways. They all had long high foreheads, and heavy lower jaws; their slanting black eyes were dark and inscrutable. They wore either long calico shawls or bright-colored bandanna handkerchiefs over their heads, black and brown wrinkled stockings covered their legs, and on some of them it was easy to see three or four layers of old dresses, one layer upon the other, hanging torn and dirty over their knees. Worn, grease-stained, ill-fitting moose-hide outer skirts and jackets covered the bulges of cloth beneath them.

I saw no young bucks and assumed they were out on a fishing or hunting expedition. The old men were moose-hided from toe to neck and some of them incongruously wore grease-stained, wide-brimmed cowboy hats.

They stared blankly at us—their long, sharp, cruel-looking faces were pockmarked, wrinkled, icily expressionless.

Pan said "howdy," waved his hand, gesticulated a minute, then seeing no signs of friendly reciprocation, he snorted loudly and spat on the ground.

Over the whole camp hung a rancid smell of dried fish, rotten meat, old moose hide, and whatever the stuff is that they use for tanning hides. The old men and women hadn't changed their positions or blinked an eye since our arrival.

Seeing that the horses were on the verge of stampeding, Pan snorted at the group once more, and held up his hand in a farewell but unappreciated gesture. Tommy rode up alongside Pan to help him hold the panicky horses back to a walk.

Looking over my shoulder, I saw the whole Indian clan gathered before the caved-in buildings silently watching our departure.

Pan called back to me, "A nice friendly bunch of neighbors."

Heavy willow brush now bordered the riverbank. The black, slow-moving water looked dangerous, but we had to get to the other side to keep our east-by-northeast direction.

A few miles beyond the Indian camp we came to a spot where the riverbank dropped off gradually. On the opposite side it was not too steep to make a landing.

Pan held the horses up for a moment and called back to us,

"Here's a crossing, boys; I'll try her first, and if you see I'm gonna make it all right, shove those cayuses in behind me."

He crawled down off his horse and started to loosen up his cinch, then called to us, "You boys has swum enough to know you should loosen up your cinchas—enough to give your horse lots of lung room when he hits the cold water; and I don't have to tell ya not to pull up or tighten your bridle reins when your horse hits swimming water. The smallest pressure on his head will make him roll over on top of ya."

"What the hell do you think we are? A bunch of schoolboys?" I retorted in a loud shaky voice.

Tommy and I took off our chaps, hung them over our saddle horns, adjusted our cinchas, and crawled back on our horses. Now we watched the Top Hand ease Piledriver, the Pete McCormick Hamiltonian he'd been breaking, into the water.

The river here was about sixty feet wide, murky black in color, deep and almost still. Dead water on the surface with a slow undercurrent is dangerous horse-swimming water. This didn't look good to me.

Pan had kicked his feet out of the stirrups and was now leaning forward on the horse's neck. His left hand held the bridle reins slack but not dangling, and he had a grip on the black's mane.

The Piledriver moved cautiously out towards the slow current. The water reached the saddle skirts, then suddenly deepened, and with a cold hollow gasp, the horse dropped into the swim. Only his head was above water when he hit the undercurrent. Pan, feeling the violent tug of the current beneath him, stretched out in the water alongside his horse, his left hand holding the reins and mane.

For an instant I thought the current would roll Piledriver up on his side. But now I learned another trick by watching Pan, and I thought to myself, as I often did, "What kind of past life has Pan had to give him his vast source of knowledge?"

The Top Hand reached forward his right hand, and pushing the side of Piledriver's nose, forced him to head at an angle into the current. Almost immediately the horse righted himself and swam powerfully forward with his head and the saddle above water, and Pan gliding happily along by his side.

Now Tommy and I fought the loose horses into the river, and

splashed in single file behind them. I drew in my breath as the cold water struck me above the waist. Ahead of us loud-breathing pack horses, colts and loose saddle horses were climbing up the bank.

Stuyve bobbed up and down like a cork. Gradually he got into his smooth easy swimming stride. As we hit the undercurrent, I felt him start to lift up on his side. I turned his head into the current with my hand the way Pan had done. Moments later we were dripping on the bank.

The following day we had climbed several hundred feet above the willow bottom when Pan pulled up his horse at the base of a sharp knoll, crowned by a single jackpine tree.

"I'm gonna climb that telephone pole," he said. "We ought to be close to the Blur by now. Maybe I can get a look from up there."

We watched Pan go up through the branches, pausing occasionally to grip the trunk of the tree with his legs, while with both hands he fought a losing battle with the mosquitoes. Finally he completely disappeared above the heavy green growth. We could hear dead branches snapping, and once in a while his heavy breathing.

I yelled up at him, "You better not take any chances. If you fall out of there, we'll leave you where you land. Can't fight these swarming eagles and bury you, too."

"I'm above the mosquitoes, boys," called Pan. "Climb on up here and rest your tired faces."

Tommy started hurriedly for the tree. One of his eyes was swollen shut. He squinted through the slit of the other fast-closing one. He reached the trunk, then looked up.

"To hell with you, Pan. You're not foolin' me one bit. The mosquitoes are worse up there than they are down here. What do ya see?"

I could tell from the silence at the top of the tree that Pan was looking through the field glasses, and then I heard him begin his descent. He scraped down through the branches into sight, dropped awkwardly to the ground, and started for his horse. The Top Hand didn't glance in our direction. I knew he had seen something from the top of the tree, and now would keep us in suspense. He got on his horse. I turned to Tommy.

"Good old Pan," I said.

Taking the lead, Pan reined his horse halfway about, and from the position of the sun, I judged he was now traveling due east. We plunged along the edge of a slough grass swamp, almost bogging down. Then we hit through another wet green pothole.

By now Tommy had learned that it was no use to pump the Top Hand for information, but I decided to approach Pan in a different way. We had started to climb up the face of a steep windfall-covered hill.

"It won't be long now," I called to the silent Pan. "I'm glad the grass country lays over the top of this ridge."

He didn't answer.

"It's lucky you climbed that tree, Pan. We might have missed the opening by a couple of miles."

"Yes," said Pan. "Lucky."

This enlightening talk went on back and forth between us until we rode out on a long neck of open grassy meadow. The horses raised their tired heads and sniffed in the air. The bunch of them began shaking themselves.

Apparently we were now above the floor of the mosquito country. The atmosphere seemed to have changed suddenly and only an odd buzzer whined in the air. Looking back I could see grassy necks extending down into the timber behind us. The gut we were traveling on ran in an easterly direction.

The jackpines began to thin out. The horses started to trot up in a bunch behind Pan.

Where the narrow neck suddenly widened, we surprised a herd of mule deer, who ran in high graceful bounces into a grove of jackpines, turned about, and stood wide-eyed, with their heads held high, watching the pack train. There were twenty or more of the animals in the band.

Game trails ran in every direction. The horses shied at groups of long-headed cow moose and little, buckskin-colored, humpbacked calves that trotted awkwardly away through the tall grass in front of the pack train.

And then the last vestige of fog and cloud vanished suddenly in blue sky, and we stared in amazement at a wide greenish yellow world that dipped in a great low curve into an empty horizon. We were on the edge of a gigantic hay meadow. Its immensity struck us speechless, but we still had no realization of the magnitude of the cattle country that we had discovered.

Nobody spoke. The horses lowered their heads to smell the grass and bite hungrily into tender shoots.

"Keep the horses going," Pan barked at me. "We'll head for that little red butte over there, stickin' up out of the grass. Looks like there's a crik or lake below it, and a good place to camp."

The line of horses moved jerkily ahead, trotting, stopping to snatch up mouthfuls of grass.

On the butte, as dusk settled down about us, we ate, talked little, and rolled into our beds, groaning with exhaustion, but freed from the nightmare of the previous days.

Pan spoke once from his bedroll. His voice was cracked and tired.

"There was nothin' to it, boys—nothin' to it at all."

Then he started to snore. Out in the grass, under the starlit night, horses' bells rattled for a while and then stopped.

CHAPTER XV

Fury on the Hoof

IN THE COLD PINK DAWN, the sudden snorts of the horse herd and the wild clanging of horse bells snapped me out of a deep sleep. I sat up in my bed.

Through the vague pinkish light I could see the horses racing fan shape out into the opening; at their heels trotted the dim figures of three moose. The fast-moving mass vanished in a thin mist rising off the bottoms, and the bells became faint in the distance. It was as if the tail end of a strange dream had flashed across my mind.

I yelled, "Moose running horses out of the country!"

Pan turned over in his bed and snorted.

"Let 'em run, let 'em run."

He started to snore again. Tommy hadn't stirred.

"What an outfit!" I said. Then I thought, "Both boys are right. We can't outrun either the moose or the horses, and they won't quit this country for the mosquitoy back trail—so why get excited?"

Two hours later I dragged out of bed, crawled into my clothes and started a fire. A small creek splashed over a gravel bar below the red butte. I slid down and dipped up a bucket of water. Soon I sat before the fire with a steaming tin cup of coffee burning first one hand, then the other.

From my comfortable position beneath a scraggly bullpine, I looked out at the wide grassy opening. At least a mile out on the flat, a group of black dots stood out in marked relief against the yellowish green of the grass. It was the horses who had finally stopped running.

I refilled my coffee cup and focused the field glasses to my eyes. With the first sweep of the glasses I picked up five groups of moose. A closer look revealed that they were cows and calves. They seemed to be feeding on low clumps of brush. The eight power glasses brought into view three indistinct groups of tiny black dots, possibly four miles distant. They were still more moose.

An odd mosquito floated up out of the bottom and came in my direction. I paid no attention to these stragglers, but swung the glasses completely about and gazed in the direction of the Itchas. Not far off I saw a flash of water through the high green spruce. It looked like a wide creek or river. On the other side of the water the country appeared to be partially open between huge spruce trees.

The sun showed that the time was nearly nine o'clock. I walked to the Top Hand's bed. He was flat on his back, his mouth wide open, a happy expression on his face. Grabbing the foot of the bed firmly with both hands, I lunged backward. The force of the sudden pull rolled the struggling, woolen-underweared figure of the Hand out to the ground.

I yelled at him, "The sun's behind the hills—the herd's broke over the big mountain! Boots and saddles!"

I waited expectantly for his barefooted charge as I stood happily on a mound of sharp broken rock.

Pan paid no attention to me.

"Nice day," he said. He stood up, yawned and stretched his wide shoulders and long arms above him.

"Nice day," he said again.

"Nice day," I answered disappointedly.

The Hand slipped into his pants and boots, and stepping over to Tommy's bed, pulled the foot of it suddenly above his head. He shook out the contents. A hundred and sixty pounds of Tommy Holte came kicking into view. I saw that he hadn't removed his shirt or pants but was barefooted. He struggled to his feet and went for the Top Hand, who now stood beside me on the sharp rocks.

"Nice day, Tommy," he said.

Tommy stopped, looked down at his feet and the rocks, spat on the ground, then grinned back at us.

"Nice day," he chuckled.

"Now," Pan said, "everybody together—one—two—three."

In unison we all chorused:

"Nice day!"

A bunch of ducks were frightened up out of the creek below camp, and an irritated squirrel chattered down at us from the bullpine.

By the time breakfast was disposed of, a hot sun burned down out of a clear blue sky. This was to be our first real summer's day.

We got out our map, and began to chart our approximate position on the big blank space. Calculations were made by using the position of the rising sun, the compass needle, and an estimate of approximate miles traveled since leaving Anahim Lake.

To the southeast of us a high granite peak towered above a pale blue and white glacier. Its summit split the sky thousands of feet above the timbered slopes at its base. We were almost sure the pinnacle was Itcha Cairn, the triangulation point on the map.

After walking a short distance to the water seen through the spruce, we were at first confused to find a small river that flowed in a westerly direction. But we knew that somewhere to the west of us, the creek would have to make a right-about-turn, and then flow east, for the gentle rise of land in that direction ended at the base of the high Coast Range, at least a hundred miles west of us.

Therefore this whole vast terraced basin must be the Blackwater watershed.

With our approximate position established on the map, we were amazed to find that our camp could not be over sixty miles due north of Anahim Lake. The devious roundabout route we had taken from Anahim must have been well over a hundred miles.

That first day on the Blackwater we counted 117 cow moose and over a hundred calves, but saw no bulls, and came to the conclusion that we had invaded a vast moose calving ground. Main-traveled game trails took a north and south course. We figured that these were the migration trails crossing the Blackwater country to the Itcha Mountains.

We didn't bother bringing in the horses, and late in the evening the bunch came into camp on the run. Here they settled down to feed on the Canadian bluegrass that spread for several hundred acres around the butte. Tommy walked easily up to Old Buck and Stuyve, caught and staked them out below camp. Nimpo's hobble-burned ankles were badly festered. It would have been sheer cruelty to have staked or hobbled him. We took a chance and left him loose.

Night dropped down upon us. Out in the dark—beyond the light of the fire—horses grazed contentedly. The air grew crisp and cold. A quivering blanket of stars settled down, split by occasional flares of the aurora.

Suddenly the horses' bells stopped. A breathless silence followed —and then I heard it. The sound drifted down the wind to us— it must have come from a long distance. But there—it came again! A noise different from anything I had ever heard. Uncanny, unreal, a wailing whistle, plaintive, clear as a bell, high-pitched— floating off into the silence and the space of an unknown land.

The horses pounded up the flats, snorting. Tommy rose to his feet, and looked out into the night.

"Moose calf," he said. "It's calling its mother. Hope the old lady ain't around here."

He threw a stick into the fire and sat down again.

Pan laughed, "Yes sir, Tommy, that's a real spooky sound. I sure don't crave to be out there near that doggie—not tonight."

The horses quit running and fell to grazing a short distance up the meadow, as we could tell by the sound of the bells. The calf didn't call again.

The next day the three of us repaired equipment, and took a swim in the icy river. In the afternoon Pan made a scabbard for his 250-3000 Savage rifle. He was great for streamlined ideas, and with a piece of tanned moose hide, produced something entirely new and different. His long face beamed as he proudly exhibited the finished product.

"Look at it, men," he said, flourishing the strange-looking moose-hide object above his head.

"Looks like a flute-holder," I said disgustedly. "Where does the gun go?"

Pan reached for his Savage, which rested against the bullpine, and jammed it down into the receptacle. The barrel fitted tightly up to the sight. The Top Hand showed us how quick he could jerk gun from scabbard.

"It don't take a pile of extra room under the stirrup leather, and it will last a lifetime," he concluded, tying the flute-holder in place on his saddle.

The next morning we decided to see just how big this grassy feed country was. I rode west along the big creek, and Pan and Tommy trotted off in the opposite direction.

My trip was uneventful, so I shall confine myself here to reconstructing Pan's and Tommy's adventures from what I learned later —and at great length.

The boys rode along the edge of the opening for several miles. Groups of cow moose with calves alongside stepped out from behind brush clumps and stared intently at them. Tommy rode his short-legged bay up to the first bunch of cows, but when the animals made no move to get out of his way, he veered off to the side and went around them.

Once a little humpback calf left its mother and walked towards the riders. The cow immediately charged past the calf and stopped between the calf and the men with her ears laid back. Tommy walked his horse away at a slightly faster pace. Pan followed and, looking back over his shoulder, saw the cow standing motionless watching them, while the calf ran to her for lunch.

Later the boys rode onto a long open neck of green slough grass; water struck the horses between the ankle and the knee. Two hundred yards to the left of them, a small round butte covered with down timber rose above the surrounding country, and from its proximity sticks began to crack. Both Pan and Tommy turned in their saddles looking in the direction of the sounds.

"Look," said Tommy, "three cows comin' our way!"

"What the hell?" said Pan.

Three cow moose were trotting towards them out of the windfall. Pan's mount, Piledriver, shied to one side and stood quivering under him.

"Let's get going," snapped Tommy. "You couldn't hit the broad side of a barn from that colt you're ridin'—he'd throw you a mile. Better give me that gun and I'll shoot in the air—it might turn 'em."

"Those critters don't scare me," said Pan. "Why not rope and bust that brood sow in the lead?"

"You're crazy," Tommy rasped. "I'm gettin' out of here right now." He spurred his nervous horse into a run.

As the moose kept coming, Pan thought, "I wonder if the crazy fools really ain't gonna stop. If I let go a blast, Piledriver here will dump me sure—I got my hands full ridin' him when nothin's scarin' him—and if the shot didn't turn 'em and I lit in the water, that's where I'd probably end."

He looked quickly around—Tommy was already fifty yards out on the soggy opening, his horse's short legs churning water and mud. Pan took his eyes off the three cows, mentally noting that he hadn't seen their calves; then he estimated the distance across the watery opening to three lone jackpine trees to be about a mile and a quarter.

"I'll trot in that direction a ways—maybe they'll turn," he thought.

He trotted a hundred yards before bothering to look back, but when he did, what he saw caused him to let Piledriver break into a lope. The lead cow was approaching the opening; her long legs jerking awkwardly across the ground. The other two cows were immediately behind her.

Pan thought, "In a second I'll know the answer—if that moose don't stop when she hits the open meadow and the water, I better start travelin'."

The big black colt was trying to reach for more ground, but Pan still held him in. He spoke to the horse.

"Piledriver, you old swamp-eater, there ain't no hurry. Sure in hell ya can outrun a lousy bunch of moose. Ya can run the legs off the best horse in the Chilcotin."

Pan turned again in the saddle. The big cow splashed water at the edge of the opening; her long jerky strides propelled her forward at astonishing speed—faster now it seemed. A few paces behind her the other two animals spread out fan shape. Pan spoke again to Piledriver.

"Friend," he said, "it looks like a test. We've got a hundred and seventy-five yard start, and a mile to go. They're out to get us—but you can show them trotters how to run."

Slowly Pan pressed his knees into the side of the horse as he let him have his head. The black shot ahead under him like a bolt of light. Pan leaned low over the horn of his saddle and put as much weight as possible forward on his horse to keep hindquarters from bogging.

Now he studied the ground ahead—if Piledriver stuck his foot in a hole—if he lunged into a real boggy spot—if he tripped—"Well, what the hell!"

Tommy was a hundred and fifty yards ahead of him. "The kid's lost his hat." Pan grinned. He spoke to his horse.

"Look at that head of long blond hair wavin' in the wind up ahead, and to think Tommy's dropped his Stetson and won't turn round to go back after it. I'll look back in just a couple of seconds more and see how our girl friends are comin'. We've made three hundred yards since I looked back last; now I'll be able to judge how much ground we're gainin' on 'em."

When Pan looked over his shoulder, his darkly tanned face turned ashen gray. He gasped. With ears laid back, the horrible nightmarish head of the cow moose jerked methodically up and down less than a hundred yards in his wake.

"My God!" breathed Pan. "They're gainin' at every step, and Piledriver's doin' his best."

He looked ahead. The black had moved up at least thirty paces on Tommy's bay. There was nearly a half mile to go to the trees. The jackpines looked small. Now he was flanked by the other two moose. They gradually moved up on the black, out fifty yards on either side.

Piledriver, not yet hardened to the saddle, was breathing hard. Sweat ran from his laboring body—bits of lather sprayed back into Pan's face. Once more he spoke to his pounding horse.

"It's my fault, old-timer—it's sure my fault. I never knew a trotting moose could go as fast as a fast-runnin' horse."

There—in that unknown land, hundreds of miles from civilization—the weather-beaten, snow-streaked granite face of the Itcha Cairn looked down on her land, on a world of green grass and red willow and black water, and watched a drama of life and death, of courage and heart. Saw two white-lathered horses, with aching bodies and bursting hearts, plunging heroically forward through the mud; saw two tense-faced men leaning forward in their saddles, making the ride of their lives; saw three crazed moose cows swinging ahead at a long trot, as they closed the gap between the horses, the men and themselves.

Pan looked back again, and at that moment Piledriver faltered, stumbled on some object beneath the mud, and almost went down. All the Top Hand saw behind him was a brown streak coming closer, and he heard a grunting piglike noise. He pulled up hard on the reins to save Piledriver from falling, and as the ground came up to meet him, kicked his feet out of the stirrups, and reached across his saddle for the gun butt.

But the Piledriver didn't go down. He stumbled and staggered and plunged yards through the mud, and then caught his feet to save his rider and himself.

"Good boy," said Pan. "Good boy—I couldn't get the gun out."

Now Pan dragged hard at the butt. It was still stuck fast by the sight onto the top of the buckskin lacing.

"Flute-holder—flute-holder—it's a flute-holder sure as hell!" He gritted, struggling and shaking at the butt.

Pan's shock and surprise when he had discovered how fast the moose were running him down was now replaced by his habitual calm. He thought fast as he watched the center cow move up longleggedly behind him. He realized that Piledriver could never beat the moose to the trees; that actual body to body contact with her was inevitable. What would she do? How would she attack?

His mind flashed back to the cow-moose talk at Anahim. He remembered Andy, on the mountain, telling that moose had been known to slash a horse to ribbons with their sharp front feet; and then he remembered the night at our horse camp when Alfred had told us that a trotting moose could outdistance a racehorse in mud or windfall. He visualized Alfred standing before the two of us, waving his hat and loudly proclaiming, "Make the son of a bitch break from a trot to a gallop—make 'em break that trot—and a good horse can move away from them!"

Pan swung in the saddle, jerked off his hat—faced the oncoming

horror. He swung his hat wide and fast—and yelled, like a maddened beast. With a piercing cry he snapped the hat full into the
face of the animal.

The moose swerved to the side, lost the swing of her trot, and
fell back into a labored lope.

"By God—you're right, Alfred," Pan whispered as he reached into
his pocket for his jackknife.

A few yards ahead Tommy struggled from the back of his winded
horse into the branches of a spindly jackpine tree. Riding low on
his faltering horse, Pan held his jackknife to his teeth and bit the
blade open. As Piledriver swayed to the tree, Pan slashed the scabbard free, jumped to the ground, jerked the gun loose, swung it
in an arc to the center, pulled the trigger, and jumped to the side.
At this moment the jackpine tree broke in the middle under
Tommy's weight, and Tommy lit with a groan on his back beside
Pan, who pumped another shell into the chamber.

At their feet, the dying brisket-shot cow kicked at the dirt. Pan
swung the rifle towards the cow on the right as she stopped in her
tracks.

He yelled, "Come on, critter—come on just one step closer—and
we'll have more meat in camp than we can use."

The third cow circled the trees, joined the hesitating one, and
both of them whirled and trotted off.

Out of the distance—from beyond the mud-churned flat—came a
long clear wailing whistle.

Pan listened.

"Too bad," he said, and leaned his gun against Tommy's broken
jackpine tree.

That night at camp I ate tough moose liver, listened to both
boys' version of the moose race, and told them of seeing a big grass
country, several herds of mule deer, caribou tracks and an old black
bear with cubs.

I told them about the many flocks of grouse and prairie chickens
I had scared up, and groups of brown and white ptarmigan that
waddled across the ground looking for cover. I then said that I had
seen several groups of cow moose and calves, added that none of
them had paid any attention to Old Scabby White and myself, said

that Pan had just gone out to antagonize the old cow, and I ended by giving them both the raspberry.

Pan looked thoughtfully at me and said, "Well, friend—I didn't pay much attention to this cow-moose-in-June talk myself; but I learned one thing today. When a moose is after you, look for a tree, but make damn sure it's a big one."

He turned and grinned at Tommy.

A few days after the cowboy versus cow moose event, I hurriedly left my fishing rod on the bank of the river, and to the high-pitched tune of a whistling calf, ran the hundred yard dash in nine and three-fifths seconds, barely beating an irritated cow moose to a spruce tree. It was the only tree in sight. It was a real big one. I cleaned the dead branches out for twenty feet up its trunk before coming to rest on a green limb. Here, for three hours, I listened to the calf calling its mother, and watched the cow run to the calf, and then back to my tree again.

After dark I slipped timidly down the denuded trunk, and ran the mile into camp in four minutes flat.

I am convinced that any man can equal or beat world track records, either in the short dashes or the longer distances, if he first gets a real good look into the eyes of a cow moose in June.

CHAPTER XVI

Indian Drums on the Blackwater

TOMMY KNEW HOW TO JERK MEAT. With him as instructor, we fell to work on the cow moose. We cut the meat in strips, about ten inches long, an inch wide, and half an inch thick, and hung them over rows of green willow sticks suspended four feet off the ground. Above the poles we built a crude bark wickiup roof.

A green willow and alder fire in a pit beneath the hanging meat was steadily replenished, and a cloud of gray-blue, sweet-smelling smoke filled the hut and kept off flies.

It took three days for the strips to harden and turn black. This moose jerky would keep indefinitely when sacked and hung up. I made some top mulligans by boiling the meat for about six hours in a kettle with salt and pepper, then removing the contents to a heated iron pot or Dutch oven—juice and all—and adding a mixture of dried onions, washed rice and a couple of strips of pork or bacon.

I left the Dutch oven simmering in the coals of the fire about an hour. When the lid of the iron pot was removed, the fragrance of the Blackwater stew would draw a man hurriedly into camp from almost any given distance.

One morning when Tommy was wrangling the horses, he found a perfect location for ranch buildings and corrals about a mile west of the butte. The site centered around a long narrow neck of blue-grass. Lofty spruce and bullpines bordered a slow moving, half-moon-shaped pool around the other three sides of our future home site, affording shade in summer, protection from the wind in winter, a handy water system, a swimming pool at the front door, and trout fishing from the bedside.

We caught the horses, packed up and trotted in a body behind Pan who proudly took the lead on Old Joe. Joe's huge palm-leaf ears slanted expectantly forward, and his feet twinkled across the ground in his fast-running walk.

At our new-found home-ranch headquarters, we began con-struction of our first and most important edifice. It was to be an octagon-shaped corral with seven panels and a gate. This corral was fast becoming a necessity, since the horses, after a few days on wild Canadian bluegrass, were hard to catch, and we couldn't leave hobbles on the cayuses for more than ten hours at a time or it would stiffen their ankles.

Pan and I, using our saddle horses to snake the logs in, soon found that this was impractical. In fact, after our first round of seven base logs were dragged into position, Stuyve and Roanie had had it. They were dripping with sweat.

Tommy was cutting notches in the logs. The metallic steely clang of his axe sounded strange and incongruous here in the stillness of these backlands.

Stepping down from Roanie's back, Pan slipped the hondoos off the logs. He looked at me.

"Why don't you use that head of yours? Do you think we're gonna play out these cayuses, and take a week to snake in these sticks?"

I got down off Stuyve. His shoulders were quivering.

"That's the last corral log Stuyve is going to tie on to," I said. "You figure out something. We've got no horse collars, harness, chain or doubletrees."

Pan snorted disgustedly, then spat on the ground.

"That's what you think," he answered, and walked over to our rigging pile and began to rummage around.

"Come here and give me a hand," he said.

After about an hour's work, much to my amazement, Pan had

rigged up a makeshift harness and a horse collar. The collar consisted of two breast-collar straps hung together, circling the horse's neck, and hanging down on his brisket. Two cotton cinchas were used for the back band. Tugs were made of two seven-foot lengths of half-inch rope, twisted together and run through the cinch rings to connect with the breast collar. A few moose-hide strings were used to hold the rigging in place on the horse's body, one of them going over the neck and holding up the breast collar.

Pan had never made such a rig before, but knowing the principles of a harness, he figured it out, and it worked. For the logging chain, a lariat rope was doubled and twisted, and adjusted through the rope tugs and back to the log.

Soon Big George, sporting the Blackwater type of harness, with Pan leading him by the halter shank, had the log pile beat.

It was while we were rolling the logs up into place that I began to sense rather than hear a strange rhythmic throb in the air. I had grunted and strained up one end of a particularly heavy log, and thought for a while that the vague pounding noise in my head had been caused by my overenthusiastic lift, but the sound persisted.

When the round of top logs were resting in their grooves, the Top Hand snapped the sweat off his forehead with his finger and barked at me for a smoke.

"Why don't you pack your own tobacco?" I asked him, as he reached into my shirt pocket for my pouch. "I've always got to tote your tobacco as well as my own."

Tommy crawled down off the top log and leaned his axe against a jackpine.

"I hear some kind of a noise," he said. "Sounds away off."

"I've been hearing the same thing," I responded, "and for a long time. What the hell is it?"

The Top Hand blew smoke through his nose, and handed me back my pouch.

"Indian drums," he said. "They're poundin' away at 'em all afternoon."

"What the hell's on their mind?" I said hurriedly.

"Well now, friend, my guess is that those boys are workin' themselves up to pay us a nice quiet little visit. On the other hand, maybe it's a medicine man chasin' the bad spirits out of some Injun that's dying."

That night the wind must have shifted very subtly, for not a twig or a branch stirred, and an oppressive silence hung over the meadows and forests like a smothering blanket.

We sat around the campfire listening.

Out of the darkness floated the creepy, nerve-tingling, unrelenting beats. *Tum tum tum—boom, tum tum tum—boom* went the Ul-gatcho drums. A side eddy of the creek made a weird gurgling noise against the distant beat of padded moose bone on taut hide.

Tum tum tum—boom rang the throb until it got right inside of you. I was unconsciously swaying in unison with the beat. The wide-branched spruce trees in the black shadows beyond the fire began to fall into the sway and the swing of the beats. The water's gurgle seemed to be getting thin, barely perceptible, far away.

Tum—tum—tum—boom——tum—tum—tum—boom—getting louder. Gradually my body, my mind, my life were throbbing with the rhythm. *Tum—tum—tum——*Pan got up to his feet and began to chant and step and step and sway around the fire in time and tune with the throb.

I don't know when the tom-toms quit. They were still pounding when I fell asleep. In the morning I had that strange subconscious remembrance of drum beats running through a dream. But now, with the birds singing, the sun shining, and squirrels chattering in the trees, the black throbbing night-before seemed fantastic and far back in my past life.

It was the day after the irritated cow moose had been responsible for my record-breaking performances, in the hundred yard dash and the mile run, that Nimpo and Stuyve turned up missing on Tommy's before-breakfast wrangle.

Tommy ate, changed horses and rode out to cut off tracks. I wasn't worried for the inseparable pair had a habit of grazing a short distance away from the main body of the horses, thinking that the grass they found themselves was of a superior quality. But at noon Tommy rode in and crawled worriedly down from his sweat-covered brown cayuse to report that the two horses had quit the country.

"Those damn range-quitters have took a short cut," said Tommy. "Tracks are headed in a straight line for Anahim, and they're on the trot. Nimpo must be in the lead. I'm gonna have one hell of a time catchin' up to 'em now."

"Okay," replied the Top Hand. "There's nothin' to worry about. Saddle up Old Joe and throw a pack saddle and your grub on Scabby White. Old Joe will running-walk those two trotters to death. When you get on the tracks, turn Scabby loose. He'll never quit Old Joe. Those old-timers have got more in their heads than those damn dim-brained colts, and when Joe smells their tracks, he'll stay on 'em."

A short time later, Tommy, riding philosophical Old Joe, whose ears flapped backward and forward, and leading a lightly packed but reluctant Scabby White, splashed across the creek below the pool and into the timber.

Pan had a strange kind of sixth sense—but he covered it up well. He also depended a great deal on his knowledge of the workings of the other man's mind. He was a combination of psychologist, psychoanalyst and salesman. His thinking processes were uncomplicated and based on the fundamentals of right and wrong, black and white, and on a logical sequence of cause and effect.

Pan had repeatedly warned Tommy and me that within two weeks of our arrival on the Blackwater, we would be visited by the Ulgatchos—that we must be mentally and physically prepared to meet them. The drums had prepared us mentally at least.

Pan had it figured that the Indians would have to be handled with mighty thin kid gloves. They would not only resent our moving into their country, but would probably resort to almost any method short of murder to make us move back to white-man land on the other side of the mountains.

Pan had said, "Let me handle those boys when they come in. I'm gonna watch 'em awful close, and maybe I can figure out how they do their thinkin'. If I once get a holt on that, us fellows will have something to work on. Sure as hell we can out think 'em.

"Maybe they'll need some bluffin', maybe a little bit of scarin'— and then there's got to be some kind of a truce made with 'em. I'll do the leadin' and the talkin' and you boys follow me."

Pan and I rode in early the afternoon Tommy left on the horse tracks. We were rummaging about in the tent looking for fishing tackle when the Top Hand suddenly straightened up. He grabbed my arm. I looked around at him. He had his index finger to his lips.

Then I heard the sound. Horses' hoofs were padding softly across the pine needles towards the back of the tent.

Pan's Smith & Wesson 44 was in a pack box in the front of the tent. He stepped over and like a flash pulled out gun and holster, and swept the cartridge belt around his waist. My gun was under the head of my bed—I didn't have time to get it. Sounds of horses' hoofs had stopped, and Pan was barking from the tent flap.

"Make big noise when you stop this camp! Make big noise—you hear? Maybe next time I kill somebody!"

Through the open tent flap I saw a moose-hided Indian on a short-legged, shaggy-haired horse. I knew instinctively that if I moved for my gun it would start something.

I stepped out beside Pan in time to see a second Indian slip down off a low-set hairy-legged pony.

Pan said to me, "Coffee."

He didn't look away from the mounted Indian who sat stoically on his horse, his right hand on the butt of a small pearl-handled revolver of some kind.

"What's a matter?" I laughed at the Indian. He looked blank. I turned my back, scraped together my pile of pitch shavings and lit a match to it.

"Take your hand off that gun," I heard Pan bark, "or you're gonna get killed—see!"

I threw a stick on the fire and turned around. The one Indian was dismounting and the other was standing at the side of the tent, his dark treacherous eyes roving over the camp site.

I set four tin cups on our homemade table and opened a can of milk. Pan was sitting on the butt of a log watching the Indians who squatted down between the fire and the table in complete silence. Now I had a quick but good look at them.

They were dark-skinned. Both had wide slanting eyes in narrow bony faces. One of them had a flat nose that spread almost to his cheekbones. They looked to be between thirty and forty years of age. Jet-black hair hung almost to the shoulders of the one with the pearl-handled revolver. The other Indian with the flat nose had wide bulbous jaws, a long narrow forehead and his hair was shaved off so short that he looked bald. They were an evil, nightmarish-looking pair.

I filled the coffee cups and turning to the Indians pointed at them. Pan got up and sauntered slowly to the table. He poured in milk, added sugar, and handed each Indian a cup. He helped himself and squatted down on one of our log stools facing half sideways to the Indians.

Now we all drank in silence. Pan continued to stare at the visitors. I thought, "Pan's first bluff has worked." His blasting verbal attack on these men for sneaking up quietly on camp was one of Pan's well-thought-out acts.

When moving into a strange and possibly hostile Indian country it is smart to make it absolutely clear at the start that to approach your camp or cabin without yelling or making some kind of a loud noise means lead for breakfast. Up here in the sticks, when we approach an isolated camp, we bellow in a loud voice from a safe distance: "Who stop this place?" or "Somebody stop this house?" or "Howdy there."

While Pan and I sipped our coffee with the savages, I laughed, gesticulated and tried talking to them. They ignored me completely and glared icily at our tent. I had never before seen Indians who gave one such a creepy feeling as these Ulgatchos.

Suddenly one of the Indians looked quickly at his partner and then at Pan. He grunted out the words low and harsh.

"This country no good for white man." He spat on the ground, set his empty cup on the table and growled, "Maybe something happen to white man this country."

I could feel the atmosphere tightening, and knew the Indian was working up to something. I was more than aware that both Indians wore six-shooters. Mine was still under my bedroll.

The Indian stiffened on his stool. His black personality shot out into the atmosphere.

He said, "Indians he hold potlatch Blackwater. He watch this camp. He come Ulgatcho. He tell us. Now we ride long ways."

His eyes narrowed—he spat out his ultimatum:

"White man, you go—this country belong Ulgatcho Indian."

Pan said nonchalantly, "Can you shoot good with a six gun?"

The long-haired, pearl-handled Indian looked contemptuously at Pan.

"We Ulgatcho fight man. We shoot good and we use hands too." He held up his right fist. "We use 'em gun and we use 'em hand fight."

I felt sweat pop out on my forehead.

"Let's see," said Pan.

His right hand moved like greased lightning to the Indian's gun. He jerked it out of the holster, spun the small, old-fashioned 25 calibre revolver around in his right hand, then grinned at the startled Indian.

"Haw, haw," laughed the Top Hand. He pointed with his left hand to the gun.

"Peewee," he said. "No good for fight this kind—big gun he more better."

The Indian didn't move. His eyes bugged out.

"Look," said Pan.

He shifted the small pistol to his left hand, and leaning forward snatched the milk can off the table with his right hand and flung it at the river.

Pan's draw for his beloved and much-used gun was swift, and as the tin can hit the water, the 44 Smith & Wesson boomed—the tin can bounced—the gun cracked again—the can popped out further in the channel. Once more the gun went off, and the can bubbled down out of sight.

"Big gun more better." Pan grinned. He handed the man back his little revolver.

Now the shaved-headed, flat-nosed Indian rose to his feet. He grunted, then shook a gnarled, dirty fist at me.

"Me best fight man Ulgatcho. I show you. Then you go."

My father, who had been both a fencing and boxing champion at Annapolis, had roughed me around with boxing gloves from the earliest days that I can remember. At our home in Los Angeles he built a gym with a regulation ring and heavy bag for my brother, myself and the neighborhood kids. In those days the smell of the gymnasium and glove leather clung as natural to my nostrils as the smell of horses and saddle leather did now.

Later, along with Fidel La Barba, Joe Salas and Jackie Fields, I boxed on George Blake's Los Angeles Athletic Club's boxing team, worked out under Arthur Donovan in New York, and in the meantime coached the San Diego Army and Navy Academy's boxing team. My last legal workouts were with Bob Pastor as one of his New York sparring partners, when Joe Willing Welling was training him for his first bout with Joe Louis.

However, all this had been some years before and the only workouts I'd had for a long time were mild sparring practices with Pan. We used my set of Everlast twelve-ounce practice gloves which I toted around with me wherever I went—even here to the Blackwater. I knew that I had not only slowed down but that my timing was away off.

I looked the wide-jawed Ulgatcho fight man over as he walked threateningly towards me. "About a hundred and sixty-five pounds," I thought. Twenty pounds lighter than I, but all bone and muscle, probably fast and cruel as hell—dangerous in close. If he knocked me down, would he tear me apart with his bulldog jaws and dirty sharp fanglike teeth?

I knew I'd have to be cagey and use every bit of boxing training I was lucky enough to have picked up. I stood up, tightened my belt and stepped around the table.

Pan flashed to a pack box and was between us with the gloves. He talked fast out of the corner of his mouth.

"Use the mittens, boy. You cut him up with your fist and there's trouble later. They don't forget."

The Indian was staring hard at Pan.

"What's a matter?" he growled. "You stop 'em fight. More better you go now."

"He thinks he's backed us up," I thought.

"Off with the shirts and the guns," Pan barked. "No use get clothes all dirty." He waved his arms around to show them what he meant. Then he gave me the wink and I slipped out of my shirt. The guns and shirts were piled against a bullpine.

The Indian objected to the gloves.

"Bedrolls he no good. You scare," he snarled at me.

"Try 'em with the mitts first," said Pan, "then take 'em off and use hands." He gesticulated. Both Indians grunted. Pan hurriedly tied on our gloves and stood to the side.

I stood with my gloved hands by my side. I doubted whether the Ulgatcho fight rules resembled those of the Marquis of Queensberry's.

The Indian came at me with the savage fury of a wild animal. I ducked, stepped back, and tripped over a root. I rolled fast to one side, avoiding his downward, mouth-opened plunge at me.

I was up before he was, and met his next rush with a light long-distance straight left to his nose.

"Now go after him," rasped Pan.

I thought to myself, "This scene is sure one for Ripley. Stetson-hatted Panhandle Phillips, fight manager and trainer, giving me advice from my corner. Long-haired Ulgatcho fight trainer in the other, and the Bow and Arrow boy and myself boxing it out on the untrodden headwaters of the Blackwater River."

I stepped back and ducked under two terrific haymakers, but was too slow to slide away from a third which slid by my eyebrow, glanced off my forehead and kept on going into space. I was dazed for a moment—then suddenly snapped out of my stage fright. He was almost on top of me again when I landed a left shovel hook about four inches below his solar plexus, too low to be really effective, but I could see it slowed him up.

Now I felt better. As he rushed in again with wild clublike swings, any one of which would have upended me, I hopped to the side, and then stepped into his head-on charge with my whole weight behind a straight left. It missed his chin, landed on his forehead, was too high, but his knees sagged. Now I didn't give him a chance. I measured him quickly with a light left jab and then smashed my right hand to his jaw with everything I had behind it.

He groveled and kicked in the dirt, rolled over on his face and lay still. A thin trickle of blood spewed out on the sandy loam.

Sudden panic grabbed me.

"My God, Pan," I cried, "I've killed him."

I knelt down beside him. The other Indian was staring unbelievingly at the motionless figure. Pan grabbed up a lard pail and sprinted to the creek. I rolled the Indian over. The Top Hand ran back with the water, splashed it over the Indian's face

Blood ran out of the corner of his mouth. His eyes rolled. He shook his head, grunted, looked around.

"Wowie," said Pan.

I took a deep breath and raked the sweat off my forehead.

It was growing dark. We watched the two Indians ride out of camp headed for distant Ulgatcho, their saddles bulging with gifts from the Blackwater outfit.

Reaching skyward from the shaved head of the swollen, bulbous-jawed Indian proudly sat my old New York collapsible opera hat. Around his neck, tucked happily and neatly into his moose-hide shirt collar, glared an old white evening scarf, while tied to his saddle were a few handy items such as packaged chicken noodle soup, oxo cubes and tea.

(The reader may be curious about that opera hat. I don't think there is a top hat alive today that has lived a fuller, more adventurous life. After its dignified existence in New York, the topper traveled with me to Wyoming, where I remember seeing it at the Lander Rodeo, perched precariously on the back of Pan's head, then waving wildly in his hand as the Top Hand rode out a crooked, high-pitching bronc.

(On the Anahim frontier it had caused a sensation. Indians were excited and mystified by the way it could be snapped open with a pop, or smashed shut, apparently without hurting its dignity—and I doubt that any top hat has spent its last days in a weirder setting than on the lice-infested head of an Indian in Ulgatcho.)

I was the recipient of a moose-hide stretched and braided half-inch stake rope.

Pan had presented the long-haired Indian with a pair of silk stockings for his klootch, some silver-plated conchoes and snaps, an old pair of silver-mounted Crocket spurs, and an old Wyoming bucking-horse car license, as well as his assurance that white man would not bother the Indians' beaver and other fur.

"Ya see, friend. It's just like I told ya. There's been a truce made. Those Ulgatcho fight men are ridin' away from here full of coffee and happy as boys. There was nothin' to handlin' 'em at all. Nothin' to it, boy. Nothin' to it at all."

I looked sourly at Pan through a blackened and partially closed eye.

CHAPTER XVII

Cowboy Carpenters

Pan threw a spruce stick on the fire. Sparks popped up into the night. Somewhere out in the darkness a horse whinnied. For a moment I could hear water splashing in the ford below camp, and then Scabby White and Old Joe appeared out of the shadows.

Scabby stopped abruptly, his long bony head stretched forward on his neck. He stared incredulously at the campfire and the tent, the same scene that he had so often witnessed. He snorted wildly, whirled in his tracks, and with flapping-eared Old Joe close behind him, dashed through camp towards the meadow.

"They're just like a couple of colts," observed Pan.

Tommy rode into the firelight on a glaring-eyed Nimpo, leading a chastened Stuyve.

"Good going, Tommy," barked Pan. "I knew damn well you'd bring 'em in."

Tommy crawled out of the saddle. He dropped his bridle reins and stepped to the fire spreading his hands out over the blaze.

"Long, long ride," he grunted. "Got around 'em in a draw some place up in the mountain. Changed onto Nimpo. I give him lots of ridin'. Maybe he'll stick around for a while now."

"Yes, he'll stick close to camp," said Pan. "He'll be right inside that round corral."

We picked out a likely spot for the wrangle-horse milk-cow pasture. This enclosure would contain about twenty acres of Canadian bluegrass and was dotted with clumps of silver spruce, and here and there a scattering of giant diamond willows. A small creek flowed through its center and emptied into the main river. The proposed bunkhouse would face the big half-moon-shaped pool and be inside the pasture. This would be the most-used piece of ground on the ranch, with the exception of the corral system. The fence surrounding it would have to be foolproof, with horses like Nimpo and Stuyve in our cavvy.

Tommy cut the timber down, I trimmed it into eighteen-foot lengths, and Pan, using Big George, who was now well broke to work, skidded the logs into position. We decided on a worm fence, a type of log fence that requires no nails and would stand for a short lifetime. The logs were notched at both ends, and the first round rested on big blocks.

This kind of a frontier fence takes a long time to build, especially if the logs have to be hauled for any distance—and men must work steadily in order to see any results. I shudder to think what the average city contractor of today would charge to put up a mile of this fence. As it was, Pan, Tommy and I, not having a watch, worked the daylight hours through. We found out later that at this time of year it got dark at ten-thirty P.M. and daylight came shortly before three A.M. No wonder we seemed to be perpetually tired.

A group of Indians dropped into our camp while we were working on the fence. One friendly old Indian, wearing a moustache and a golf cap, spoke understandable English. When he found out that Tommy was Andy Holte's son, his face brightened up and he warmly shook hands with each of us. He was Andy's old friend Alexis.

His two sons, Peter and George, were immaculately dressed in fancy cowboy regalia. They reminded me of Thomas Squinas and the easygoing, good-hearted Anahim Lake Indians.

Peter was tall and happy-faced. George Alexis was hunchbacked and built on a wide scale close to the ground. Later we learned these were Kluskus Indians, whose tribe made their headquarters about thirty-five miles east of us. There was no resemblance between these pleasant-looking Indians and the narrow, bony-faced, bull-jawed Ulgatchos.

The Alexis men spent the night with us. We enjoyed their easy Indian humor, and celebrated by drinking so much coffee that I burped the stuff up for several days afterwards.

Peter and George, it turned out, were dolled up for the Quesnel Stampede. They were riding more than two hundred miles through the bush to the event.

The day after the Kluskus Indians rode out of sight on the wide surface of the meadow, I watched Pan skid a fence log into place. He dropped Big George's halter shank, unhooked his rope singletree, and walked over to me.

"Sit down, friend," he said. "The time has come for a pow-wow."

"I'm good for that kind of stuff any time," I told him.

"We've got to do some heavy thinkin' and some fast actin'," said Pan.

I looked at his copper-colored, expressionless face, and asked him what the hell he meant by "actin'"—told him that action had been the only thing I'd seen for a long time.

"It's like this," said Pan. He broke a splinter off the fence log, and pulling out his jackknife started to whittle.

"We've got a mighty lot to do before snow flies. It must be along about the middle of June, ain't it?"

"I don't know what date it is," I answered, "but it sure can't snow us in very soon."

"Look, friend," continued the Hand, "we've got to get a pack trail through to Anahim, land a mowing machine which weighs nearly eight hundred and fifty pounds, a ten-foot rake, iron stove, nails, wire, tools, even windows, on this ground before haytime. We'll have to pick up this equipment in Bella Coola—that's a long ways away when it comes down to pack horses, cuttin' a new trail, and totin' in heavy machinery."

He stopped whittling for a moment and looked at me.

"I'll get a pencil and we can figure out the time and the help it will take to get this outfit set up and hay in the stack before those Itchas and Algaks fill up with snow."

"That means about October first, if we're lucky," I said.

Turning his head, Pan looked at the distant glacial-rimmed peaks. He walked over to a pack box, pulled a pad and a pencil stub out of his shaving kit, walked back to the log, and began to figure.

"Tomorrow the three of us will cut a trail through the heavy timber across the creek. We'll swamp it out due south towards the mountains. Our special map figurin' says that Anahim Lake ain't any more than sixty miles from here as the crow flies, and that's the way to get there—not around those mountains and the muskeg the way we came in here."

The Top Hand asked for the makings, and remained silent for a moment looking at the toe of his boot.

"That timber is heavy for a couple of miles. Beyond that it thins out enough for a pack train to get through. I figure I'm the boy to hit that country. I'll drive fourteen head of horses south towards the split between the Algaks and the Itchas, and I'll get to Anahim. Bronco Bryant will be ready to throw in with me, and we'll pick up a few head of extra horses around Anahim and pound them on the rump to the coast. If I leave day after tomorrow, I should be on the ocean in maybe fourteen days' travelin'. Andy Christenson said he'd have a Massey Harris mower and rake, anvil, forge and stoves and all that kind of stuff put aside for us in Bella Coola.

"Bronco and I should make the trip back from Bella Coola to the Blackwater in twenty days. That means I'll be gone a month and a week, countin' packin' up, and restin' the horses in Bella Coola."

I looked gloomily at the Top Hand.

"What about the money, boy? It takes some of that kind of stuff to buy an outfit like that."

Pan snorted.

"Money? What do ya mean, money?"

He spat on the ground and snorted again.

"Money? What's that? I'll get back here with that pack-trainload of machinery. There ain't gonna be anything to it at all."

I shook my head at him.

"One of these days you're going to trip over this nothin'-to-it business." I was irritated with Pan's self-assurance and noncommittal airiness.

"Now let's face the facts. Where and how are we going to get all this cash?" I asked him. "There's no bank down in Bella Coola to rob or any stagecoach full of gold bullion to hold up. What have you got on your mind?"

Pan looked blankly at me. He reached in his pocket for his lighter, fumbled a moment, then held out his hand for a match.

"Damn you," I said. "Why don't you tie that lighter down where you can find it?"

I handed him my own lighter, and he lit the butt of his half-chewed cigarette.

"I got ten top cow horses and brood mares at Stanley Blum's. You ain't forgot them, have ya, friend? And that Palomino stud, run it out of the wild band? Those horses are worth money to any cow outfit."

Pan paused, cleared his throat, then spat between his feet.

"I'll get Stanley Blum to sell 'em for me."

I had forgotten all about Pan's string of well-broke rope and cutting horses. He had spent a lot of time training them and there was no snappier cow string in that country, but on the other hand, Wyoming was topheavy with light horses. The high draws of the Wind Rivers, the Bad Lands of the Red Desert crawled with broomtails of every color and description.

I had my doubts about getting enough money out of Pan's string to pay our tobacco bill, but I didn't mention it. It was an idea anyway, and it certainly wouldn't hurt anything if Pan made a pitch in that direction.

The Top Hand continued, "You and Tommy will be workin' every hour of daylight to finish up the horse pasture fence, and build the cabin. When Bronco and I get back, we can slide right into the hayin' job.

"You'll be out of grub for maybe three weeks, but that's nothin' to worry about; there's lots of meat and fish around the country, and you've still got lots of salt—that's the big thing."

"Yes," I snapped at him, "that's the big thing—salt."

And so it was that around June seventeenth, I waved and yelled, "Good luck—good riding," to the old Top Hand, far up the timbered slopes at the base of the Box Canyon, and as I swung my horse about, I saw the sun-blackened, eaglelike face of the first white man to push off alone into that awesome scramble of glaciers and peaks sprawling across the southern sky.

Pan turned in his saddle, held his hand over his head, then whirled about to the south. Long after Pan and his fourteen horses vanished in the scattered timber, I could hear his swear words urging the horses ahead.

Little did I know what the Hand had tackled and what lay ahead of him in his venture. I suspect that he knew what he was in for and was mentally prepared to overcome any obstacle that lay in his path.

Few men that I know of would have or could have tackled this undertaking. It is an entirely different proposition for a man to start into an unknown country, headed for a distant objective, in a boat, or with a pack on his back, than it is for one man alone to drive a bunch of loose horses into such country sight unseen. Feed and water must be found for the horses. Windfalls and swamps can block the way. Rivers must be swum, and a man must sleep with his eyes and ears open, be able to outride the loose horses, hold them together, and keep them headed in the desired direction.

I rode on back to camp through the jackpines, and the same lonely spooky feeling, that sinister, lifeless jackpine spell seemed to reach out and grip me as it did when I first looked out on this vast empire from the Algak Mountains.

We used a battered calendar to keep track of the date. Each evening I crossed off the preceding day. We started this system the day after Pan left, calling it the seventeenth. Actually our timing was a week off.

According to our calendar, we threw two wrangle horses, Stuyve and one of Tommy's cayuses, into the completed pasture on the twenty-seventh. The following day we leveled off the ground for the foundation logs of the bunkhouse.

We cut the base logs twenty-one feet for the long sides and seventeen feet for the short. The building would measure fourteen by eighteen feet inside. We rested these base logs on big rocks to keep them off the ground so they wouldn't rot.

Tommy had helped erect several log buildings and he really knew his stuff. I'm not saying anything against Pan's brilliant cabin-building demonstration, for as the Top Hand had said we had laid her up on time and that old cabin at Anahim would always be there to go home to.

We had notched and rolled up about ten rounds of logs on the cabin when both of us took sick—and, of course, about this time it started to rain. The tent leaked, and our beds got wet.

Tommy rallied on the third day, and staggered about camp trying to cook up a hot meal. Our grub had run out, all but dried moose meat and rice and a little sugar. The thought of, or vague smell of, these edibles simply turned my empty, bile-filled stomach over again. We never found out what gave us this violent form of ptomaine poisoning. I have been told recently that we might have had the dreaded cholera.

Tommy recovered enough to go weakly about skidding in cabin logs, but I grew steadily worse. On the sixth day Tommy had to force me up to a sitting position with his arm around my back, to feed me some thin rice gruel soaked in moose gravy.

"You've got to get something in your belly, Rich—you've just got to down something. You can't go on this way—you're near done."

He forced the cup to my lips and poured some of the gruel into my mouth. I retched and threw up violently against the wet tent wall and on the corner of my bed.

Tommy shook his head and let me down easily onto my back again. I remember telling myself over and over again, "You're not going to die boy—you're not going to die. You can't die now when you've found the great new range."

Then I remember doing a bit of praying and also a bit of re- penting for some of my bad acts in the past. After that I was in a semiconscious daze.

The next day Tommy made a discovery that quite possibly saved my life. Rummaging through the pack boxes, he found a large-size can of Pacific milk. He let out a yell and rushed to the fire where he poured a third of its contents into about that much warm water, and added a teaspoonful of sugar. He brought it almost to a boil, and came anxiously into the tent holding the warm cup of fluid carefully between his hands.

I remember him lifting me to a sitting position. I was conscious of the warm mellow sensation as the canned milk spilled down my throat. I was able to swallow the entire cup by degrees. Tommy held me up for a few minutes after the cup had drained. Sitting there I fell asleep. Hours later I came to, with Tommy pouring more of the milk brew down my gullet.

For days I hadn't been conscious of whether it was night or day. Now I suddenly noticed that it was dusk outside the tent, and I heard horse bells in the distance, and the crackling of the campfire. I knew then that I had made the grade.

Tommy rationed the last of that wonderful life-giving can of milk into two more feeds. The next evening I could sit up without help. A week later I was able to lead Big George by the shank and weakly roll the top bunkhouse logs into place. July had advanced to the twenty-fifth before I felt anywhere near myself again, and it was on this date that Tommy and I finished the roofing job.

We had laid tight-fitting poles about three inches in diameter across the frame of the gable ends. On top of this pole platform we spread a foot of slough grass. With a homemade derrick we hoisted bluegrass sod, with the dirt side up, onto the top of the slough grass. Over that we constructed a pole frame that extended out two feet beyond the cabin walls.

For several days thereafter we split up a straight-grained dry jack-pine tree into three-foot shakes, then tacked them on the roof frame. We chinked the cracks in the walls with swamp moss and fitted small peeled poles over the moss-filled openings.

Now we had a weatherproof cabin completed, all but the windows and the floor. Pan was to have the windows on his pack train. But the floor problem was Tommy's and mine.

Have you ever seen a whipsaw—or heard of one? I hadn't made the acquaintance of this sinister-looking, seven-foot, saw-toothed blade until I arrived at Anahim. There I listened to lots of wise-cracks and laughter having to do with whipsawing. I never could understand why all the whipsaw joking, nor could I see why whip-sawing would be much harder than ordinary two man crosscut sawing. Now, face to face with the real article, I suddenly found out the answer.

Tommy had built a frame between two trees about eight feet off the ground, where, after some difficulty, we hoisted a fifteen-foot dry log about sixteen inches through. Now Tommy balanced above me on the frame holding the whipsaw handle with both hands. One end of the log reached several feet beyond the frame. Tommy made a few scratches about two inches in from the end of the log.

"Now," he said, "I'll pull the saw up—and you pull her down."

We jiggled the saw up and down a bit until it had made a groove. Tommy heaved upward with a mighty effort. The saw reluctantly ground up through the log. I grabbed the bottom handle and, by putting every bit of weight and strength on that end, pulled it back down. Tommy's, the frame man's job, is the harder—but after a three-minute round of heaving, tugging and struggling, I yelled up at him,

"Bell!"

Tommy didn't know what I meant. He fought the saw up again. I pulled it down and yelled,

"One-minute rest."

Sweat was running off Tommy's nose, and I could feel mine trickling down my back. We looked at our work. We had made one inch.

Tommy got down off the platform and looked at the saw and then at the sawcut.

"Something's wrong," he said. "Shouldn't pull that hard. I don't think the damn saw is set."

He looked closely at the teeth.

"No," he said, "it's not."

"Have you ever set a whipsaw?" I asked him.

"Never," said Tommy.

"Well, go ahead and set the ripper any way that's different from the way it is now."

"Okay," Tommy said, "it sure can't get any worse."

An hour's work with a hammer, a file and a little steel wedge, and the face of the whipsaw vaguely resembled a crosscut saw in places. Now we started again. It drew through the wood slightly better than before.

We made one slab that day, and for six days thereafter averaged a board a day. Each night both of us dropped exhausted into our beds. It didn't occur to us to rest up the seventh day, for Tommy suddenly had an idea.

"What's the matter with us?" he said. "Here we made six cuts and only get seven boards. I wonder if the Top Hand would have thought of what I've just figured out?"

"Forget that brilliant-minded genius," I said, "and tell me what you've got."

Tommy let out a whoop.

"As old Pan would say, there's nothin' to it at all, nothin' at all," Tommy said happily. "All any outfit needs is one man with brains."

"Forget those Panhandle poems," I said. I thought to myself, "This is about the most talk that has come out of the kid since I've known him. The Top Hand's influence is beginning to show."

Tommy said, "We saw one log through the middle and get two boards—one sawing, two boards. Get it? All we have to do is· to set the sawed side of the log flush with the rest of the floor, by notching out the undersides to fit over the stringers. Three more sawings and we've got the floor."

I thought a minute. The impact of the simple manoeuvre sank in. There was certainly no need to have the floor boards flat on both sides. One log sawn down the middle would give us two flat surfaces—and those were what counted. Our labor would be cut in half if we quit sawing up our logs into full boards. "Nice going, Tommy," I said. "Let's try it."

Three days later the floor was finished.

A year later, when old-time whipsawyer Lester Dorsey and his helper, Ole Nucloe, took charge of whipsawing fifteen hundred feet of lumber for the floor and furniture of the main ranchhouse, they stared unbelievingly at the set of the teeth. Lester still can't believe that we sawed the floor of the bunkhouse with that saw. He set the teeth the proper way, and he and Ole sawed out an average of twenty boards a day.

With the bunkhouse completed, Tommy and I built two double-decker pole bunks against opposite walls. It was now the tenth of August, and Pan was ten days overdue. I was worried. I thought of a score of accidents that could have happened to the Hand on his lone venture.

Tommy and I saddled up and rode towards the mountains. We reached the mouth of the long Box Canyon, and found impressions of old shod-horse tracks across a strip of dried gumbo land near the creek. From here on tracks had been obliterated by rain and weather. We rode up the canyon till dark, and still found no horse signs.

Suddenly Stuyve shied hard to one side. Tommy's brown cayuse snorted, and both animals fought their heads away from a shallow wash.

A monstrous grizzly bear, with long shaggy silver-streaked hair, reared up in the draw. We let our horses have their heads and raced away. Looking back over my shoulder, I saw three more full-grown grizzlies and several cubs amble out of the draw to watch our disappearing act.

We started back towards camp through the night. Cold frost seemed to rise up out of the ground—an occasional shooting star flared across the brilliantly lit sky above us. The horses' hoofs made a hollow cracking sound across patches of rock—and then—from somewhere along our back trail, floated the spooky moan of a northern wolf.

We splashed the horses across the creek behind the bunkhouse as a yellow light crept up out of the east.

CHAPTER XVIII

Pan Meets a Grizzly

O N THAT DAY IN JUNE, after Pan waved goodbye to me near the mouth of the Box Canyon, he pounded his pack train steadily south towards the distant glacial rim.

As he advanced, he was surprised to see the canyon widen. In places a narrow redtop meadow spread out on both sides of the gravel bottom creek. The rest of the open floor was dotted with bunch grass. Pan looked often at the rainbow-colored sand and gravel beneath the water, and wondered if it was a placer gold proposition.

Clusters of strange, cone-shaped, lacquer-red and lemon-yellow buttes rose in desert-like splendor on the borders of the canyon, some of them reaching up a thousand feet towards the granite peaks and blue-green glaciers that towered far above them.

An hour before dark, Pan rode quickly around the line of horses, holding up their advance. They ducked their heads to feed on bunch grass. He quickly tied two ropes together, and strung them around a group of bullpines, staked out Nimpo and Old Buck, left the two camp followers, Scabby White and Old Joe, loose, and hobbled the rest.

The Hand hurriedly cut a willow stick, tied on his fishline, baited his hook with a small piece of moose meat. He advanced hungrily but cautiously to the creek bank. A school of small trout shot across a pool. In a half hour Pan grunted happily, stood up, and walked into camp with a lard pail of brook trout averaging about eight inches in length. He hit his bed while it was still daylight.

Before dawn the horse bells stopped rattling. Instinctively Pan eased up and out of his bag. He got the fire started, coffee boiled and consumed, and started for a picket horse. The bells started clanging again a short distance below camp. The horses had roused from their brief two o'clock sleep to feed again. All was well.

Pan was much encouraged by his progress so far. He figured that he had made a good twenty miles the day before.

Now he had some trouble driving the pack train, for the horses didn't want to move ahead through the grass. They stopped often to feed. Pan knotted the end of his lariat rope, and kept up a steady rump-snapping, loud-cursing procedure that moved the outfit to the end of the valley—to the base of granite walls and rock slides.

Pan made camp. In the evening he saddled up Piledriver, and led him by the bridle reins up through a rock slide towards a wide ledge. The Top Hand climbed up the ledge, and found himself on another rock slide that appeared to level out above him into a pass.

He mounted the Piledriver, and rode him up through the broken rock. They were nearly two thousand feet above the floor of the canyon, when Pan put a slight pressure on his bridle reins and brought the big bald-faced black to a stop.

"Take a breather, old boy," said Pan. "You'd never quit pluggin' ahead if I didn't stop ya. Look around ya now—this here is a whole world of rock we're in."

Pan dismounted and looked north.

"Look, Piledriver, ya knothead—look back there. Can ya see that big open country? Well—that's the layout, boy—that's the old Blackwater Lost Range. Sure is a fine sight from here. Look at those buttes stickin' up out of the sides of the canyon, every color of the rainbow. Boy—what a plumb beautiful country this here is."

Pan patted Piledriver on the shoulder.

"Aw—what the hell's the use of me tryin' to show ya the country. Yer just thinkin' about that bunch grass down in the valley—ya ain't looked at all."

Pan studied the high pass above him, and was finally satisfied that this was the route through the peaks. He sat down and rolled a smoke, and watched dusk creep up into a pale sky. A vague moaning wind sprang up out of the north.

Above him a rock broke loose. Piledriver plunged wildly off to the side. Pan swung about.

He gulped—then gasped.

On a flat rock, fifty paces above him, a great, moth-eaten grizzly bear swayed from side to side, his beady eyes staring down unblinkingly at him.

The Piledriver, dragging his bridle reins, crashed down the rock slide.

Pan knew grizzly bears. He froze where he sat. His heart pounded wildly. "My God," he breathed through his teeth.

Below him Piledriver started a rock slide. The clattering of loose rocks rose to a deep rumbling roar. The black flashed struggling out of sight.

Pan rose slowly to his feet and reached carefully for his Smith & Wesson 44. He steadied himself.

The monstrous bear shuffled several steps down towards him over the rocks, then suddenly rose up on his hind legs. He towered above Pan, his mouth open, slime drooling out of the corners.

Pan eased the gun muzzle up till it pointed to the bear's open mouth. The wind swept stinking bear stench to his nostrils. The Top Hand felt sweat break out on his back and his forehead. Then he spoke low and soothingly to the big animal.

"I can shoot ya twice through the mouth—and two times in yer ornery heart—and I know you'll keep comin'. I'm too close to stop ya."

A slow paralysis seemed to numb Pan's mind, choke the strength from his body.

The huge animal swayed on his hind legs. Now his leering mangy head stretched forward on his shoulders. He peered intently at the motionless figure of the man.

Pan gripped himself. Again he talked to the savage, drooling monster before him.

"Yes, grizzly—yer twenty steps away—I'll get four shots into ya before ya reach me. You'll kill me all right—you'll kill me dead— but you'll die too. Jest take one step closer—and you'll die—and so will I. Take that last step, Mr. Bear—'cause I ain't afraid to die— and I'll take ya with me when I go."

He waited. Now his gun hand steadied. His eyes squinted along the polished barrel through the gun sight into the gaping jaws. Across the high rocks above him, the low moaning breeze was split by the high shrill whistle of a mountain marmot.

Pan had the strange feeling that the grizzly understood what he said. The animal appeared to be thinking—then to have made up his mind. The great bulk of him dropped to all fours, paused a moment, smelled into the breeze, and then he shuffled heavily over the rocks at an angle away from Pan.

He turned once again, and looked back at the motionless figure of the Top Hand, then swung on out of sight behind a wall of rock.

"Wowie!" said Pan. "Jumpin' bullfrogs! Whew! I sure done put up a bluff." He sat heavily down on a rock. His gun hand started to shake violently. "Did I tell that bear I wasn't afraid? I sure am one hell of a good liar."

He wiped his left hand across his forehead. Sweat ran off his fingers. He looked off in the direction where the grizzly had vanished, took a deep breath, dropped the old 44 back in its holster.

"Hell," said Pan. "What's the matter with me? There was nothin' to it at all."

There is little doubt that Pan's deadly calm in an emergency and his knowledge of the workings of a grizzly's tiny brain saved his life.

If the Top Hand had turned to run away, if he had shot in the air, or run towards the big bear waving his arms in an attempt to bluff him; or if he had poured lead into the animal, the chances are that a one-sided wrestling match would have resulted.

We've all listened to bear stories, and many of us have had bear experiences, but I doubt if any accurate analysis of the workings of a bear's mind can yet be set down on paper. Pan followed a few known grizzly-bear rules, rules that seem to prove out in about eight cases out of ten here in the North.

First, one must realize that grizzlies, ranging over isolated areas where they have never come in contact with man and his firearms, are lord and master of all they survey. A grizzly bear puts the run on all other animals. He doesn't know the feeling of fear, he travels where he pleases, and when he ambles down a path he takes it for granted that the right of way is his.

Pan knew that the grizzly bear is a curious animal, and that he will often watch and study a man with no intention of attacking. Up in this north country, men have been killed when they excitedly fired at a curious grizzly.

A startled or surprised grizzly will charge nine times out of ten. That's why packers in the north country often leave the bells on their horses when they travel through grizzly country. The clanging sound warns the bear of the approaching train.

If a hunter is hidden, three or four well-placed shots may bring the animal down, but take that same bear, shoot him in the same spots with the same lead while he is looking at you, and he will travel a terrifying distance in your direction.

The next morning, with a lame but game Piledriver limping behind his saddle horse, Pan pushed the pack horses up through the steep rock slides and slanting ledges towards the high gap.

The day was spent when the thin line of horses struggled up onto the height of land, and Pan looked off through the rocky pass.

Ahead of him stretched a jagged precipitous land of rock and snow. The pass was a false lead. On the other side it dropped off in a sheer wall more than a thousand feet into a rocky gorge, where a line of tiny blue lakes mirrored the tilted rise of a great gray-green glacier reaching skyward on the north face of the next mountain peak Far in the distance the high rock world ended abruptly, and beyond it a billowy range of snow mountains stood forbiddingly against the horizon.

Pan and his pack train were in a critical position. There was no horse feed, water or firewood. He would not hobble his horses here in this precipitous rocky land. There was only one thing to do. Turn the train about, and hope that by good luck and by the grace of God, the horses would be able to penetrate the dark, and feel and sense their way down the ticklish back trail to the valley floor, thousands of feet below.

As Pan gazed in awed silence down upon the cliffs and chasms about him, night suddenly fell. Far below a faint clattering rose into a deafening roar as a great avalanche, loosened by melting snow, swept down into empty space. And then the whole land seemed to shudder as the mountain of falling rock crashed with a terrifying detonation. The noise was like a thunderclap. Up out of the depths the booming crashes echoed—back and forth between the peaks the sound was flung—until they died in space.

An empty penetrating silence seemed to pervade the world. The tired pack horses stood frozen and trembling in their tracks.

"It's a nightmare—sure as hell," spoke Pan, trying to get a grip on himself. "This sure can't be real—we're havin' some kind of a bad dream."

His words gave him assurance. He turned Croppie about and yelled at the herd.

"Hit the back trail, ya swamp-guzzlers. Hit down the mountains, ya ornery bunch of bunch-grassers. We've been up here in the stars and found it ain't for us."

The Top Hand kept yelling until Nimpo shook himself, smelled into the night, and took the lead down over the rocks. The other horses fell in behind him. Piledriver limped behind Pan and Croppie. Steadily and cautiously down across the darkened face of the heights, the black line of horses picked its way.

Cagey, sure-footed Nimpo led the pack train through the dark mountain night, down the rock ledges and the slides, and finally safely onto the grassy floor of the valley.

After taking care of the horses Pan walked wearily to his bed. Around him dawn was breaking. The horses stood with their heads down where Pan had turned them loose. They were too tired to eat. The creek gurgled soothingly over a gravel bar below camp.

The sun was near the middle of the sky when Pan finished his coffee and hotcakes, and getting out his map, began to figure out where he was, and where he would drive the pack train from here.

Using our Blackwater map and the compass, he made a pencil mark on a dotted line with an arrow pointing north. He assumed this was the creek running through the Box Canyon. The pencil mark he made was some thirty miles due south of our Blackwater camp on the Blur. South of this line was the winding line of Corkscrew Creek, beyond that was Anahim Lake. Although he couldn't see it, the Itcha Cairn would be east of him.

Yesterday he had traveled too far west. The pass he had climbed into opened towards a spur of the Algaks, and beyond them to the Coast Range. It was now clear to Pan that he would have to find a pass through the Itcha peaks to the southeast of him.

He tied a couple of slabs of jerky to his saddle and struck blind up a rock slide. Late in the afternoon he found himself at the edge of a slanting glacier that reached above him towards an opening.

"If that's a pass through," he thought, "this route will be hard to beat."

He led Croppie the last hundred yards over the slope into the narrow gap. He held his breath as the country beyond came into view.

The Top Hand let out a yell—turned to the uninterested Croppie and pulled the animal's mane with a happy flourish.

"We've cracked her, boy—we've cracked the wall This is the cattle trail to the outside—and down there is old Anahim Lake."

CHAPTER XIX

Pan Meets a Girl

Pan and Alfred Bryant broke through with the machinery pack train the day before Tommy and I planned to strike towards Anahim on a searching party.

I was stirring a moose-meat and rice mulligan in an iron pot on the campfire, when I heard a continuous series of yells coming closer through the spruce jungle across the creek. It was now the middle of August. The sun had dropped into the bullpines behind camp, leaving a yellowish twilight, the smell of pine—and deep silence.

Stuyve had been acting mighty strange, pawing the ground, whinnying, trying to get out of our newly finished horse pasture. For some time I had been conscious of a faint staccato sound breaking the stillness. Now I knew what it was. I pulled the pot out of the fire, grabbed up my battered old Brownie, swapped ends, and splashed waist deep across the creek into the spruce.

I stopped to get my wind on the edge of a long brushy opening. I could hear the noise of horses' hoofs on the hard ground, and the raspy ripping sounds that tired-voiced men make at tired-out horses —and then a pack-laden cayuse came into view, and behind him another one—and still another—until a long snakelike line of slow-moving horses, carrying on their backs strange and awkward loads, strung out across the opening.

The feat of manoeuvring this heavy and ungainly tonnage, with our inadequate string of horses, through the unmapped muskegs and jungles that cling to the southern slopes of the Algaks and Itchas, and finally across the tangle of peaks and glaciers of the summit to the Blackwater, was a stupendous one.

Now two riders appeared out of the bush behind the pack horses. I could hear Panhandle's voice. It sounded like a horse rasp on hard steel.

I raised the camera—looked through the lens.

Big black Piledriver is in the lead. He stumbles every few steps. Look at his pack—a great bulk of rake teeth, mower knives, parts of a hayrake.

Two hundred pounds is a heavy load for any horse to pack in this kind of country. Piledriver is toting nearly three hundred.

His long Roman nose turns in my direction. I click the shutter. He pauses a moment, looks at me curiously, then pulling himself together, he moves on by.

·I wind the film. Another horse.

"Buck!" I yell. "You ornery old buckskin bastard."

The game old horse follows close behind Piledriver.

"What a load," I say out loud. "A whole damn rake frame and the wheels."

Old Buck flicks one eyelid at me as he passes, then he pretends not to see me. I snap the lens.

A big chunky black horse steps easily on Buck's heels. He is Nigger, Pete McCormick's much-written-about pack horse who climbed Mystery Glacier, on the famous first ascent of Mount Waddington, the highest mountain in British Columbia.

I draw in my breath as the big, sure-footed black reaches my side. Two cast-iron, heavy-duty mower wheels and parts of the frame—more than three hundred and fifty pounds—are lashed down on his back.

More horses, more big packs follow. A picture of their back trail flashes across my mind. Three hundred miles of bush and timber and rock and mud. Torturous miles over narrow passes and mountain summits, with back-bending loads, sore backs and sore feet, scorching heat and sweat, silent shivering nights on mountains near the sky.

There's Little Roanie. He moves jerkily ahead—dead tired. His eyes have a blank look. On one side of his back leans an iron stove. Roanie shuffles by me. I click the camera.

Next comes a big rack of windows. Almost hidden beneath this load is Old Scabby White. I pretty near bust down and cry. Old Scabby isn't confused by my step in his direction. His load isn't too heavy, but it's bulky and looks like a terrific tonnage. Scabby kind of shrinks back under his burden and pretends he's moving a terrible weight. He glances sideways at me, then looks straight ahead. Beyond me he turns halfway around, groans and proceeds on his way.

A long faltering whinny floats up from one of the horses in the drag. It's a special kind of a whinny, sounds like a donkey stuck in a mudhole. Only one horse can make that noise. Nimpo! From the horse pasture across the creek comes Stuyve's high nasal answer to his pal. And now Old Buck's voice breaks the sound of thudding hoofs.

These horses are coming home—these conquerors of the rocky trails—these unsung heroes of the silent lonely lands. These cayuses whose strong backs and brave hearts have made possible the opening of a new frontier. Horses who carry within their flesh and hold within their souls, the untold deeds and the unrewarded greatnesses of their ancestors, the ghost horses from frontiers of the past.

Here comes Nimpo in the drag. The little black cayuse with the crooked blaze sprawled across his dished face is thin, and he's awful tired.

Here he is now. Look at his pack. High on one side he is toting the unbelievable bulk and weight of a Massey Harris oil-bath mower frame—weight approximately three hundred and fifty pounds. On his other side, to balance this terrific weight, is slung a hundred-pound anvil which hangs down even with the bottom of his belly.

As he stumbled towards me across the opening, his head swaying from side to side, there was nothing except the great pack he was toting, and a certain glint in his eye to indicate that some day this nondescript little black range horse was to become a legend on this last cattle frontier—that his fame would reach across Canada—and that his indomitable will, his heart that couldn't be broken, and his feats of endurance in the face of great odds, would earn for him the title of "The Horse That Wouldn't Die."

And there—grinning down at me—were Pan and Alfred.

I barked at them, "Mulligan's burned—the rice has died—you're late for dinner!"

After we had unpacked the leg-weary, trail-worn horses, Pan, who was as trail-worn as the cayuses, dragged himself around the new horse pasture. He was pleased with the high horseproof enclosure, and after a light supper lay down on his new bunk to test it out. He fell asleep almost instantly. I pulled his boots off and let him lie.

Alfred managed to crawl out of his dusty clothes before trying out his bunk, and before he started to snore, said, "Boys, we've got a real good one on Pan this time. I'll tell you about it in the morning—but whoever wakes up first, ask Pan how he likes the Bella Coola girls—or was there just one girl he saw? Kid him about the Blackwater being a real nice sociable place to bring a wife to."

Tommy and I were up early. We dug around with a great deal of pleasure through the packloads until we found a hundred-pound sack of flour, a four-pound tin of baking powder and a can of dried eggs. We uncovered a slab of Swift's premium bacon and a can of strawberry jam. Tommy picked up his hackamore and started for the wrangle pasture and I went happily to the cookfire with the delicacies.

Alfred and Pan were still dead to the world when I went to the bunkhouse, picked up my fishing rod and headed for the creek. I made a clumsy cast into the big pool in front of the cabin, and the Royal Coachman fly lit heavily on the water. There was a swirl as a shiny body flashed to the surface from the black rocky bottom.

The Coachman vanished. I jerked, and felt the hook set in a heavy body. My reel screamed—line ran off. I slipped on the bank, fell, got wet to the waist, came up out of the water cursing.

My line was tangled on a snag, but I finally landed him—a rainbow trout weighing about five pounds. He was fat.

Back at the fire I cut the trout through the middle into two-inch pinkish red steaks, and dropped them into the sizzling pan of bacon grease.

I had been the camp cook so long that I had acquired all the annoying habits of one. The only difference between me and the average cook was that I sported a large appetite, an appetite that never seemed to be appeased. When I had the grub to cook with, and I don't mean rice and moose meat, I ventured forth into new and untried fields. Some of my Blackwater mulligans made history, and the fame of my specially constructed hotcakes traveled beyond the Canadian National Railroad.

During the summer of 1936, after a particularly rough encounter with two big hotcakes, Ole Nucloe and Tommy Holte nailed the third one to the doorframe on the bunkhouse. It was still strongly in evidence several years later, having weathered all kinds of storms, thaws and freezes.

The last time I saw that old cake, he was staring down at me unmoved, hard as the Rock of Gibraltar. Recently Andy Christenson told me that Pan had shot a number of holes in the old boy with his six-shooter, but that it had withstood the lead, and still looks down from the doorway of the Blackwater bunkhouse.

Now, with my mouth drooling from each corner, I brandished a hotcake turner in one hand, and a homemade wooden spoon in the other. I was overdoing myself in the preparation of a super-meal.

When all was ready, I walked hurriedly into the cabin and rolled the Top Hand out onto the floor. I returned quickly to the fire and our rough-hewn log table. I heard Pan mutter that he had picked up a splinter on the lousy floor, and then heard another thud, a groan, and Alfred asking what had happened.

It was a sunny pine-scented day. Pan and Alfred charged nude out of the bunkhouse and plopped into the creek. Their loud cold yells echoed away in the spruce across the water, and then, with towels wrapped around their middles, the packer and the Top Hand advanced upon the breakfast table.

Tommy came around the corner of the bunkhouse saying that the horses hadn't moved far from camp, but that there were some sore backs and big swellings, and two horses were lame.

"That's good," said Pan, as he sat down on a log stool and reached for the hotcakes. "They told us in Bella Coola that whatever horses packed that Massey frame and McCormick rake would have to be put out of their misery before we got over the Itcha Mountains.

We'll go over the whole bunch of 'em after we eat; but it won't pay to do no worryin' about those cayuses now. Look what that bald-headed old cook has produced for us."

While he talked the Top Hand had filled his wide tin plate to the brim with golden brown hotcakes, fat trout steaks, bacon and a load of strawberry jam. He sniffed into his coffee cup. Tommy made for the table in a hurry as he saw the grub disappearing at such an alarming rate.

While Pan and Tommy talked, Alfred had concentrated on his meal. I stumbled about between the log stools scraping out pans, pushing bowls and pots around the table.

Finally Alfred gurgled happily into his coffee cup, reached for the coffee pot, filled his cup again, stirred in sugar and canned milk; then shoved himself contentedly back from the table and spoke to me,

"You know, Rich, this spot here on the Blackwater is mighty beautiful—but there's something lacking."

I took it up quickly.

"All it lacks is the soft touch of a woman."

"That's it," said Alfred. "This place would be just about complete if one of us boys would break down and marry the right little woman."

The Top Hand coughed up a fishbone that had hung up in his throat.

"Too many bones in these trout," he said.

"Eat your breakfast," said Tommy. "We're talkin' about women —not fishbones."

Pan snorted loudly. He carefully gulped down a mouthful of coffee and setting down his cup, pointed his finger at Tommy.

"Now, Tommy—just what do ya know about women?"

He looked sternly at the kid.

"Have you ever seen any women except your own mother, and the three other Anahim ladies?"

"Sure I have," said Tommy. "I seen lots of 'em—and I've talked to 'em too. I've been to Williams Lake."

"That's right, Tommy—you've been to Williams Lake," Pan said seriously. "I'd forgot about that."

I could see that Pan was swinging the conversation away from

Alfred's and my lead. He was turning the talk to Tommy and he would have us sidetracked before we knew it. I thought this over. Why was the Top Hand steering away from Bella Coola woman talk?

This wasn't in keeping with Pan's usual habit of making the boys envious of his good luck and his happy times on a trip.

I said to Alfred, "Say, Bronco, you fellows haven't told us anything about your trip. Tommy and I want to hear all about those pretty Bella Coola girls, and about all your parties down there. What kind of a figure did the Top Hand cut on his first appearance?"

Pan broke in.

"Boys, we better cut the talk and get after those horses. There's got to be a lot of doctorin' done."

He pushed up from the table, retucked the towel about his middle, and strode seriously for the cabin. I watched Pan walk to the bunkhouse, Tommy got to his feet and followed the Top Hand. I turned to Alfred, "What's eating Pan? I never saw him act like this."

Alfred looked knowingly at me and said, "Pan didn't go on any parties while we were in Bella Coola; he wouldn't even take a drink—said the stuff dulled a man's brain. I finally left him altogether. He spent his time taking the prettiest and smartest little girl in the village out riding. You met her when we took the pack train down last winter."

Alfred paused a minute and carefully relit his cigarette.

"Well, I'll be damned," I said. "You mean that beautiful little Shorty?"

"That's the one," replied Alfred. He drained his cup. "I think Pan has fallen like a ton of bricks. Maybe it's too bad for him. She's a smart girl—been outside to school, and she doesn't spend much time at her family's home in Bella Coola—been away a lot in the city—you know the kind, Rich—wears swell clothes and looks real slick in them, talks about books and music and things that folks in the outside world talk about. She's about as different from that horse-minded snorting old Pan as a red rose is from a cactus bush."

We used two forty-five-foot straight-grained spruce trees as our hay stacker. These two limber poles were joined together at the top with a chain. Guide wires held the A frame up in place, and a set of center-breaking slings were constructed. With this rigging and several blocks and pulleys, we sweated up the first stack of hay in the country beyond the Itchas. Alfred helped us up with the first stack, and then struck for Anahim and his own hay problems.

Something on that trip to Bella Coola had changed Pan. He wasn't the easygoing, smart-cracking, practical-joking character of old. He seldom laughed, and only once did he pull off his "nothin' to it" remark. That was when I asked him about finances.

"Why, hell, man," said Pan without snorting, "there was nothin' to that. It was just like I told ya. Those saddlers of mine was worth money. Stanley Blum and Ashley Williams just drove the bunch up to the Diamond G. Dude Ranch. It was just what they were lookin' for—well-broke, snappy-lookin' mounts for their dude wranglers and dudes. I had to wait a week in Bella Coola before Stanley cleared me for a thousand dollars."

"I was just wondering why the trip took you so long," I said lightly. "How did you spend your time? Roping those Bella Coola farmers' calves?"

The Top Hand gazed off towards the mountains. He looked sick.

"Well, friend—I guess it done those horses some good, restin' theirselves before that tough trip back. Those ten days in Bella Coola didn't hurt 'em a bit—and then there was that machinery to take down—every nut and bolt of it, to lighten up the main parts. I was busy enough all right."

Pan stood up from the table and went out of the cabin.

"Somethin's wrong with Pan," observed Tommy. "He must be worryin' about gettin' his hay up in good shape before it rains."

One evening we were topping out our third stack of hay. I had been complaining to Pan about working after the moon was up, and the Top Hand was grunting something at me when my slip team, Big George and Baldy, threw up their heads and whinnied.

"Look," exclaimed Pan, "here comes a cowboy ridin' a pinto pony."

I glanced up and saw through the twilight a flashy-looking black and white pinto dancing across the meadow. Tommy drove his team to the stack, yelled "whoa," and hooked the stacker snatch blocks to his load of hay. He unhooked his horses and turned to Pan.

"That's Dad. He finally musta got the nerve up to ride that Redstone pinto wild hoss of his."

"I'll be damned," said Pan. "Seein' a white man in this country jolts a man up."

Andy Holte let out a yell as he approached us. Riding in close he held up his side-winding pinto as he lashed out hard at Pan for using the teams at night.

"Sure as hell," rasped the Teamster, pointing his finger at the bunch of us, "you've fog-heaved every last one of them cayuses."

Big George took a kick at Andy's pinto. It had been biting him on the rump.

"See there," grated Andy. "That petrified-boned, lumber-footed, pinch-backed swamper is fog-heaved and he's stretched. You've killed off your horses, boys," he hollered. "Where's the cookhouse? Me and my Morgan ground-gainer here have got to tie on the feed bag. Unhook—you horse-killers."

Pan snorted for the first time in days.

"Who ever saw a pinto Morgan? What the hell ya talkin' about, Andy? There's a thousand carloads of them little painted ponies down in the deserts—and they call 'em broomtails in that country."

Andy let out a high whining wail—snatched off his golf cap, and the big leggy pinto sprung high in the air.

"Wowie," yelled Andy.

Straight up and straight down went the pinto. At each jump Andy let out a wild piercing yell and lashed his legs forward in unison with the horse's pitches. Finally the pinto raised his head and looked about him. Andy reined him over to the haystack.

"Them little U.S. pinto desert rats," he rasped at Pan. "Did ya ever see one of 'em lope fifty miles over the mountains and pinnacles in a day and then start shakin' the hump out of his back?"

"Come on, Andy," I called, as I swung my team and slip about and headed them across the meadow towards the bunkhouse. "It must be near ten-thirty. Leave that damn slave-driver and his yes-man back there. We're going home and eat."

Andy trotted up alongside of my slip and we moved across the opening. The Teamster turned in his saddle and yelled at Pan,

"I've packed in your mail—and there's a nice sweet-looking little letter for ya from Bella Coola."

Pan and Tommy must have gone into action then, for Tommy's hay slip, with Pan at the ribbons, caught up to us before we reached the wrangle pasture.

Back at the bunkhouse Pan moved fast. He lit the lantern, shook the pile of mail out of Andy's gunny sack, and scattering it hurriedly about my bunk, snatched up the letter he was looking for, and without a word of explanation, dashed out the door where he crashed head on into the Teamster who dropped his golf cap in the sudden confusion.

Andy looked bewilderedly after the disappearing Top Hand, and stooping over, picked up his headpiece.

"He's fog-heaved and he's brain-fevered hisself," exclaimed Andy, shaking his head. "Night life in the swamp bottoms will do it to man as well as horse."

Andy sat down on a bunk and I went to work on the supper.

"How's it going back here in these muskegs?" he asked. "Figured I'd better check up on you boys, and it's a lucky thing I did."

"How you making out, Andy? Which way did you come in?"

"Over the mountain on Pan's pack trail. There's a high slanting glacier above a rock slide on top. Don't know how those boys ever got that machinery train over it."

The Teamster fumbled for makings, and I pointed to an opened tin of tobacco. Andy helped himself.

Tommy stepped through the open door.

"I'm hungry," he said, sniffing at venison steaks that sizzled on the griddle. He threw his Stetson at Andy who neatly ducked it.

"How's haying going?" he asked his father.

Andy looked sheepish.

"Well, I'll tell ya something, Tommy. I'm not supposed to be here, so don't ever tell your mother you saw me."

I started to laugh, but Tommy looked serious. Andy waved his arm carelessly.

"I busted my mower knife up on a rock. Had to get a new batch of sections, so I saddled up and rode out to get some."

There was a moment's silence. Andy glanced furtively at Tommy and then stared hard at a crack in the floor. Tommy looked incredulously at his father.

"Rode out?" he said. "Out here eighty miles to Blackwater for mower sections?"

Andy looked apologetic.

"Well, I rode to Anahim for the knives and got the word that gold is going up to thirty-six dollars an ounce—and there's prospectors in the country."

The Teamster took off his golf cap and scratched above his ear. He looked shrewdly at me.

"I figured I'd look over that Box Canyon on the mountain before those prospectors got in there first—so I brought you boys' mail along. I've found a placer proposition, and hard rock as well. That crik up there is filled with gold."

"How did you find that out?" I asked.

"I used my cap for a gold pan, shook out some sand along the crik." The Teamster showed his cap to me. "See the black sand in there?" he asked. "It's still stickin' inside the band."

Andy now spoke in a high-pitched voice.

"It's a placer gold proposition sure as we're livin'—anybody can see that. There's copper, silver and zinc in that mineralized belt too, but I'm more interested in the gold end of the proposition, even though the copper and silver will pay the operatin' costs of the whole thing."

Pan came through the doorway. He slapped the Teamster a resounding blow on the back, and yelled at me to snap out of it and get the dinner on the table. I noticed immediately that his personality had reverted to its old state with the reading of his letter.

After cleaning up our supper, Pan asked if any of us had writing paper and envelopes.

"This here jumbo pad," said Pan, "ain't very stylish to write a business letter on."

"There's some brown wrapping paper over in the corner," I said. Pan looked sheepish.

"No—not that kind of paper."

Tommy looked admiringly at the Top Hand. "I wish I was good enough to write a real businessman's letter," he said.

Pan snorted, and started upsetting bags and coal-oil boxes in a vain effort to find writing paper.

I got up, put everything back in place, and told him to stop trying to be so high tone.

"Use the jumbo pad," I snapped at him. "It's paper isn't it?—and good enough for any man to write on. If the receiver of that letter judges you by the paper you write on, that person is no good anyway—and you've found him out. You can mark that guy down as a small-minded ignorant son of a b."

"You betcha life," chimed in Andy. "You're lucky to have any paper at all."

Pan was visibly impressed by Andy's and my sound logic. He carried the big schoolboy pad to his bunk, sat down, said, "Maybe you boys are right."

Then he ducked his head to his work. I thought over his last remark. This kind of a statement from Pan was out of character.

While Pan was writing, I turned to the Teamster, who was carving on one of the bedposts with his jackknife.

"I'm leavin' my brand here," explained Andy without looking up.

"That's a good place for it," I said.

Pan spoke from his pad, "Say, Rich—I guess I am not a very good hand at writing."

"Your English is improving," I answered. "You're getting so you can talk like a professor."

The Top Hand looked embarrassed,

"Say, Rich—how do ya spell 'forever'? Is it one word or two words?"

I looked at him closely.

"Two words," I said.

The Top Hand was now obviously confused; he glanced in the direction of Andy, who seemed to be deeply engrossed in his job of carving up my bed.

The Top Hand wrote something down on the pad, and then looked back up at me. He cleared his throat.

"Are you plumb sure that 'forever' is spelled with two words? I've got to get this thing right. You know how it is, Rich—when you're writin' a real business letter—well—ya just got to get the thing spelt right."

I was staring hard at the Top Hand.

"One word," I said.

When Andy rode south into the jackpines the following day, he carried in his pocket Pan's "business letter."

CHAPTER XX

The Great Grassy World

EARLY IN SEPTEMBER we topped out our fourth and last stack of hay. Our twenty-five head of horses were now insured against the toughest kind of northern winter.

The day Tommy saddled up and started for the Holte swamps to help Andy finish up his haying, Pan and I inspected our long hard summer's work. We sat on the top log of the round corral and the Top Hand's face wrinkled into a broad grin.

"Friend," he said, "I told you away back in June that before the snow blew down on this outfit, we'd have all these improvements done. You said it couldn't be did in one summer. Now I'm saying I told ya so. We're right on schedule. Ya see—there was just nothin' to it at all. Nothin' to it, boy. Everythin' was easy."

"It sure was an easy summer," I answered.

The Top Hand continued with his talk.

"Now it's just a question of time and a little money before we're dodgin' our cayuses among a herd of rustlin' whiteface cows. But now we've got to do some ridin'. We're gonna see just how much grazin' country and hay meadow we're sittin' on. Let's get our saddle horses and a pack horse and ride."

That afternoon we struck down the big grassy opening in a northeasterly direction, and camped on one of the many pothole meadows beyond it. The following day we came out on old road slashings, blazes and last fall's wagon tracks. We swung our horses east down the indistinct trail. We were on Paul Krestenuk's slashings that ran some 225 miles from Quesnel, at the end of steel on the P.G.E. railroad, to the Indian village of Ulgatcho.

The Top Hand talked of cattle prices in B.C.

"Ya know, friend, we're startin' in at the right time. For five years good Hereford beef cows has been sellin' at market for ten dollars to fifteen dollars, and good beef steers has only been bringin' ten dollars to eighteen dollars in Vancouver. It's been shown on the books of the cattle companies in the States that you've got to get forty dollars fer steers to break even on a cattle operation.

"Now is the time to buy stock cheap. Beef sure ain't gonna stay at two cents a pound forever here, and the next generation ain't gonna be like their dads—in the game just fer the fun of it. Right now herds are bein' cut down, nearly every outfit in the Chilcotin is ready to sell out. They're into the banks and the mortgage companies. The rancher ain't got anythin' to show for his long tough ten-year fight to live except his rheumatics and his busted bones."

Pan jumped Piledriver over a windfall, ducked a jackpine limb, and called back to me.

"You watch her, boy. Beef is gettin' scarce—you'll see a ten-dollar cow worth forty dollars inside two years."

I trotted up to him.

"That's a big jump in price, Pan."

"What the hell," he rasped. "A twelve-hundred-pound cow sells over the butcher's counter fer twenty-five cents a pound—so three and a half cents to the rancher ain't callin' the cards very high."

We rode through great sweeps of meadow lands with the willow-fringed river winding through them like a writhing snake. Dense jackpine forests and stretches of lava-strewn volcanic-like country made tough traveling in spots.

We rode east more than a hundred miles to a creek marked on the map Batnuni River. We swung our horses west up the Batnuni. It was a beautiful lush land of many-colored wild flowers; clumps of poplar and fir grew on benches, lost in a seemingly endless stretch of low south-facing bunch grass and pea-vined hills that dipped into blue lakes at their base.

"Wow! What range!" exclaimed Pan. "Never seen the beat of it."

Leaving the Batnuni River, we led the pack horse up over a high rocky mountain, heading back towards the Blackwater. Finally we came to a volcanic ridge. A red and gray lava bed reached south to a low rolling poplar and pea-vine country.

Pan and I crawled down off our horses and spread the map before us. We came to the conclusion that we were now somewhere in the Poplar mountain range.

Herds of deer sprang up out of the tall grass, and bounced away, with their white-patched tails rising up and down above the vegetation. Grouse and prairie chickens flew out of the grass in swarms, their wings making a purring noise.

Above the dense growth of grass, pea-vine and wild flowers, the pale green bushy tops of gigantic poplar trees hummed and vibrated with the cries of all manner of birds. High over the trees we saw the brown and gold flashes of great golden eagles.

"Lots of country for two men to handle," I said to the Top Hand. He didn't answer, but started fumbling for his tobacco pouch.

Back at the Home Ranch, we changed horses, replenished our grub supply, and struck southeast towards the benches under the Itcha Mountains.

The first day out we ran into a dense tangle of bush growing up through a tumbled mass of windfall. We sweated for a day and a half, axing out a trail to get the horses through, and then broke out on to a gravel-barred creek flowing north through narrow bunch grass hills.

As we rode along, the open slopes widened to nearly a mile. We noticed that the soil was sandy and in some places rocky and graveled, growing a large type of bunch grass. Some bunches were a foot in diameter, with fine silky heads standing two feet above the ground. Two of these bushes made a good feed for a horse.

Pan chuckled and wet his lips.

"Real old-time Montana bunch grass," he said. "Just like what used to grow on the Crow reservation before it was grazed off. Best feed in the world for a cow."

As night fell we could see open prairie reaching into distance.

It was too dark to be absolutely sure, but I asked the Top Hand if he could see trees at the other end of the opening.

"No trees," sighed Pan, "just grass, and more grass. It's a hell of a country—by tomorrow we won't be able to find enough wood to start a cookfire."

Pan took care of the horses, and I got a fire going. Pan shot the heads off a mess of ptarmigan, peeled off their hides and gutted them. While I spitted the tender birds over the coals, he talked of the empire of meadow and range that we had already seen in the Itchas and country to the north and east of them.

The horses grazed close to camp. At daylight we hit east into the great open spaces. Ahead of us the wide grassy prairie swept off into treeless distance, walled on one side by fantastically shaped, brilliantly colored domes, crags and glacier-dotted peaks. Small graveled creeks flowed from the high mountains out on to the prairie, and here and there pale blue rock-bottomed lakes mirrored the red, yellow and white colors of the Itchas.

We hadn't gone far when a herd of about thirty cariboo trotted up out of a dry wash ahead of us, wheeled about to get a good look at what was coming, then struck off single file towards the mountains.

Pan and I rode for two days through the prairie and tree-dotted grass lands before we gave up looking for the other end of it, and turned our horses in the direction of home.

It seemed incongruous that, with the shortage of range and pasture in Canada and the western States, such a vast world of grass was still waiting here under the Itchas, untouched and unknown.

Back at the bunkhouse, reclining on his peeled-pole, double-decker bunk, the Top Hand rolled a smoke, then lit it with his bullet-shaped lighter. He stared meditatively into the rising smoke as it bounced against the upper bunk and mushroomed outward. The immensity of the lonely grass country we had traversed had made a deep and awesome impression on us both.

Now Pan said, "Ya know, I've been tryin' to figure out what to do. Our whole damn future rests on what we decide now. I've thought of every angle, friend—and I still come back to our first idea of startin' out here small, and buildin' this spread up through the years ahead of us." The Top Hand sighed. "And yet—on the other hand—I don't know."

He puffed for a moment on the butt of his cigarette, but it had gone out. He started fumbling in his pockets. I got out my lighter and lit his cigarette.

During moments of deep thought Pan would fumble around for his lighter or his matches and, although these articles were nearly always some place on his person, he never seemed to be able to locate them. His aimless and fruitless search for a light irritated me, so rather than break up his line of thought, I either handed him my lighter, or at a time like this, when I feared the Top Hand couldn't take the top off the lighter, I took no chances, and hurriedly lit his cigarette myself.

Now he inhaled thoughtfully, and continued with his talk.

"I guess ya realize that we've rode through a whole new frontier. We've rode more'n a hundred miles in one direction, and seventy in the other—covered more than five million acres of country, and we still don't know how much farther she runs.

"The map shows us that west of where we've traveled this country still runs on for another hundred and fifty miles, and goin' north from where we quit, there's a empty land reachin' out a hundred miles to the Canadian National Railroad."

I had done a lot of thinking as mile after mile of the new cattle frontier opened out before us, looming ever larger across the horizon, until now it seemed limitless. I had shuffled and reshuffled plans and ideas around in my head, trying to figure out what we should do about our fabulous discovery.

I knew that it would take many years for Pan and me to tie up and stock all the country we could handle, and it was only reasonable to assume that, during that time, news of our discovery, and an almost certain rise in the price of Canadian beef, would send cattle company operators, small ranchers, and 160 acre homesteaders into the area.

This ranching country was located farther from railroad and town than any ranching district in the United States, and as far as I knew, in Canada; and yet I had ugly visions of other cattle countries I had seen, where, soon after settlement, they became overgrazed pasture lands with soil erosion cutting away the top soil, the range fenced in, truck roads, and then the maze of red tape of herd laws and government supervision.

Why wasn't it possible to keep this wild stretch of land in one huge block, I thought—a modern cattle empire similar in magnitude to those that once existed on this continent. A land that except for a few lonely cattle stations, and a scattering of drift fences, would remain in its wild natural state through the years to come—an immense made-to-order cattle land where great herds of Herefords would transform the idle grass into beef, to help feed a world whose production of meat and other foodstuffs was not keeping pace with the relentless growth of its population.

For days I had tried to figure out how Pan and I could tie up and hold this great chunk of land together; and had finally come to the conclusion that there was only one way to do this.

We would have to form a cattle company to get the proper financial backing, and then purchase as well as lease, for long terms, strategical areas across the entire country. I knew that the whole business of forming a cattle company, with all the red tape and strings attached to it, would require a lot of time, management and know-how. Pan and I didn't have any of this.

It was after Pan had spoken that a picture suddenly flashed across my mind.

I saw George Pennoyer standing iron-jawed before us—a successful cattleman, admired and respected across a State—a man who had not only been general manager and part owner of one of the biggest cattle companies in the West, but who was also recognized as an authority on cattle and range management.

Quickly I said to Pan, "Say, boy, do you remember what George Pennoyer said to us before we left Wyoming?"

The Top Hand sat suddenly erect on his bunk, and the butt of his cigarette fell from his mouth.

"You've got it, boy," he snapped. "You've got the answer sure. I just now can't remember exactly what he said, but I remember what he meant when he talked. Just what in hell did he say?"

I stared at the Top Hand with a thin grin on my face. I let him dangle for several moments, then bit off each phrase slowly and distinctly,

"George said: 'If the layout up there looks big—if it's really big and you think it's a cattle company proposition—I'll come up there and throw in with you fellows—and we'll start a real frontier cattle company!'"

A few days after our decision to contact George Pennoyer and form a cattle company, Pan suddenly doubled up with a severe attack of appendicitis. Neither of us could remember whether to use hot fomentations or cold ones, so we tried both. The cold-water towel baths seemed to give Pan the most relief, so we stuck to these.

I was far more worried than Pan appeared to be. The Itcha Mountains suddenly took on a sinister and formidable appearance. I was struck with the hopelessness of our terrific isolation, and knew that, if Pan's appendix broke, there wasn't one chance in a million of getting him out. To ride fifty miles to Anahim and send for a plane and a doctor was our only chance.

Pan spoke unemotionally from his pole bunk when I suggested this idea to him.

"Friend," he said, "somehow I have the feeling that nature will provide. When this here gut-ache is over, we'll be able to tell those doctors all about it. I'm too damn mean to die. So stick around, son, and we'll write up a article on how to handle a appendix."

I thought this over—and came to the conclusion that Pan was right. If I rode to Anahim, Pan would be alone and helpless for at least three days.

The following morning Pan's right leg cramped and pulled up towards his stomach. He was violently ill. His face was a pale gray color, and his eyes sank back in his head.

I was panicky. I let go a silent prayer asking the Lord what I should do to save Pan's life. I was looking down at the Top Hand when he said, "Friend, I've got to tell you somethin' just in case. Just in case—you know what I mean. There's a little girl down in Bella Coola—her name's Adelia, but they call her Shorty—well—I'm afraid I've plumb slipped, boy."

He paused a moment. "Light me up a smoke," he said. The Top Hand remained silent while I rolled him a smoke, lit it and stuck it between his pale lips. He inhaled, then coughed.

"Ow—that sure didn't tickle none, friend—it's like a knife going into my belly."

"You're crazy to smoke," I told him. He didn't answer but perversely took another drag, and this time didn't cough.

"Go ahead," I told him. "Finish up what you're telling me. It won't go any further—anything you tell me."

"Well—just in case I bog down here, tell Shorty that I plumb loved her more than anything in the world."

For a moment Pan's dulled eyes opened wide. I thought I saw a steely glitter come to them. He cleared his throat. I could see he was struggling for strength and for words.

Now Pan gritted his teeth against the pain that was stabbing him towards unconsciousness.

"God, friend," he rasped. "Adelia and I were gonna get married green-grass time. This thing can't bust on me now. It just can't happen now."

Sweat was running down Pan's face onto the folded horse blanket beneath his head. I patted him gently on his wet shoulder.

"Easy boy—easy," I said.

A long sigh heaved up from the Top Hand's throat. His eyes closed. His body seemed to slump down in the blanket. I thought Pan's breath had stopped.

I got fighting mad. I yelled up at the bunkhouse ceiling, "God—give this guy a fighting chance. Damn you—give just one man that's trying so hard a break!"

I doused an old towel into the water bucket. It came out dripping with the cold glacier meltings. I threw back Pan's sweaty blanket and slapped the towel over his naked side.

His eyes opened up. He looked at me, a faint grin on his gray sunken face.

He spoke weakly. "That's tellin' 'em, friend. Give 'em hell."

He paused. "Somethin's just come to me. There's a can of olive oil ditched away some place. Oil—that's it. Olive oil—appendix."

The Top Hand sank back.

I dashed for our miscellaneous pack boxes and junk—a large tin of olive oil came up miraculously out of a cow-hide alforkas. I slashed two holes in the top of the can with a hunting knife—knelt by Pan's bed and poured it into his open mouth. Pan gurgled—gulped more oil—lay back—fell asleep.

I heard horses' hoofs pounding in the yard. I stood up from Pan's bed.

Scabby White's bony head peered anxiously in through the open door. Behind him Old Joe whinnied. I could see his long ears bent forward on his head. Scabby whinnied softly into the house, then turned about, and he and Joe walked on down to the water hole.

Hours later Pan opened his eyes again. They were smiling with renewed life.

"Oil," he said. "More oil." His voice came out reassured, strong. "That's the stuff. The pain's nearly gone, friend."

I handed Pan the can. He swallowed several times, handed it back to me.

"I dreamt those two colts of mine were here standin' by the bed," said Pan. "They were talkin' away at me just like white men. Old Scabby was a-tellin' me that the knife stickin' me in the guts was gonna quit—and a funny thing—Old Joe, he kept sayin' to me, 'There's nothin' to it, boy—nothin' to it at all!'"

I stared unbelievingly at Pan. "Scabby and Joe were here all right," I said.

Pan grinned knowingly at me. "Ya know—sometimes a man gets the goddamnedest dreams."

CHAPTER XXI

The Night the Horses Raced with Death

IT WAS DEEP INTO SEPTEMBER when Tommy rode into the Blackwater. While Pan was recuperating we had powwowed up our immediate plan of action.

Before the winter cracked down on us, the Top Hand was to strike for Vancouver to have his appendix removed. I was to head for Wyoming, pick up George Pennoyer, and carry on to New York to finance our embryo cattle company.

To start the ball rolling I was to ride out to Anahim immediately and send off via pony express our long, detailed letter to George Pennoyer, and one to the B.C. Department of Lands, mapping out the approximate area we were interested in—some four million acres across whose titanic area were scattered meadows and range lands which were strategic to our proposed operation.

Among other important letters that I carried in my saddle pockets was a carefully written one from Pan to Adelia.

That day in 1935, as I rode south through the wild heights of the towering Itchas, I naturally couldn't foresee the future and know that our dreams would come true; that Pan would marry Adelia; that the grand old cattleman Pennoyer would become the general manager of our proposed Frontier Cattle Company; that great trail herds, chuck wagons, horse remudas and cowpunchers would soon be strung out across the land, moving from distant railhead and town and ranch across the vast lonely lands in northern British Columbia into the last cattle frontier.

But I did know in my heart that I had found my country.

A country as yet unspoiled by man's bright new ideas.

A land where clear, calm, direct thought—based on the Golden Rule, the principles of Christianity—takes the place of the worried, confused and subconsciously frustrated state of mind that exists when economic considerations decide every move or act.

A land where action takes the place of talk.

During the next forty-eight hours I was to be a witness to one of the most grueling ordeals a human being can undergo.

I was to see the resourcefulness, stamina and courage of the handful of men and women and their horses at Anahim.

And I would see the invincible power that a man's mind can exercise over his body—in this instance not in just one individual but in several.

Late in the afternoon, the tracks of Pan's pack train, and the more recent ones of Andy Holte's pinto, disappeared in the high granite rocks of the Itcha summits. Reining Stuyve, and dragging my pack horse Alec up a narrow pass at the edge of a slanting blue-gray glacier, I looked off into the colored contours of the vast lonely Anahim country.

Anahim's yellow meadows crept octopus-like into the silver of spruce and the brown sweeps of willow bottoms, and far beyond them the Mystery Mountains, the highest in British Columbia, stood like white marble statues against the purple evening sky.

I couldn't see tracks or signs on the rocks on the other side of the pass, but picked out what I figured would be the natural route down the steep slopes towards timberline. It was growing dark when Stuyve threaded his way through a slanting alpine country below the heights. A narrow timbered gulch twisted like a snake below us. We slid by degrees down into the bottom, where a dense jungle growth cut off any progress in this direction.

Soon it was too dark to see where we were going, and we were completely rimrocked by windfall piled five and six feet high around us.

It was a dark night. Clouds obscured the stars. I did the only thing I could do—let the horses stand between the piled-up timber, while I took off my chaps, huddled into my moose-hide jacket, and sat down under a windfall, where, in a cramped position, I waited for the long night to spend itself.

The hours passed slowly. Clouds lifted and shifting stars blinked coldly down. A faint breeze out of the east made a strange hushed noise in the high tops of the jackpines, and far in the distance the mournful call of a loon was broken by the spooky high-to-low chant of a rutting bull moose.

At last a faint light lit the cold land around us, and, after some difficulty, I got the horses through the sticks and carried on to the south.

It was broad daylight when we crossed fresh blazes, horse tracks, and here and there the stump of a recently cut tree. We were on Pan's pack trail. Two hours later I was happy to see old and familiar landmarks about me, and to know that I was about two miles from the Christensons' on a well-worn trail.

It was at this instant on the trail that a strange and still unexplained phenomenon occurred.

The forests seemed to be deathly still. I could feel the silence. A heavy growth of thorny bushes and jackpines stretched west of me some four and a half miles to the Behind Meadows. Now—from that direction—a strange human cry floated up. It was kind of a low moaning wail.

Stuyve pricked up his ears and shied off the trail.

The noise came again—I swung around and tried to crash the horses through the bush in that direction, but we couldn't get through. I glanced up at the sun—about eight o'clock I thought—too early for any of the Christenson kids to have left the house and be caught in a trap or hung up in a windfall; and it hadn't sounded like a cry for help.

Again the forests seemed to drip with quiet. The noise had not been made by a cougar, wolf, a coyote or a lynx. I knew those sounds well. No—that wail was human.

I didn't have to touch Stuyve—he eased into a long lope. A few minutes later we slid into the Christenson yard. I jumped off, tied the horses to the corral and strode hurriedly to the house.

Fair-haired, blue-eyed Andy Christenson greeted me at the door,

"You must have spent the night in the bush, Rich. It's not eight-thirty yet. Come on in."

Dorothy came forward. "Glad to see you, Rich—it's been a long time. Come in—you're just in time for breakfast."

I said quickly, "Are all the kids home? Is everybody around here accounted for?"

"Why, yes," answered Dorothy. "Why?"

"I heard a strange noise back there in the woods," I said weakly. Andy started to laugh.

"Rich has been in the bush too long. He's hearing things. Look at him—he's red as a beet and just as shy and scared as a yearlin' deer."

We sat down to bacon, eggs, hot cakes, fresh milk and coffee on a gingham cloth. Shiny brass vases filled with many-colored wild flowers centered the long table.

"How's your haying going?" I asked Andy.

"All the hay is up, here on the home place," he replied. "Dorothy's brother, Vinney Clayton, is up for a vacation. He loves to run a mowing machine, so he's over at Behind Meadows now running the hay crew."

Suddenly a sick feeling crept up over me.

"We can't keep Vinney still," said Dorothy. "Andy has been trying to get him to take it easy, but no, he's going to keep on haying right up to the last few days. Then he wants to go after grizzlies in the Itchas and goats in the Rainbows."

At this moment two things happened. The three Christenson children came laughing into the room from their bedrooms, and through the window I saw a white-lathered horse, streaked with mud, fall heavily to his knees. From his back a wild-eyed Indian jumped and ran for the house. We all jumped up from the table.

"Something's happened," snapped Andy.

Dorothy rushed the children into an adjoining room.

The Indian plunged through the door. Outside I saw his horse stagger back to his feet and sway jerkily from side to side. I recognized the man at once. He was Louis Squinas, oldest son of Chief Squinas.

"Vinney!" he gasped for breath. "Vinney—he's die!"

I expected to hear Dorothy scream, or see her faint. Not Dorothy.

"Easy, Louis," she said. Her face was gray. Andy steadied himself on the back of a chair.

Dorothy said, "Now, Louis—tell us—what has happened?"

"Mowing machines he run away. . . . Vinney catch in mower knife . . . cut 'em off both legs. Lots blood . . . now he dying . . . can't live. Thomas he see him . . . ride for me . . . I ride like hell."

I have never been able to figure out the strange wails both Stuyve and I heard at the exact time of the accident. Vinney made no outcry of any kind, and even if he had, the noise could not have traveled across four flat jungle miles.

I didn't want to eat, but I quickly stuffed fried eggs into my mouth. There would be need for energy this day.

Andy spoke fast: "Quick, Dorothy, get the disinfectant. I'll saddle up." He ran for the door.

Louis flopped panting into a chair and held his head between his hands.

"Poor Vinney," he moaned. "Poor Vinney."

Dorothy ran out of a back room with a quart bottle of mercurochrome and several clean pillowcases. I stood at the door.

"I'll take those things, Dorothy. There's no horse in Anahim can step on that bay's heels I'm riding."

She thrust the stuff into my hands. I said, "Get me a couple of pounds white flour."

She was almost instantly back with the flour and a small ball of heavy braided cord.

"Tourniquets," she said.

I whirled around to Louis who was now back up on his feet.

"I get fresh horse," he said. "I come behind."

"Yes, Louis," said Dorothy. "Pick out a fresh horse, but ride like the wind for Jane Bryant. She's home now. Been training for a nurse. You know where the horses are, Louis?"

"I go like hell. I kill one more horse!" he snapped.

Dorothy turned to me.

"Tell Vinney I'm going to try and get through to Ashcroft on the phone. They may be able to connect me up with Vancouver and send a plane and a doctor."

Dorothy was as calm as a precision machine. I moved out of the door as she lifted the receiver and rang for the operator in distant Kleena Kleene. Louis Squinas followed me through the door.

"Where is Vinney?" I asked him.

"Two miles other side Behind cabin. Two meadows he come together."

I knew the spot. I tied the bundle in back of my saddle, untied Stuyve, and swung aboard as Andy came riding out of the corral on a buckskin mare.

"I'm packing the stuff," I called to him as Stuyve shot out of the yard.

"Take it away," he yelled back.

A hard-packed, well-traveled hay road reached ahead of me. Stuyve was a typical Arabian. He was a horse ready to stretch into a run any time you gave him his head, and he could feel the excitement or the tension of his rider. Now he sprang into his bit and I held him down to an ordinary run, faster than a lope.

I figured out the distance to the connecting meadows from Christenson's. Six miles, I thought. No horse can go at race-track pace that far over rough country. We swung through a gate at the edge of a long lane and I reined Stuyve into a heavy-timbered stretch. I looked back—Andy was only a few lengths behind me—but I could see the buckskin was running at her limit.

I planned out the run before us. Three miles at a held-in run— then a quarter mile holdback to a long trot, to give Stuyve a change in the use of his muscles—then I'd turn Stuyve loose.

We shot out of the timber and across a meadow. Now Stuyve was heated up. He ground his mouth into his bit, fighting to get his head. The meadow disappeared behind us—I looked back. Three hundred yards behind us the buckskin was moving onto the opening.

Fresh clear wind swept past my face—now and then a fleck of horse sweat spattered back—a patch of black mud loomed up ahead —I sawed Stuyve down as quick as I could. He slugged with short running steps through the mud and came up fast on the other side.

He was breathing hard—another quarter faded behind—more timber ahead. A half mile through the timber and I pulled the bay back into a lope. He was heaving. Three and a half miles lay behind us, three and a half miles and not many minutes. I eased Stuyve back into a trot, but he fought for his head. His chest heaved and his sweat turned to lather.

Ahead of us meadows and occasional clumps of jackpines dotted the landscape. Stuyve's breath was evening up. I let him into his ground-reaching run again.

I looked back across the opening—no sign of the buckskin. The Behind cabin came into view. We veered around the horse pasture. Stuyve fought for more bit.

Now I let him reach out farther and faster. His neck strained ahead. Far up ahead twin jackpine islands jutted out of a sea of green meadow. "We're nearly there," I told Stuyve.

The islands were coming closer. Meadow stubble flashed by like light. We shot into the neck between.

Three men were packing a coat-made stretcher; on it more coats covered a huddled figure. Snatching off my bundle I ran towards the group. Stuyve stood foam-covered in his tracks.

I thought of Vinney as I ran forward. I had met him in Bella Coola. He was the kind you wouldn't easily forget: a tall, clean-cut, brownish blond man in his late forties, a mountain climber, big-game hunter, sportsman. He came through the thickest of the fighting in World War I unscathed. What irony, I thought.

I steeled myself.

"Hello, Vinney. Squinas got through to us. I've got some junk to put on your wounds."

Vinney's face was green. A strange light shone from his eyes. He looked steadily at me and spoke slowly and weakly.

"Hello there, Rich. Never expected to see you here."

The Christenson cowhands, Billy Dagg, Stanley Dowling and Mac MacEwen, set the stretcher down. None of them had spoken.

I bent down over Vinney and carefully withdrew the boys' bloody coats and shirts.

Brown-haired, square-jawed Stanley Dowling stepped up and I handed him the bundle.

"Dorothy has already got through to Ashcroft," I lied to Vinney. "There'll be a plane in with a doctor before the sun sets."

Vinney was staring up into the sky.

"I'm going to make it anyway," he grunted. "I only did two

things right. After my team ran away and I fell in front of the cutter bar, I never let go the lines or my whip. I stopped the team and then used the whip for tourniquets."

I was looking at the whip tight in the flesh above the knee. The leg was gone just below the knee. The whole other leg was lacerated and looked to be beyond repair.

"How long since you loosened up the tourniquets?" I asked.

"It's fifteen minutes," spoke up Dowling, looking at his watch. "Time to loosen up again. He hasn't lost much blood—he was too fast with his whip."

Stanley and I loosened up the bullhide whip; blood squirted in a long thin line. Quickly, Stanley tightened the second tourniquet, the blood flow eased off, then back with the first tourniquet.

"I'm going to clean this up a bit," I said.

I opened my jackknife, stuck it into the bottle of mercurochrome to sterilize it, then carefully slashed off dragging grass-covered flesh.

Vinney gritted. "Go to it . . . I can't feel a thing . . . just empty space down there."

Stanley turned gray and stepped quickly behind a tree. My head started to swim.

"Damn it," I said to myself, "haven't I got any guts? Look at this guy lying here—he's got more nerve and guts than I'll ever have."

"Bottle," I said. Stanley was back; he quickly handed me the quart of mercurochrome.

"Here she comes, Vinney," I said.

I carefully poured the entire bottle over his one mangled leg and the stub of the other one.

I heard a thumping of hoofs across the meadow stubble. Andy Christenson leaped off the foamed buckskin before she came to a stop. He had called at Behind Meadows cabin and gathered up an armful of blankets. He stepped into our circle. Sweat ran down the lens of his glasses. Vinney didn't look away from the sky.

Andy came straight to the point.

"Vinney," he said, "we're going to rig up a comfortable stretcher with these blankets and you'll be home before you know it."

Andy was already moving for several old fence rails close by. The boys followed him.

I reached for the sack of flour and poured it all over the lacerated flesh. This would help clot the blood in the many arteries and tiny veins that were exposed.

Andy called over from his work. "You've got to have two tourniquets on each leg. You know that, do you?"

"Vinney and Stanley have already done that," I answered.

The stretcher was made. Vinney was moved carefully onto it. Clean pillowcases torn into wide strips now were wrapped about the wounds. We were ready to start on the long trek towards Christenson's.

Andy remounted his horse. He caught Stuyve by the hackamore shank. "I've got some errands to do and I'll bring back more help."

He trotted off leading Stuyve behind him.

We picked up the stretcher, a man on each corner, and started forward. We made a mile, and then rested.

"Roll me a smoke," said Vinney. "I don't smoke much, but I could use one now."

Stanley produced a tailormade, lit it and stuck it in Vinney's mouth. I looked at Stanley. He was dripping sweat; it ran down his face on his shirt front.

"I'm soft," he said. "Been down in Vancouver too long."

He touched me on the arm, and I stepped off to the side with him. He whispered, "I don't think he can make it for long, his eyes are glassing up."

"I noticed that, too," I whispered. "He's putting up a terrific fight."

Hoofs rattled across the opening.

"Jane Bryant," said Stanley. "Now there's a fighting chance for him."

A tall, willowy, intent girl snapped off a lathered horse, like a man; she carried a small battered suitcase in one hand. I could hear her gasping through her teeth as she ran past us.

"It's Jane, Vinney," I heard her say. "I'm going to do everything I can for you. A plane is expected in by nightfall, but in the meantime you'll have to take doctor's orders—no breaking the rules like a bad boy."

I saw Vinney smile faintly. I thought, "This is the first time light has come to Vinney's face."

"First order is that you do absolutely no talking. We're going to do all of that." She spoke softly to Dowling, "Stanley, give me a hand for a moment."

She had been taking Vinney's pulse. Now she and Stanley loosened and tightened tourniquets. Then she gave Dowling the wink and they walked off to one side. She nodded her head at Billy Dagg and pointed to Vinney. Billy and Mac stepped over to him and began to talk. I followed Jane and Stanley.

"Boys," she said, "I guess you both know Vinney may not live until the plane arrives."

We nodded.

"The terrific pain of the cuts hasn't started yet, but he has lived through the shock of the amputation. In another hour the pain he will have to endure will be unbelievable. And there's no way we can ease it till a doctor arrives with morphine.

"I'll have to tie up the main cords and arteries immediately and I've only got a pair of wire pliers to hold them with, but I can't wait until later when the terrible pain hits him. I want you boys to line up behind each other, and when you feel sick, step back and let the next man take your place. I don't want any of you crashing down on top of Vinney. Don't study what I'm doing—just do what I say."

Silently we followed Jane back to the stretcher.

"Vinney, I must do a little work on you now." I saw her look for a moment into Vinney's eyes and then swing her glance away from his to look into the blue of the sky.

She took a deep breath and strong lines came into her face; her jaw set in a straight line. She opened her suitcase.

Here, on this lonely meadow, hundreds of miles from civilization and scientific aids, this young and only slightly experienced woman performed a most difficult surgical operation.

She must have worked for nearly forty minutes, using the crudest of instruments—razor blades, a jackknife, a set of small pliers, scissors, silk thread, two bottles of some kind of disinfectant, several rolls of gauze, and finally pillowcases.

Occasionally she talked to Vinney—of music, of books, and of faraway places. I marveled at her quiet efficiency and great courage.

It was late in the evening when we lugged the stretcher into the

Christenson house. Dorothy had turned a back room into a ward. Vinney's bed in the center, a big oak table, trays, flowers, a chair and another bed across from it.

Andy had arrived with a bottle of rum during our long trek with the stretcher. But although Vinney was ordinarily as much of a drinking man as the rest of us, he steadfastly refused to take even a sip of the stuff. Through tightly clenched teeth, Vinney said: "No, I don't dare take even a small taste. I've got too big a fight ahead of me. I can't take a chance—it might weaken my will."

Andy asked Jane what should be done. "The plane won't get here till tomorrow," he said. "The prolonged pain Vinney's enduring is enough of a shock in itself to kill him. If he could get even momentary relief with the aid of the rum, it stands to reason it would be some help to his system. What do you think, Jane?"

Jane answered immediately, "I've been thinking about that, Andy. Vinney's chances of living look so slim that he should not be deprived of any hunch or any clear thought or decision he has made. It will be a miracle if he doesn't get blood poisoning, or tetanus, or die of the shock and the pain."

"Jane is right," Dorothy spoke up. "Vinney is a straight thinker. He knows now that his only chance of living through the ordeal rests on his will, his faith in God, and his clear mind."

Every few minutes now the jangle of two long rings and one short sounded in the house. A telephone-telegraph line stretched three hundred and twenty miles from Williams Lake through Anahim to Bella Coola. Only a few phones were installed along its long course, but the Christensons had one of these.

Adolph Christenson, Andy's active and dynamic father, a well-known frontier character, had called up three times from Bella Coola, ninety-six miles away on the other side of the mountains.

We were just finishing our supper when the phone rang again. Geraldine Christenson lifted the receiver, listened for a moment, then turned and said, "Dad, it's Grandpa for you again. He says he's in a big hurry and for you to get to the phone quickly."

Andy hopped up.

"Why yes, Adolph, Vinney's still fighting. What did you say? Oh—you can't do that! You're off your ticker! That plane should be in here by ten o'clock in the morning.

"What's that? You can beat an airplane with saddle horses! Now listen, Adolph, don't try one of your wild stunts at this stage of the game. For God's sake—don't take the doctor out of Bella Coola before the plane gets there; he'll never make it horseback."

Andy returned to the table and pulling back his chair, said, "Boys, we all might as well realize that we've now got another problem on our hands."

Billy cut in. "And that problem is 'Emergency Adolph Christenson.'"

"Correct," replied Andy. "Adolph and his brilliant ideas will be a threat right up to the time the plane gets in here. He's prancing around Bella Coola like a caged-in wild horse; says there's only one thing that counts and that's action. Lord knows what he'll think up next!"

Vinney was still fighting desperately for life when an orange-red sun rose.

"It's an absolute miracle," Jane said to me. "God grant him the few more hours needed until the plane lands on Anahim Lake."

Billy Dagg was Andy's ranch foreman. He and the new hired man, blond Dick Higgenson, left early to keep the hay crew clicking. Stanley, Thomas and I rode three miles over to the shore of Anahim Lake to build huge bonfires to act as beacons for the plane —it would be the second plane ever to wing into the country. We led extra horses for the doctor and the pilot.

While we trotted toward the lake, Thomas told us about the accident.

"We both drive mowing machines," said Thomas Squinas. "I come behind in that little neck. My team he run away . . . I try to throw machine out of gear . . . I slip . . . I fall. I won't let go my lines . . . he drag me fast like the wind . . . my mower knife he gonna cut Vinney in two. Vinney jump fast, but he slip and fall in front of knife."

We cut and snaked in roots and trees, lit the fires, and staked our horses on good feed. Soon the smokes puffed skyward.

The day dragged slowly on. Ten o'clock passed—no plane. Our eyes were held like magnets to the western sky. At two o'clock there was still no plane.

At five o'clock Stanley said, "In two more hours it will be too dark for a plane to fly in and land blind in a strange country."

Thomas grunted and cleared his throat.

"I think about it," he said, "that white man's bird he can't make it. Saddle horse he more better; that cayuse he can get there."

A horse whinnied from the trail to Christenson's. Hoofs thudded across the ground. Andy rode to the fire. His face was drawn and his eyes were bleak.

We all called at once, "How's Vinney?"

Andy got dejectedly down from his buckskin. He shook his head. "Vinney still lives. Why, I don't know."

"The plane," said Stanley. "Where the hell's that plane?"

"The plane landed in Bella Coola at twelve o'clock," Andy answered. "The pilot had to pick up the doctor and he flew around for an hour before he could land. The water was very choppy. Now he can't take off, waves are pounding on the dock. They say it's absolutely impossible to get off the water tonight and weather reports are not favorable for tomorrow.

"Jane says she's afraid Vinney will go by sunup tomorrow without morphine. Come on men, there's no use waiting here now."

Thomas grunted loudly. "I think about it long time. This country too tough for any white man machine. More better somebody he shoot 'em that bird now, then he can't fool nobody again."

We rode silently back to Christenson's.

As we arrived, Billy Dagg, Mac and Dick were getting down off their horses. Thomas, usually stoical and self-contained, had worked himself into a mad rage during our ride home and now burst forth to the boys. The last thing I heard was, "We go to Bella Coola. Saddle horse . . . ninety-six mile there and ninety-six mile back . . . bring 'em back medicine."

When they came into the house Andy snapped into action.

"How many shod horses have you got in, Billy?"

The Christenson foreman thought a moment. "I've got shoes on string 1, all but Betsy. There's twenty-two head in that bunch."

"Good," said Andy. "The plane deal hasn't worked. Now we're going to back Adolph to the limit. I want you, Billy, with Mac and Dick, to pick out six of the fastest shod horses from string 1—drive the bunch west, dropping off and picketing two horses on the meadow this side of Pelican Lake—two on top of Precipice—Mac, you stay with the horses at Precipice and be ready to help or relieve Adolph and the doctor there. Billy, you and Dick lead the other two loose horses down the precipice and keep going till you meet Adolph.

"In the meantime, you fellows will need two changes of horses yourselves. So that means you'll be starting off with six loose horses for the rescue party, and six for yourselves. Twelve of the fastest shod horses, Billy. When you're saddled up and ready, come for your lunches."

"Okay," said Billy, "twelve loose horses—six for the party, two staked at Pelican and two at Precipice. We keep going till we meet them. If we don't meet 'em, you can count on us being in Bella Coola soon after sunup."

Mac, Billy and Dick shoved through the door. Thomas Squinas spoke from the far corner of the room. "More better, Andy, I go with those boys, too. Maybe some kind trouble that trail."

Andy nodded his head.

"Yes, Thomas—maybe something happen that trail. That's why I want you and Stanley here on deck, ready for any other emergency that might crop up."

Andy moved like a cat to the phone, made several rings and snatched off the receiver. Dorothy and Geraldine hurried about in the kitchen.

Someone answered at the other end of the line.

Andy snapped, "Get Adolph on the phone at once—this is Andy Christenson."

There was a short pause—then a thin voice:

"Adolph and the doctor are outside trying to start up Adolph's car."

Andy snapped back, "Tell Adolph I want to speak to him at once."

Another pause over the line—then the voice came back:

"Adolph wouldn't listen to me—he said there was too much talk and not enough action. He and the doctor drove away."

Andy set the receiver down.

"Well—Adolph is off," he said. "He and the Doc got away in

that old Model-A of his. I guess he's planning to leave the wreck and pick up horses somewhere along the road."

Dorothy and Geraldine came into the room with trays of sandwiches, three huge paper lunch bags and a coffee pot. They set them on the table. Dorothy said,

"Andy, those boys should have a good hot meal before they start on that long trip. It won't take me twenty minutes to get it ready."

"No, my dear," said Andy. "Those boys won't take time out for that—every minute counts from here on in."

Now the three riders ran single file through the door, their tanned faces set with the tension of the night ride ahead of them. Dorothy and Geraldine shoved large cups of coffee into their hands.

The men paused. Their eyes glinted. They drank slowly. Billy looked at Andy.

"We've got the cayuses in the corral—put halters on all of 'em. Won't lose no time catching and staking 'em out."

Billy finished his coffee.

The boys started for the door. Billy turned halfway round. His dark eyes twinkled.

"Twenty-five dollars says that the horses beat the plane."

"Taken," said Andy. "Go to it, boys—good luck—and good riding."

The door opened. The men moved out into the dark. The door closed. A moment's silence—and then the thundering of hoofs. The vibration died slowly in the distance.

Andy stared for a moment at the closed door. He took a deep breath and turned to us.

"I'd like to see a moving picture of this night's ride. It will be terrific—the fastest ever made across to the coast—and the whole distance in the pitch-dark. Billy will crowd those loose horses through the jungle and the windfalls just as fast as they can run. Those boys are going to take some awful chances—but it was the only thing we could do—the only hope now for Vinney.

"I still want to get hold of Adolph and tell him about the relay horses," said Andy. He stepped briskly to the phone and rang for the Hagensborg trading post. He asked the trader to flag Adolph when he came through.

"I'll tell the telegraph operator in Bella Coola to keep the line open until after I've spoken to Adolph," concluded Andy.

While we waited we ate.

Andy said, "Boys, we might as well figure that the doctor is not going to make it through. I don't know the young Doc very well, he's only been in Bella Coola a year, but I do know that he's only been on a saddle horse a couple of times in his life."

Andy struck a match and held it up to his cigar. He inhaled and blew out a cloud of smoke.

"That's ninety-six miles, more than fifty of it a mighty tough horse trail," he said. "It's lucky Jane knows how to handle a hypodermic needle, for the doctor and Adolph will never make it. My guess is that the boys will meet them some place below the precipice—relieve the Doc of his kit and be in here tomorrow afternoon."

The phone rang. Andy answered it.

"Hello," he said. "Hello there. What's that? Say it again—this line's not clear. Speak louder there. No—I said—speak up loud, man—I can't hear you."

Andy listened for several minutes.

"Well—can you beat that!" he said. "Thanks."

He replaced the receiver and turned towards us.

"Picture this—" he said. "Adolph and his passenger just chugged past the Hagensborg store. The trader tried to flag them, but Adolph was looking straight ahead and paid no attention to the man—nearly ran him down. He said the tires were flat and the car was running on the rims, and the motor was making a sputtering sound. The trader said he could still hear the car banging and crashing up the valley."

Dorothy and Jane hadn't slept for more than forty hours. Now Andy insisted they get some sleep. While the women rested we washed the dishes, then took turns reading to Vinney, who lay motionless, his dull eyes partially open, his face a long gray shadow.

The house seemed very quiet. A dozen candles threw a strange flickering light across the walls in Vinney's room.

Looking down at him, I noticed his eyes were closed. I had a spooky feeling. I looked at my newly purchased Big Ben pocket watch. It was three o'clock. Some place beyond the walls of the room I heard the faint tinkle of an alarm clock. A few moments later Jane moved quietly into the room, her slacks making a rustling sound as they brushed against Vinney's bed.

Jane looked down at Vinney. She held his pulse for a long time, then with her fingers pushed back his eyelids. Her face was white. Stanley and I both stood up. Andy, followed by Dorothy, tiptoed into the room. Jane picked up Vinney's wrist again and stared at the black curtain of night in the window. Finally she laid his hand gently under the covers. We walked quietly out of the room.

Dorothy followed immediately behind Jane. The tall nurse turned and looked for a moment at Vinney's sister.

"Dorothy," she said, "there is still a faint flicker of life—but he hangs by only a thread—you must prepare yourself. The pain is taking it's toll, and I don't think he can hold out much after daylight without relief from it."

Stanley and I shiveringly saddled up and rode abreast through the dark towards Anahim Lake to start the beacon fires going. Water along the lakeshore glowed brown and muddy, a vague wind rustled the marsh grass, and from somewhere out in the weeds came the weird bubbling gurgle of a northern bittern.

Stanley and I worked in silence. The big fires finally cracked and blazed up in the dark. We sat down and waited. I held my watch up to the firelight. The hands pointed to five o'clock. A fresh light out of the sky was beginning to touch the dull watery land around us.

"It's beginning to light up," said Stanley. "I wonder if Vinney is still alive." He looked into the west. "There's a pile of horses that's running like hell across that country over there."

"Yes," I said. "There's some great runs and some great rides being made tonight."

"If only we hadn't counted on that plane," said Stanley. "But then nobody could have told the bad luck it would have."

We lapsed into silence again.

Shadows and strange shapes were fading into the realistic light of day. Far out across the lake floated the mournful call of a loon.

My mind traveled down the long trail to Bella Coola—to the precipice chasm—to the towering mass of broken rock across the cliffs. I could see a relentless old man and a tired younger one urging sweat-streaked ponies on and on through the night and the silence.

I could see many horses—dark masses of them—thundering west across the land. Darkness rushing by—snags and sticks and fallen tree limbs lashing out of the night at the tense faces and the moose-hide-covered bodies of hard-riding men.

And with these thoughts I felt always the constant pounding of horses' hoofs. I thought to myself, "The undertone of a new frontier —the music of horses' hoofs cracking across the silent lands."

I looked unconsciously at my watch. Six o'clock it read. A tragic chapter of the North's story was drawing to a close—and in my ears still rang the dull noise of horses' hoofs pounding across the ground.

Stanley sat suddenly erect.

"Do you hear anything?" He cocked his head at an angle listening.

"I can't get the thudding of horses' hoofs out of my head," I told him. "It kind of keeps on humming in my ears."

Stanley sprawled flat on his side, his ear to the ground. He lifted up his head.

"Put your ear to the ground," he said excitedly. "I'm damn sure I can feel a vibration."

I fell flat beside Stanley. I listened—then jumped up.

"There's no question about it," I said. "Horses coming in fast from the west."

We got to our feet and stared across the wide meadow along the Bella Coola trail. Out of the jackpines a quarter of a mile to the west of us, a horse shot into view—and then another one.

"Good God!" said Stanley. "It's unbelievable! Someone's broken through already."

We strained our eyes across the flats.

The horses were running stiff-legged, reaching out low to the ground. The lead rider, his hand waving in a wide arc, was swinging a whip down on one side of his horse and then on the other. He leaned low over the horn of his saddle.

The horses came racing across the flats—their loud hollow breathing sounded above the thud of hoofs. Stanley let out a whoop.

"I can't believe it," he yelled. "It's Adolph!"

We cheered and jumped up and down.

"Change of horses here," I called at Adolph's dust-covered sweat-streaked face, as his horse came pounding in close with the doctor's satchel tied over the horn of the saddle.

Adolph's glinting eyes didn't leave the trail ahead.

Like a harsh breath of wind, man and horse swept by us,—and behind thudded the other horse—and on his back, with both hands gripping the horn of his saddle, his eyes glazed, his tense mouth gasping for air, swayed the white-faced, dirt-covered doctor.

We kept on cheering and yelling as the riders pounded out of sight. Then we sprang for our horses.

We raced towards the ranch. Fifty yards ahead of us, I saw Andy Christenson run from the house to the doctor's horse—saw the doctor sway uncertainly in his saddle, and then fall heavily to the ground.

Now Adolph staggered from his horse towards the house, carrying the precious satchel. The doctor regained his feet with Andy's help, and took the satchel from Adolph, then shoved unsteadily through the door.

I watched his thin, mud-spattered figure sway behind Jane and Dorothy into Vinney's room.

For the following ten minutes the doctor and Jane worked over Vinney like a well-trained team. Then the doctor walked out of the room and fainted.

Later, when he revived, he told Andy Christenson that there were four reasons why Vinney lived through the ordeal: the accident taking place on clean, uncultivated land saved him from tetanus and blood poisoning; Vinney's quick thinking in using his whip for a tourniquet before he lost much blood; Jane's skill in cleaning and suturing the wound—and, above all—Vinney's will to live.

Now Adolph walked into Vinney's room. I heard him say, "Good going, Vinney—you've cut the mustard, kid!"

He returned to the living room where he let out a war whoop. "Who says a plane can beat a horse in this country! Give me a string of quarter horses, a quart of overproof rum, and I'll beat any relay of planes in the country!"

Down onto the sofa went Adolph with a thud. He, too, was out like a light.

And thus ended one of the fastest and most remarkable rescue rides ever made in the north country. Unbelievable night rides made by three cowhands driving loose horses ahead of them down narrow jungle trails; a man in his late sixties; and a young doctor unused to the saddle. Rides that not only beat the traditional mercy plane, but cracked into objective in time to save the life of Vinney Clayton.

Adolph told me a few of the facts.

He and the doctor made the first twenty of the ninety-six mile journey in the flat-tired, broken-down Model-A. When it collapsed completely they dogtrotted to the nearest farm where they borrowed two work horses and battered saddles.

Despite the fact that the next twenty miles through inky black night were covered on these clumsy animals, these miles were fast ones in accordance with the accepted standards of riding. But the terrific ground-eating speed made by the doctor and Adolph began when Billy Dagg met them below Precipice with the first of the relay horses.

At this point the doctor was tired out, blistered and saddle sore. He told me that when Billy met them he couldn't see how he could possibly hold out for even one of the fifty-odd miles still confronting him. A five-minute rest and a cup of hot coffee laced with rum revived him.

From here on in, Adolph, followed by the doctor, made incredible time. The three sets of relay horses were in turn held down to a fast trot, and then pounded into a full gallop. As Adolph switched saddles at the relay points, the doctor mixed the coffee and the rum.

The plane settled on Anahim Lake early in the afternoon, and the next day carried Vinney and the doctor straight to Vancouver where surgeons saved Vinney's mangled leg.

As the plane rose into the sky above Anahim and purred over the distant mountains to the south, Thomas Squinas turned to the bunch of us, grunted loudly, and said:

"I think about it. White man he's some kind of man—I don't know what kind!"

CHAPTER XXII

The Four Million Acre Cattle Company

IF GEORGE PENNOYER DECIDED to throw in with us, we would try to raise enough capital to finance our first objective—the tying up of strategical lands, the swamping out of a wagon road to Quesnel, B.C., the enlargement of our pack train, and the purchase of a small experimental herd of cattle.

In the meantime Pan was to have his appendix removed, and then go to the Parliament Buildings in Victoria to discuss our plans with officials of the Lands Department, the Survey Branch and the Grazing Commissioner.

Early in December, 1935, I climbed a train headed for Cheyenne, Wyoming, while Pan headed for a hospital room.

George Pennoyer went over the whole proposition with me. The great cowman threw himself whole-heartedly into the venture, and the next spring and summer he ate up more than three thousand saddle-horse miles through the formerly unexplored territory.

The adventures we had, discovering and tying up vast meadow lands, valleys, entire watersheds; the many difficulties we encountered, including the raising of money for the enterprise and forming the cattle company, took two years, and is a story in itself.

It wasn't until the spring of 1937 that Pan finally received a wire from George in New York, giving him the go-ahead to purchase an experimental herd of Hereford breeding stock, and instructing him to drive them to the headwaters of the Blackwater.

In accordance with a prearranged plan, Pan, with a string of saddle horses, was in Williams Lake when he received the wire. Far north of Pan, I was camped with a pack train on the outskirts of the frontier town of Quesnel, at the end of steel on the P.G.E. railroad. At Quesnel I received a letter from George explaining our future course of action.

A group of sportsmen in New York had agreed to finance the year's operations, and the purchase of the experimental herd. The herd was to be trailed over the mountains to the Itcha prairies, where they would be held during the summer. In the fall the cattle would be driven to the swamp and meadow area in the vicinity of the Home Ranch. In other words, the summer and fall ranges were to be tested out.

The plan then called for the cattle and horses to be trailed to the distant northeastern boundary of our proposed cattle range, the Batnuni Lake country, where they were to be wintered. Pan was to handle the Home Ranch area operations, and I was to operate the Batnuni end of the country.

If the cattle summered and wintered in good shape; if the range turned out as well as we anticipated it would; and if we had no losses; this group agreed to arrange for the backing of the great new cattle company.

As I pushed and yelled my pack train west across the narrow bridge spanning the Fraser River, my voice must have been heard in Bella Coola.

The pack train, with Nimpo walking slowly, proudly and with great authority in the lead, and Old Buck crankily and uncompromisingly biting the horses ahead of him as he brought up the rear, hadn't progressed many miles before I stopped yelling and gave thought to the immediate future.

I began to realize that we were about to tackle a cattle proposition that for inaccessibility and remoteness from town and railroad has no parallel in our times.

Our operation would not run into thousands of raw acres, or into hundreds of thousands, but into the millions. Between our two proposed main ranch headquarters, the Home Ranch and the

Batnuni, our cattle company would control something over four million acres. Beyond those points I knew not how much more.

The western end of our range, near Tetachuck Lake, lay nearly three hundred miles beyond Williams Lake; the first two hundred were dubious mud-holed car-road miles for only six months of the year; the remaining hundred were as yet only game trails over mountains, canyons and muskegs.

We estimated that there were at least 130 miles of trail connecting Batnuni on the far eastern end with Quesnel at the railroad. It was probable that Quesnel would be our shipping point, and that was why I had shoved my outfit north of the Itchas to this town.

I realized many things could happen during the coming year that could terminate our operations in a hurry. I thought of the tricky, almost superhuman task that now confronted Pan in driving the first herd of cattle over the high snow-crusted summits of the Itchas; the cattle drive that I would have to make in the snow and the freezing temperatures of early winter, across the dark, uninhabited, wolf-infested lands that reach from the Home Ranch to the Batnuni Lake country.

"Here is the big test," I thought. "Our big test."

Success lay across the horizon, but it was a success that could only be gained through luck and the use of every bit of energy and headwork that George, Pan and I could produce.

CHAPTER XXIII

Starvation Drive

THE DRIVE STARTED inconspicuously enough early in May, 1937, when the Top Hand, Alfred Bryant and Mac MacEwen started the horse remuda and seventy-five big raw-boned whiteface cows and calves, a bull and an old black and white pot-bellied milk cow, west through the Chilcotin. The grown stock had cost Pan thirteen dollars a head, and the calves were thrown in on the deal.

As Pan herded a group of lead cows down the road ahead of him towards the remote Home Ranch, he had no idea that this unpretentious bunch of cows was to become famous.

This was the gallant herd that trailed hundreds of miles into uncharted, uninhabited country; crossed great mountain ranges and swam ice-choked rivers; faced wolf packs and raging blizzards. These cattle were to know the gnawing pain and the aching belly of creeping starvation on frosted bodies, for they were starting on the incredible trek that almost ended in disaster. The trek that is known in northern British Columbia as "Starvation Drive."

That year the grass was late in starting, and Pan was forced to make short drives, covering not more than ten miles a day. The first week the drive passed beyond the Chilcotin, and then for many days through the dark jackpine land between Tatla Lake and Cariboo Flats, a network of sloughs and highland meadows.

Here Pan looked north and saw in hazy distance the towering Itcha mountain range, over whose dizzy summits he would soon have to drive. As he looked at this dreamy white world splitting the sky thousands of feet above the surrounding country, its face cracked and broken by jagged peaks and sheer granite walls, the first feelings of doubt about this new venture entered his mind.

The drive reached the muddy shores of Anahim Lake in June, having covered more than two hundred miles without mishap. The cattle and horses were held on a strip of slough grass along the lakeshore for nearly two weeks, while the men axed out a trail through the twenty miles of heavy bush to the base of the Itchas.

Through the newly cut trail the drive moved into the foothills, and then up onto a high open swamp at the base of the main range. On the north face of the summit, Pan's pack trail skirted the upper edge of a slanting glacier. Snow often lay deep around this ticklish crossing. Now Pan decided to make a brief reconnaissance. He left Alfred and Mac with the cattle, and just before daybreak rode up towards the peaks. At more than two thousand feet above timberline, he zigzagged upward through a foot of snow. Higher, his horse floundered brisket deep in the heavy wet stuff.

The sun had dipped beyond the world of rock and snow when Pan and Piledriver finally broke through into the pass. He looked north in agonized silence at a vast snowfield stretching towards the distant valleys, and realized that the ten- to twenty-foot drift would probably not melt all summer.

Here at nearly seven thousand feet above sea level, Pan spent a shivering night. Piledriver stood dejectedly in the deep snow with his head down while Pan crouched on his chaps in the lee of an ice block, where he watched the pale stars move across the sky above him, and heard in the distance the empty moans of timber wolves.

Just before dawn a faint breeze blew in from the eastern peaks, and Pan made a discovery.

During the night a two-inch crust had formed on top of the snow. Pan could walk across the crust, but Piledriver broke through every few steps.

"Here's the big chance," thought Pan. "If by some streak of luck the wind keeps up out of the east, I may be able to get the herd through at night on a crust."

Several days later, after yelling themselves hoarse, the men had pounded the unwilling cattle up the mountain to the edge of snow. Here for three days and nights they waited for the crust to harden. Sparse bunches of alpine grass, enough feed to keep the cattle alive, were browsed slick to the ground, and the men fought the herd day and night to the edge of the snow, for the cattle had made up their minds that these high mountain slopes were not for them.

On the fourth night an orange-colored moon hovered low above the peaks, and the sky was splashed by the Great White Way. Occasional flares of the Aurora streaked across the sky.

The drive hit over the snowfields.

Up through the stillness of the mountain night plunged the herd. Higher, always higher echoed the roar of bawling beef and the hoarse cries of the men. Upward through the glittering night towards the moon-splashed peaks swept the first herd of cattle. High above the wedge-shaped mass, a fine black line moved snakelike into the pass, marking the advance of the horse remuda. A vague bluish steam hung above the herd as it cracked into the pass towards the north slope.

At the edge of the slanting glacier the horses suddenly balked. The lead cattle stopped abruptly in their tracks, and those in the drag started to mill. Not an instant could be wasted, for once the cattle had made a final balk it would be nearly impossible to move them forward.

Pan yelled over the backs of the milling cattle, "I'm taking the lead. Both you guys empty your guns in the sky and pound 'em in in back of me."

Horns and hairy bodies plunged and reared about him. The narrow pass echoed the mad bawl of the cattle and the frightened snorts and whinnies of the horse herd.

Now Pan rode cautiously down the steep incline to the snowbank above the glacier. He realized that a crust, not over eight inches through, was all that held his horse above twenty feet of wet soft snow. He was conscious of a vague yellowish light creeping out of the east, the Great White Way melting into empty space above the mountain world, and the moon leaving strange shapes and shadows as it dipped behind the crags. He heard the sharp reports of guns, and saw, taking sudden life and shape above him, a wide black mass that swept over the brink along his back trail. It was as though a dam had broken, and black water seethed suddenly down over a white basin.

Soon the horses moved into the lead. The cattle followed them across the slanting snowfield; down through a land of rock into the snow brush; and then to the windswept trees at the line of timber. It was late in the afternoon when the drive stopped in a parklike jackpine country at the base of the pinnacles.

Pan's fabulous cattle drive through the dead of night, over high summits of an uncharted mountain range, on top of twenty feet of briefly crusted snow, stands out as one of the most daring accomplishments in the history of cattle driving in the North.

Early in July the drive came to the lower end of the Box Canyon. A lush carpet of strange grasses covered the valley floor, and Montana Wyoming bunch grass lined the banks of the clear creek flowing out of the glaciers. Herds of moose fed on brush clumps, and jumping deer watched the drive from a distance.

Once the cattle and horses stampeded when two mountain grizzlies and their cubs reared ugly heads above a cutbank. The herd ran in a fast-moving arc around the grizzly group, and the boys pounded their ponies in behind them. Looking back, Pan saw the big bears hadn't moved. The cubs were still up on their hind legs watching, but the grown grizzlies had dropped again to all fours, and to their serious job of log rolling.

At the northern end of the canyon the men threw together a crude drift fence to keep the stock from straying until the drive was resumed. Leaving the footsore, trail-weary cattle and horses in this grassy, well-watered stock heaven, they lashed down their now empty pack boxes on three horses, and rode north to meet me at the Home Ranch, on the headwaters of the Blackwater.

The night of the reunion was a gala one. I surprised Pan by cracking open a bottle of thirty O.P. Demarara rum; a happy-faced bottle that had traveled some seven hundred pack-horse miles unopened for this occasion. Sitting before a crackling spruce fire, braced with hot rum, fried landlocked salmon and roast ptarmigan,

I told Pan of the good luck I had had in lining up the winter's hay for the herd.

At Uncle Bill Comstock's old Batnuni Lake ranch, I had made a contract with two drifting cowboys, Bill Anderson and Mac Mac-Taggart, to put up 150 tons of hay. I had also packed a six months' supply of grub into Batnuni.

Pan and I decided to leave the herd in the Box Canyon until October fifteenth. Two men from Quesnel were coming in to help me drive.

That summer the upper reaches of the Blackwater River resounded to the metallic clack of double-bitted axes; the whine of whipsaws; the sodden thuds of mud plopping up on the banks of watery drain ditches; while on the rocky trails and distant heights towards Bella Coola on the coast, sounded the crack and clatter of hoofs, the snorts and whinnies of pack horses, and Pan's nasal tones singing "Red River Valley."

Late in the summer, on one of Pan's last pack trips to the coast, I was surprised to see Old Joe and Scabby White among the loose horses that strung out single file through the jackpines in front of him. This seemed strange to me, for Pan had been feeding both the old cayuses oats, currying them up, working over their feet, and allowing them to hang out in the bunkhouse yard all summer. Pan had allowed nobody to ride or work them, and they had not been on a single pack trip.

Although I didn't mind Old Joe and Scabby being under my feet all day, I did resent them breaking into the meat cache, pulling down a good hind quarter of moose, knocking over the privy and breaking a window in the bunkhouse.

When I complained to Pan about his lousy no-good six dollar cayuses getting in my hair, he pointed out that he was training Scabby and Joe to like home so much that they would never pull out on us. I saw there was no use arguing with the Top Hand and let matters ride.

But camp discipline went from bad to worse. The two old knot-heads began to play jokes on me. They hung around the cabin doorstep most of the day fighting flies, and pulling off my Stetson every time I entered the bunkhouse with both arms occupied with a load of wood or other supplies.

Later Old Joe would stand in the doorway swishing his tail, looking in the other direction as I approached with a couple of buckets of water from the creek. Scabby would be walking along beside me trying to get his bony head into a pail.

As I reached the door with about a third of the water already splashed away, and took a kick at Scabby, Old Joe would quickly douse his head in a pail and snort into the water. I would finally enter the house with two half-filled buckets.

Those spoiled, weevil-brained old pranksters finally spent most of their spare time thinking up new tricks to play on me. I developed a bad case of cabin fever with both horses.

One day I returned to the bunkhouse to find that Scabby and Joe had pushed open the door, entered the cabin, knocked down and trampled my newly washed pots and pans, overturned my sourdough pot onto the floor and eaten a fresh batch of bread. They had not been satisfied with this, but one or both of them had turned tail and manured the flour bin.

Neither horse was in sight as I grabbed up a stick of stove wood and went screaming out the door. Rushing towards the far end of the pasture, waving the stove wood over my head, I found the gate into the outside pasture open and Pan walking through it.

I swung the stick at the Top Hand's head, but he ducked and grinned at me. I stood trembling in my tracks, frothing at the mouth as Pan gave me a lecture on not losing my temper.

"There's nothin' to it, friend," he said. "No matter what happens always hold down that boiling point."

And so it was that I took a long happy breath when I watched Old Joe, with his ears flapping forward and backward, fighting Nimpo for the lead, and Scabby, who was now slick as a whistle, prancing on Old Joe's heels—but I did have a premonition that Pan had some important task picked out for them. Some special kind of a job that the Top Hand figured no other cayuse could do.

A month later when the pack train splashed across the creek in back of the bunkhouse, I was suddenly confronted with the answer.

In the lead of the train Pan rode nonchalantly on the tall, Roman-nosed Piledriver, while at his side, and reaching only to Piledriver's withers, Old Joe's ears bent forward with great éclat as he proudly carried Adelia, the future Mrs. Phillips, towards the bunkhouse. Bringing up the drag, Lester Brewster, Adelia's older brother came into sight riding a proud smug Scabby, and looking like the accomplished packer that he was soon to become.

To me the Top Hand's engagement to the attractive and diminutive Shorty was a miracle. I figured this phenomenon could only have occurred because of Pan's ability to make a decision and follow it up with everything he had. He must have taken full advantage of his salesmanship, his showmanship, and his never-say-die philosophy.

Shorty, whose father was a leading salesman in a large Canadian company, had had the advantages of education and travel. She was not only the cutest and prettiest little girl any of us had seen, but her gaiety, her infectious laughter and her sympathetic understanding of all of our problems soon made her the pivot around which life on the Blackwater revolved.

Early in October Pan said to me, "Friend, I sure don't like the idea of not havin' ya along to Williams Lake as my best man. But I guess we'll have to split forces this time. You've got a tough drive ahead of ya—but I know ya can do it.

"You'll have that bunch of critters into Batnuni by middle November. The two boys from Quesnel and Charlie Forrester should be enough help—and you'll see—there'll be nothin' to it boy, nothin' to it at all."

Now I looked at Pan.

"Friend," I said, "I'll make it to Batnuni all right—but how about you? I guess you're going to tell me that there's going to be nothing to handling a woman, nothing at all."

A wide sheepish grin spread across Pan's face and he slowly shook his head. I thought for a moment that Pan was going to admit that there was something to it after all, but he suddenly shook himself like a horse and snorted loudly.

"Hell," he said. "All a man needs is a little bit of brains and enough strength to carry them up off the ground."

It was along about the middle of October when I waved the Top Hand, Shorty and Lester up the trail on their long 550 mile round-trip journey towards Williams Lake.

Then suddenly the long fall days had gone; strange swishing winds carried a vague smell of frost from the north; and high in the sky, geese were honking southward, and the time had come for the drive.

But the drive didn't start for the distant Batnuni hay pile on October 15, and the herd had not strung into the north by November 15; and on the twenty-fifth of November, when the empty jack-pine world was covered by a foot of snow, and an icy blast struck from the north, the odds were not in favor of the drive ever reaching its destination, or now of even surviving.

A series of calamities had occurred near the headwaters of the Blackwater River. The two men from Quesnel never arrived. Cattle had broken out of the Box Canyon, and strayed miles back towards the Itcha Mountains. Charlie Forrester, my only hand, and I had been riding for weeks, tracking down and rounding up groups of homesick, bewildered critters. The horses had followed the example of the cattle, and lined out towards the distant peaks and their home range, and only a fierce mountain blizzard stopped them.

All game seemed to have pulled out of the country, and we had only five days' supply of grub left when the cattle and horses were finally rounded up, and moved to Blackwater Camp.

Charlie and I rode herd all night, and at daybreak on November the twenty-seventh started the drive north on its 110 mile trek to Batnuni Lake.

To the south of us towered the sinister snow-smothered heights of the Itchas, now an impassable barrier. Ahead of us stretched a wolf-infested land, uninhabited and desolate—a vast waste of broken volcanic rock, blackened charred snags and stunted jackpines.

Charlie was riding Eddie, a short-coupled, short-legged bay gelding; I rode Steel Gray, a five-year-old, twelve-hundred-pound leggy gray.

This first day of the drive the loose horses trotted hopefully ahead, believing they were headed for a haystack. I kept them lined out into the northeast, and at the same time herded a small bunch of lead cows behind them. Charlie led three pack horses tied head to tail, and drove the main body of cattle down the broken trail made by the horses and my lead cows.

Thus our first camp was reached shortly before dark, with twelve miles behind us, and ninety-eight to go. Everything had progressed far beyond expectations this first day and a new hope was born in both of us.

We made camp on the edge of a small slough grass meadow. The horses immediately fell to work pawing snow to reach the grass underneath. Soon the cattle licked up feed the horses uncovered.

While Charlie prepared our meager meal, I caught up Stuyve, and staked him out close to camp. Stuyve was chosen as my night horse. I would keep him saddled and ready for instant action during my night watch from dark to 1 A.M. Next I caught Charlie's night horse, likewise staking and saddling him. Charlie's shift was to be from 1 A.M. to 6 A.M. When Charlie had finished his meal, he grunted "good night" and disappeared into the battered tent.

I leaned comfortably against a silver spruce with my feet towards the fire, and smugly rolled a smoke. Charlie's long plaintive snores soon drifted out of the tent.

Black night engulfed the trail camp, and out in the darkness horse bells tinkled gently. The spruce fire popped and crackled, and the flames blazed up bright and cheery. With my belly filled and the stock feeding contentedly, it was hard to realize that ahead of us lay the ominous possibility of a starvation drive.

I had made up my mind to jot down a few notes at the end of each day to serve as a rough sort of diary, and reaching into a pack box, withdrew a little book and a pencil. I wrote:

"Nov. 27—12 mile drive today, successful and uneventful—temp. 2 above zero."

I had brought along a thermometer to keep a record of the weather.

It was crowding midnight when I was aroused from a doze by an intense silence. Remains of the campfire glowed dully. Charlie's snores had stopped. No horse bells clanged. I jumped to my feet and groped in the dark until I found Stuyve. We rode out to the meadow at a fast flat-footed walk.

All the cattle were bedded down in a group, and the horses stood like black marble statues against the white background. I breathed a sigh of relief, and went back to camp and woke Charlie. I vowed to myself I would not doze off on this drive again—too many things could have happened. Getting into my sleeping bag, I drifted comfortably away in sleep while Charlie took over the guard.

I was being manhandled; something soggy and wet brushed against my face. I protested, then opened my eyes. Charlie's baby face peered down at me.

"It's after six, cowboy," he said. "Roll out before I give you a panful of snow."

"Okay, sonny boy, okay. Leave me alone! Get those wet socks out of my face." I struggled up and chased Charlie out to the fire, in my bare feet.

At this time of year day breaks around eight o'clock. An hour before that time, while Charlie held the herd on the meadow, I started the horses up the trail. Three miles from camp I caught the pack horses and tied them to trees. The other cayuses walked on down the trail, stopped and looked back. I left them and trotted back towards camp.

Charlie's voice reached me long before I arrived, and I could tell he was having trouble. I touched Steel Gray with my spurs and we loped into the opening.

Cattle were breaking back in all directions. Charlie was riding furiously back and forth on their flanks, trying to keep them in a bunch away from the jungle bordering the edges of the opening. For over an hour we rode hard around the outside of the bawling stubborn critters. Now it took a good horse, a rope and a voice like a lion to make the herd move forward. Time wore on; our voices began to sound like croaking bullfrogs; the game saddle horses we rode, white-lathered and breathless, began to falter.

Suddenly to my dismay I heard a loud clanging of horse bells, and looking up, saw the entire cavvy racing past us headed for home.

"Turn those cayuses into the cattle," I yelled.

We whirled from the cattle and dashed into the lead horses, cutting off their retreat just in time. A wicked outlaw horse, a roan named The Spider, was in the lead and almost got past me. The big gelding spun on his hind feet and plunged, screaming and blowing, into the frightened cattle.

"We oughta shoot that son of a bitch now!" cried Charlie. "We've been fightin' him all summer!"

The other horses ran among the scattering herd.

"We'll fight 'em here in a circle till the end of hell, Charlie," I croaked. "I'm going to try for Nimpo with my rope. Steel Gray can't hold up much longer."

I knew that the first crisis of the drive was at hand; everything depended on my throw. I had my rope down, the loop shaken out; we were going on a gallop within twenty feet of Nimpo, on the back side of the main bunch of horses. I carefully swung the loop over my head and snapped my wrist suddenly forward with a slight inside twist, quickly got two turns around the saddle horn. Charlie yelled, the rope jerked taut, my saddle horse settled back on his hind legs. Nimpo was in the bag.

I jumped from Steel Gray, shifting my saddle to Nimpo's shiny back. I jerked my bridle off Steel Gray. He rolled over on his back, then staggered to his feet and stood to one side of the maelstrom with his head hanging down.

Charlie made a dandy throw, snaring his own big mouse-colored gelding. I looked at my watch. It was nearly eleven o'clock.

Nimpo patrolled back and forth behind the herd with little effort. The pace slackened off.

"Passive resistance," hissed Charlie, as he rode close to me. "We're too tough for 'em!"

Suddenly Steel Gray and Charlie's tired horse threw up their heads and walked resignedly down the trail towards Batnuni. The other horses quit the cattle and followed the leaders. Bully Boy, the bull, and the misfit, misshapen, off-color milk cow, Old Pot-Belly Black, stepped out and stoically walked on down the road. Other cattle followed. The trail outfit moved northeastward towards Camp Two.

Diary: "Nov. 28—Tough day today. Fought stock 4 miles to standstill. Lucky we got lots of changes of cayuses—we need them —Batnuni 94 miles—three days' grub left—temp. 10 above zero."

"Nov. 29—Wore out three horses each today—had to fight cattle out of bush with clubs—looks like cold snap coming."

"Nov. 30—Colder'n hell today—for once stock trailed good—guess too cold to fight back—made 10 miles—started rationing grub, but we got lots of coffee and tobacco left—temp. 30 below. Batnuni 77 miles."

"Dec. 1—Both of us rode all night last night—cattle and horses trying to slip back on us—fooled 'em. Made 6 miles today—animals act like being driven to their doom—bawling day and nite. Feel damn sorry for the poor critters. This rationed grub doesn't go far—could eat the hind end out of a skunk—Charlie says, 'Nothin's too good for a cowboy!' Batnuni—70 miles. Temp. 22 below."

As usual Charlie got me out at 6 A.M. However, there was no horseplay now. We were dead tired; neither of us wasted movements or spoke unless it was necessary. We hoped to make Kluskus, a deserted Indian village with a meadow and corrals this day. Our saddle horses, subsisting on frozen feed containing little nourishment, were not holding up under the heavy work required of them. Herding the outlaw roan Spider had been a one-man job in itself. I decided to catch him in a corral at Kluskus and try and ride him.

Our biggest problem with the cattle was to get at least one leader moving down the trail. Even with a single animal taking the lead others would follow.

Just before daylight I threw my saddle on Nimpo, and rode up quietly on a big brockle-faced cow. She was chewing her cud. We judged her to be as level-headed and as intelligent as a cow can be. We'd soon find out.

I got within twenty feet of her and snapped my loop down over her horns. I had tied my lariat hard and fast to the saddle horn, so that there was no chance of losing it. The cow charged in the opposite direction and came up hard at the end of the rope. Nimpo held her a minute while she reared and plunged, then quickly I rode up on her. I gained about ten feet of slack on my rope and threw this swiftly over her back. Now I swung Nimpo away at a forty-five degree angle, moving at a run.

The cow was bewildered and mad, but as the slack snapped tight on the off side of her hind legs, she was tripped and lit heavily on her back. I had "busted" her. Charlie got a figure eight around her hind feet, stretching her out. We fitted up a heavy rope halter over her head and let her up. I snubbed her up close and began dragging her first to the right side, and then to the left. I was breaking her to lead.

Charlie called our brockle-faced lead cow Broccoli. Soon she led up behind my saddle horse like an old broke pack animal. Pot-Belly Black, whom we had usually pounded into the lead position, resented this intrusion on her custodianship of the herd, and, crowding close on Broccoli's heels, maintained a hurt but dignified air. Bully Boy bawled his dissension to this new arrangement, but fell in behind Pot-Belly Black, and soon the herd was strung out single file behind me.

Dusk was enveloping the white world around us; a star or two glittered bravely down through the waning light of day, as we broke out on the sweeping Kluskus side-hill. Below us lay a frozen lake, and above and around us loomed, unreal and fantastic, a vast grotesque graveyard. Literally hundreds of graves stretched before us, marked by headstones of every conceivable shape, size and color. Markers with savage hawk heads, demon-like distorted figures, crosses and signs appeared out of the ground around us.

A score of frame and log buildings in various stages of decay and collapse bordered the graveyard, and standing alone, aloof and forbidding, towered a faded green and blue church with spires and steeples.

I shuddered and, turning in my saddle, called back to Charlie, "This sure is one high-toned city!"

He didn't quite make out what I was yelling, but nodded his head in agreement, and weakly answered,

"Yes—smallpox!"

An hour before daylight Charlie and I were drinking black coffee before the fire. It bubbled and gurgled in my empty stomach. We were shivering, nothing seemed to warm us; I could hear the horse bells down on the frozen meadow below camp. I wondered how we could all stand another day. It was strange that by now neither of us was hungry, just incredibly sleepy.

I glanced across at Charlie and noted that his big, blue innocent-looking eyes were sunken in his head, and his cheekbones stood out as he stared blankly into the fire. At twenty-six years of age, Charlie had but one ambition. That was to be a top hand.

Charlie stepped over to a pack box, pulled out the thermometer and grunted. "Thirty-four below. Are you gonna ride that roan or shall we warm up in the church?" I didn't answer.

We caught the pack horses and unstaked Broccoli, getting everything in readiness for a fast exit. It was light enough to see when we jumped the horses and headed them into a corral on one side of the graveyard. When they were all corralled Charlie sat his horse in the gateway, letting all the horses slip out past him except the Spider, then he slammed the gate shut.

The business of putting a saddle and bridle on the roan began. I tried to front-foot him from the ground and he put me over the corral, his front feet striking the corral logs under me.

"If I was you," warned Charlie, "I'd put a bullet in his ornery brain and forget him. This sure ain't no place to get crippled up or buried. That killer has crippled two men over Chilcotin way and you could be the third." He looked at me, his eyes wide and pleading.

"I'm no bronc peeler, Charlie," I said, "but I was able to stay on the roan's back a couple of times last summer. He can turn on a dime. He's one of the toughest horses I've ever seen; and, look at him, he's the only horse in the bunch that's still fat. He's worth three of these other cayuses, and if I can stay with him the first thirty seconds I think I can handle him."

I didn't explain to Charlie that this little speech was made to bolster up my courage. Charlie didn't answer. Riding Eddie through the gate, he made a spectacular throw, snaring the roan's front feet as the animal whirled in midair. It was a beautiful job of front-footing, and The Spider lit hard on his back with feet in the air. I jumped on his head and, while he was still stunned, Charlie got a figure eight on his hind feet. Quickly remounting Eddie, Charlie stretched the roan out.

I cinched the saddle down tight on the outstretched animal, got a hackamore over his head, tightened it under his chin. I felt weak —my knees were shaking and I trembled all over. Sweat broke out on me. "Must be lack of sleep," I kept saying to myself.

I stood over The Spider, gripped the hackamore shank, carefully fitted my left toe in the stirrup, took a deep breath and yelled, "Turn him loose!"

Charlie threw slack to the figure eight. For an instant the outlaw lay motionless, then with one movement sprang savagely to his feet.

I found my right stirrup as he came up under me, and shoved both feet deep into the stirrups.

The roan's head disappeared between his legs; I threw my feet forward, leaned back in the saddle, pulled up hard on my hacka-more shank. The animal screamed his chagrin, and plunged four stiff-legged jumps straight ahead. I dug my spur rowels fast into his belly and hung there. I could see nothing except the horn of my saddle, the snow immediately beneath me, and was conscious of Charlie's yells of encouragement. Suddenly the big roan shifted his stance and made three high, crooked pitches to the left. He came up sharp against the corral and threw up his head to get his bearings. I had him!

Pulling out my spurs I spun him in a circle to the right—he tried to get his head—I spun him in a circle to the left. Each time he tried to get his head I spun him to either side. The hump in his back straightened out.

I shouted, "Open the gate. The drive's on!"

Charlie quickly took charge of the lead cow and started along the shore of the lake. Spider moved like an elastic ball of fire under me. He shifted and darted in and out behind the cows, starting them into the drive. I used him hard. He moved without apparent effort. I noticed at once that he was free going. That means he could change gait or pace, shift on his feet from one position to another without the rider noticing any difference in movement. The Spider was indeed worth three ordinary horses.

Diary: "Dec. 4—It's been a long day, a cold day, a hungry day and a tired day. The Spider sure is an asset. Used him all yesterday and again today—other horses now getting a break. Both of us getting weaker and sleepier. Figure we'll have to kill a beef to-morrow—sure hate to do it—won't sound very good to have to kill beef on our first drive—but we can't last without grub much longer. Clouds gathering—sure hope no storm. Temp. 12 above—Batnuni about 55 miles."

The drive was now passing through dense jackpine timber. We were engulfed in a murky gloom. Looking up through the narrow split between the high treetops, I noticed the clouds settling down on us. Charlie was far up ahead with Broccoli. The herd was plodding along single file. Clanging sounds of the horse bells reached me occasionally.

I suddenly stiffened in my saddle. A message of doom floated out of the forest somewhere along our back trail. First a single unearthly wail rose to a peak of sadness and discontent, quivered and fell off into space. Other lonely, awesome howls, some low and throaty, echoed hollowly through the gloomy jackpines.

Soon the air reverberated with the combined roar of dozens of wolves. I knew that some of these sounds came from the throats of the dread black wolves. These animals reach the unbelievable size of a black bear, sometimes attaining the 225 pound mark. The black wolf can spring fifteen feet through two and a half feet of snow to bring down bull moose, cattle and all game with the exception of the grizzly bear.

Some of the cattle began to run; others stopped in their tracks and bawled. Far up ahead the bells clanged wildly, and I knew the horses had stampeded.

The uncanny sounds made by the wolf pack stopped suddenly, and again heavy silence gripped the forest. The wolves had picked up the smell of beef. What lay ahead of us now I did not know. The thought of the agony of hauling great piles of firewood to protect the stock at night made me shudder.

We made camp on a big open flat. Charlie had just started the fire and I was staking Stuyve, when to my amazement two Indians leading pack horses rode out of the timber. They were covering an immense trapline on their monthly circuit, and had with them extra grub and plenty of reserve strength. These two Indians must have been sent from heaven and I treated them as such.

After a big meal of dried meat, rice, bannock and tea, I vaguely remember stumbling into my bed, boots and all. I opened my eyes once during the night and saw big fires burning around the edges of the opening. I still speculate as to what would have happened that night of December fifth had not those kindly Indians, Jerry Boyd and Peter Morris, come to our rescue.

Diary: "Dec. 6—Reached the little meadow on south side of Blackwater River today. Wolves all around us—cattle and horses panicky—huge black fellows come out on trail ahead and behind us —then vanish in bush. Tomorrow we attempt to cross Blackwater—

ice conditions far worse than we imagined, possibility of stock being washed under ice into lake below crossing. Anyway—nobody can say we haven't tried. Charlie just remarked, 'He was only a cowboy, but he knew he'd done wrong.' Them's the sentiments—temp. 18 above—starting to snow—Batnuni about 46 miles."

I must have slept for some time—I came to with a start and stared groggily into the black night. Charlie had me by the shoulders and was shaking me hard.

"Quick, Rich—roll out. Hurry, there ain't a second to waste! Wake up, you bastard, wake up!"

I dove out of my bag, my boots were still on. Charlie cried hoarsely, "Cayuses have got away, camp full of wolves, we're sunk."

I staggered out of the tent to Stuyve. A fresh blanket of snow mantled the camp. It was falling so thick the nearest fire was almost blacked out. I could faintly hear horse bells on the back trail, but before I got in my saddle the sounds had died in the distance. Cattle were jammed in a circle around the tent and the fire. Some were bawling. Slinking black objects rimmed the outer edges of camp and yellow eyes reflected the glare of the firelight.

Charlie rode like mad ahead of me. He beat the horses out two miles down the trail, and drove the reluctant animals back through the dark and the hush of falling snow. With our pack ropes we quickly strung a rope corral around a group of poplar trees, and into it drove the horses. We roped and dragged windfalls and dead roots into camp and built big fires on the outside of the stock. The cows stopped bawling but stood wide-eyed and trembling inside the circle of fire.

Daylight finally came; the black bodies slunk back into the shadows of the timber; horses were packed. Charlie and I rode to the river, with axes.

Great cakes of ice, some half as big as houses, were piled high on its banks. Ice reached out from each bank towards the center, ending abruptly at a fifty-foot open channel of black rushing water. This boiling cauldron disappeared into a frozen lake just below the crossing. Charlie gazed at the sight and spoke slowly. He carefully measured his words:

"This is the real cowboy life. I wonder why everyone ain't a cowboy!"

We cut an opening in the ice from the edge of the boiling water back some fifty feet to the shore. Charlie, riding his own big Mouse, bravely settled down into the channel. The water deepened as he slowly rode out until it reached above his saddle skirts. I had my rope down and held my breath, waited. The current swept Charlie and his horse some yards towards the black hole above the lake. They came out on the opposite edge of the channel, breaking through the ice for about thirty feet towards the bank.

"Nothin' to it," yelled Charlie, "nothin' to it at all."

"You've been with Pan too long," I called to him. "Now you're beginning to talk like him."

I threw the axe over to him. He cut an opening back towards shore on his side, tested the ice on the lake and found it to be not over an inch thick, rotten and spongy. The snow had stopped. It was almost afternoon.

We had no choice but to drive the herd to their possible destruction. The feed was cleaned on the little meadow, we could not hold the horses much longer, and I knew the wolves would close in on the stock before another night had passed.

We led the horses across one by one and tied them to trees on the opposite bank. Now we faced the big moment! Driving the cattle down to the mountainous pile of ice, and leading Broccoli, I dropped swiftly into the channel. Charlie began forcing others in behind her. Pot-Belly Black kept her usual position close in to Broccoli's tail. Bully Boy hesitated a moment at the edge of the ice and then jumped in. The cold water made him gasp. Now I heard a deep rumbling sound, then a loud report. A great chunk of ice had broken free, letting all but a few of the cattle into a swirling mass.

A few ran back for safety. Charlie had his gun ready and fired several shots over their backs. It turned them. Charlie charged. The entire herd was now milling in deep water.

A seething, fighting mass of writhing brown and white bodies swept relentlessly towards the death trap below. The Spider and I crashed to safety on the bank, dragging Broccoli bodily out of the swift current. I dropped her halter shank and swung Spider about. My rope was down. Hurriedly I took half hitches on my saddle horn.

I wasn't quite on time. Pot-Belly Black had been swept down to the lake; her frightened, horror-stricken eyes showed above the water, while her struggling hindquarters were being sucked slowly under the ice.

Other animals, frantically using her as a bulwark to block the hole, were crawling up the bank. I had thirty-three feet of lariat. Pot-Belly Black was at least twenty feet from my saddle horn. I think maybe I must have let go a prayer or something as I took one desperate swing overhead and snapped the rope towards Pot-Belly's head. Some of the cows with calves at their sides were struggling to safety and ran into my taut rope.

My lariat was slipping beneath the surface; Pot-Belly was under there at the other end. The combined pull of the current and her heavy body was more than an ordinary horse or rope could withstand. Here was a test! The Spider was hard and fast to Pot-Belly Black. The half hitches had tightened solid.

The Spider seemed to sense the extraordinary circumstances under which he labored. His ears stood up straight and rigid, his body tense. He leaned forward, dug in all four of his feet, slipped, went almost to his knees, slid backward. I tried to get out my jackknife to cut the rope—couldn't get my hand under chap belt—called, "God—The Spider's going too!"

The thought flashed through my mind; this Porter special lariat is one of the strongest ropes in the world; it won't break. "Here it is," I thought. We were slipping, slipping, sliding backward. I looked down into the churning water.

At that instant the powerful, unbeatable, incredible roan made a terrific lunge to one side; got his feet under him again; crashed forward to his knees, struggled, plunged, plowed, reared, leaped against the rope. He pitched ahead screaming like a wild animal through the roar of his straining breath.

It all happened so fast that before I realized what had happened, I found myself sitting in the saddle back against the timber, with the trembling roan standing wide-legged, heaving under me, and Charlie getting the rope off the horns of Pot-Belly Black who was belching water and foam.

"Close call!" yelled Charlie. "Lucky—best damn horse I ever seen!"

I grinned back and swallowed hard. Old Pot-Belly Black got to her feet with an effort; stood dazedly looking about her. Water poured from her mouth and nostrils.

Bully Boy took charge of the cattle and herded them to the timber and safety. I made a quick count of the Herefords.

"Tally, all present and accounted for," I said. "When we get in to the ranch I'm swearing off cattle drives and cowboying forever! No wonder sane people think us bogtrotters are crazy."

Charlie snorted, "Oh hell, man, you'll never quit this life—it's good fun and a happy life to be a cowboy!"

Diary: "Dec. 10—There don't ever seem to be any letups on this drive—up all last night again—had to hold horses and cows on open side-hill or would have lost half of them. Hell of a cold wind blowing. Frosted my feet—rubbed snow into them for half an hour. Talk about fun—wolves never crossed rotten ice on Blackwater— guess we're lucky—Batnuni 38 miles. Temp. 15 below."

"Dec. 12—Cleaned up grub Indians gave us—we're out again. Stopped yesterday Chine Lake pothole to let stock fill up on good grass there and rest their legs. Cold is no name for it—no use writing about it—Temp. 42 below. Batnuni in three days. Charlie says, 'No use to worry about bein' out of grub for a few days—after all we're only cowboys!' Batnuni 28 miles."

"Dec. 13—Cold—cold—cold. Temp. 44 below. Batnuni tomorrow."

Late on the frosty day of December fourteenth, a broken, miserable line of dirty, half-frozen, half-starved cattle, horses and men dragged wearily out on an open bench overlooking the wide expanse of the Batnuni Ranch. Haystacks dotted the meadows below, and a thin spiral of blue smoke drifted skyward from a log cabin.

It had not been necessary to lead Broccoli the last two days, as Pot-Belly Black had steadily maintained the lead position without being coaxed or urged, and the rest of the herd had willingly followed.

Now the grand old black cow paused for a moment on the edge of the bench, and carefully surveyed all that stretched below and beyond. Her eyes rested for an instant on the herd of horses. They had surrounded a stackyard and were trying to break through.

Without further ado, she burned a rag down the incline to the nearest haystack, where she immediately lay down and gave birth to husky twin calves. One was a red bull calf with a white face, and the other was a little black heifer with a definite pot belly.

The horses, busily engaged since their arrival at Batnuni, had finally broken down the fence and now milled about the haypile. Led by Bully Boy, the cows and calves advanced in a body to the hay.

Charlie and I swung about and started for the bunkhouse where two strangers appeared in the doorway. Despite my exhaustion I was conscious of The Spider's elegant carriage and rode proudly forward. One of the men stepped out on the porch and cheerily waved his hat.

This was an unexpected welcome for The Spider. He plunged high and crookedly to the right. I plunged high and crookedly into the snow.

Diary: "Dec. 15—Yesterday Game Wardens Phil Brown and Cliff Atwood witnessed trail herd's arrival at Batnuni and my brilliant exhibition ride. Last night Charlie asked Game Warden Brown why he wasn't a cowboy! Told him 'Cowboy life is a good life and an easy one!' "

Telegram to New York City—sent by Game Warden Brown from Vanderhoof, B.C., January 2, 1938:

"Test herd cattle horses arrived Dec. 14 Batnuni stop no losses stop drive successful and uneventful. Signed Rich Hobson."